FRIENDS FOREVER

A NOVEL

JAN VERMEER

Published by Open Doors International
P.O. Box 27001
Santa Ana, CA 92799
www.OpenDoors.org
ISBN: 978-1-935701-01-9

Cover design by: Dugan Design Group.
Interior design and typeset: Katherine Lloyd, The DESK

Printed in the United States of America

It's a world of laughter

A world of tears

It's a world of hopes

And a world of fears

There's so much that we share

That it's time we're aware

It's a small world after all

—Theme song of Disneyland's
world-famous ride "It's a Small World"

✪ ✪ ✪

I, even I, am the LORD,
and apart from me there is no savior.

—Isaiah 43:11

To

Marjolein, Michaela and Gabriëlla,
as they make everything worthwhile

and

Susan, Jean and brother Simon,
without whom this book would not have been written

and

Joo-Eun, Kim Tae-Jin, Kim Jin-Chul, Park Joo-Chan, Lim Mose,
Hyok Kang, Kim Hyon-hi, Lee Soon-Ok and Chol-Hwan Kang,
as their life stories have changed my view of God and the world

and

Jong-Cheol,
who gave his life for Christ at the age of 11

FOREWORD

I recognize much in this moving book. In 1988, while the Olympic Games were taking place in Seoul, I was in South Korea to speak at various Christian conferences. One thing struck me. Before this Olympic year, nobody in the South spoke about North Korea. Yet it appeared that the Olympic Games had pulled South Korea out of its isolation, and they began to pay attention to their brothers in the North. The same applied to the church. Suddenly I kept coming across speakers who challenged Christians to make "impossible" plans, plans to bring the gospel to North Korea. I myself was one of those speakers.

I dared to challenge people because we serve a God for whom nothing is impossible. For many years now, North Korea has topped the World Watch List for Christian persecution. In all honesty this country is a world of its own—a world of persecution, poverty, fear and hunger. Yet even in this world, God is Almighty.

This tragic and hopeful book shows how our Lord works in this dark country. You will not understand everything, especially why people hurt each other so much and why God does not always appear to intervene. I emphasize "appear," because God's thoughts are higher than our thoughts. He can change both the North Koreans and us into other people. That is the greatest miracle. Together with the North Korean Christians, who are so strikingly described in this book, we are pilgrims on the way to His kingdom. There justice and righteousness reign.

I hope that this book will be a building block in the building of God's Church. I pray that by reading this book and by Jesus' grace you will hear God's voice calling. Pray without ceasing for your persecuted brothers and sisters in North Korea and in other countries.

—Brother Andrew

PROLOGUE

Zhang took a deep breath. The smell of the grass penetrated deep into his nose. On the other side of the hill, hidden among the trees, lay the enemy. His friend Jin and he were the only ones left. The rest had been knocked out by mortar shells, air attacks and gunfire. Now the shooting had stopped. The silence had become a friend. Was he mistaken or had he indeed heard the screeching sound of caterpillar tracks? Were the Americans approaching?

Zhang looked behind him. There lay Unsung, his village. No American would ever set foot there. Jin looked behind and gave the sign. Attack! Jin pulled himself up, and Zhang jumped up behind him. The boys zigzagged from tree to tree. The loose sand made running up the steep hill even more difficult. Just three more meters to the top of the hill.

There was that terrifying sound again. Zhang had heard it so often—the sharp whistle of approaching mortar fire. "Bombs!" shouted Zhang, while peering at the sky. As they both dropped to the ground at almost the same time, Zhang did not see the mortar shells, but there were explosions to the left and right. As long as you can hear a mortar shell, there is nothing to fear, his grandfather had once told him. But the ones you don't hear are those that kill you.

Falling on his stomach, with one hand Zhang clamped his helmet firmly on his head, while the other hand gripped his wooden toy gun.

"Don't give up, Private Zhang! We are the only ones who can still stop the imperialists! Think about the people in Unsung!"

"Yes, Lieutenant Jin! We'll get them!"

Zhang got up once more and ran the last three meters to the top of the hill—right into the enemy. There was no place to hide—no trees, no protection. They ran straight into the trap.

Zhang pointed his gun. It would not last much longer. The mortar attack would stop. Otherwise they would hit their own men. The Americans were fools, but not that foolish.

"Perhaps we'll never see each other again after this, comrade Zhang," said Jin. He took a jackknife from his pocket and made a small cut in his right index finger. "Give me your finger," he said.

Zhang let go of his gun and held out his right hand. Quickly Jin made a cut in Zhang's finger. The pain was more intense than Zhang had expected. Then they shook hands.

"Promise that you will never desert me, comrade Zhang."

"I promise, comrade Jin. Blood brothers forever."

"Forever."

The mortar attack had stopped. Jin tapped Zhang's helmet. "Ready? Attack!"

Zhang gripped his gun and ran with Jin into the valley. The "Americans" were too surprised to return the fire. Fools. They had not counted on the bravery of these two exceptional soldiers. The battle was over in minutes. The survivors fled, leaving their dead and wounded behind.

They'd done it! Zhang and Jin had turned around the war. The American advance had been brought to a standstill. From this moment on, the mighty North Korean army would drive them back into the sea.

Jin collapsed exhausted onto the dry grass. Zhang stood next to him. In the distance he could see the statue of the Great Leader. Zhang placed his right hand over his heart and bowed. It seemed that the Great Leader nodded with approval at the brave soldier who would turn 8 next week.

CHAPTER 1

If only the radio could be silent! Father Kim Il-Sung was dead. The Morning Star was no more. The glorious nation had come to an end. For the first time in his life, Zhang wished that the radio had an off button. Even though the radio had done nothing but pay tribute to the Great Leader the past few days, now only eternal silence was appropriate.

"Comrade Zhang!" Mother tapped her forefinger against Zhang's chin. Her red, listless eyes stared at him. "You're nineteen, a man now," she said, "a soldier. You're not allowed to cry. The country needs you."

Zhang nodded and wiped the moisture from his eyes. With trembling hands, Mother buttoned up his uniform and brushed away the imaginary dust from his shoulders. She was even weaker than the last time he had seen her six months ago. The illness was consuming her from within. If only they knew what it was and how to help her.

Zhang took a look at himself in the mirror. He tilted his chin up and squeezed his eyes together. *Don't give in to sorrow. A soldier does not cry.* His dark green uniform looked as good as new. Yesterday evening he had used all of his soap to get out the stains.

Wearing his navy blue suit, Father came into the living room, pushing up the knot in his tie and then straightening his lapels and his sleeves. He looked so smart it would be hard to guess that he was a factory worker.

Behind him was Hea-Woo, with her head bowed, as if she could hide the fact that tears were constantly forming rivers over her cheeks. She looked so beautiful in her neat, black skirt and white blouse. Zhang's sister deserved a good husband, a large house in the town and many children. *She has to get out of this hole*, Zhang thought. Just take a look at the bare walls, the threadbare couch and the fifteen-year-old, incredibly ugly table. Their meals were meager, always consisting of maize. In the village of Unsung, they ate rice only on special occasions, such as public holidays and funerals. *Why hadn't the Party issued rice today?* Zhang wondered.

"Are you ready to go, son?" Father's voice sounded heavy, betraying the effect of years of smoking cigars. "Have you picked some beautiful flowers to pay the Great Leader your last respects?"

Zhang heard the note of sarcasm in his father's voice. He steeled himself. *Don't respond. Not today.*

Above the radio in the living room hung the photos of Kim Il-Sung and his son, Kim Jong-Il. As always, the portraits were spotless. This morning Mother had done even more than her usual best to dust the portraits of the Great Leader and the Dear Leader. Mother was such a patriot. Father was not. Zhang feared that his "humor" would have dire consequences for him someday. And not just for him. Zhang shuddered to think that somebody from the Party might hear that Father called Kim Il-Sung "not such a fantastic president." The entire family would disappear into a camp. Even if they were to survive that, Zhang's life would be ruined for good. He could forget about a career in the army then. That must not happen. He could not allow his father to obstruct the only road he had to a better life—becoming a general, living in Pyongyang and gaining eternal fame by defeating the Americans. That was the objective.

Mother brushed her hand over Zhang's chest, to show that she was finished with his uniform. Zhang made a half turn to face the portrait of the Great Leader. It was simply unbelievable that Kim Il-Sung was no longer alive. The man who had freed North Korea from the treacherous Japanese and after that from the imperialistic Americans, the god who had turned North Korea into a paradise was no longer. The country was lost, even if Zhang were to become a general.

The death of Kim Il-Sung was not part of the plan. Zhang was to humiliate the Americans at the command of the Eternal President. How was he to do that without the inspiration and leadership of Kim Il-Sung?

"I'm going." Zhang made another half turn, as if the commander had dismissed him. He grabbed a bunch of Kim Il-Sungias from the table but thought how ridiculous it was for a soldier to walk down the street with a bunch of flowers instead of a gun. Zhang pulled himself together. He had to remain submissive to the Great Leader. He pulled his cap tight onto his head and left the house.

As Zhang closed the door quietly behind him, he saw a long procession of people slowly moving down the street. Usually the residents of the rural village were clothed in rags, but not today. Everyone wore their best clothes. Yet these clothes could not disguise the fact that they were as thin as rakes. Zhang was taller and better fed than they. This was hardly surprising since he had carried out important tasks in the army. People who served the country's interests simply had a right to more food.

The wide road proceeded steeply up to the end of the village and into the hills. At the foot of the statue of Kim Il-Sung, it ended. The right hand of the bronze twenty-meter statue pointed the way forward.

Zhang greeted several acquaintances with a nod and joined in the procession. He was engulfed by the great throng of people and felt more united with the villagers than ever before. What a privilege that he was allowed to be a member of this superior people! They were so disciplined, always willing to make sacrifices. Throughout the country, lines of people kilometers long formed to lay flowers at the statue of the Great Leader Kim Il-Sung. These images would be transmitted across the world and would make the Americans tremble.

If only Zhang could be in Pyongyang now. The capital was the jewel of the Democratic People's Republic of Korea, no, of the world. Just for her the sun would have to rise each day. Undoubtedly the lines of people there would be tens of kilometers long. Compared to that, the procession he was part of now was nothing.

"Zhang! Hey! Comrade Zhang!" A stocky young man wrestled through the mass of people toward Zhang. It took a while before Zhang saw him.

"Jin!" Zhang called. He hugged his friend. "You look fantastic, man! They certainly give you good food in Pyongyang! When did you return from the university?"

"Only yesterday evening," Jin said. "Just in time to pay my last respects to the Great Leader in my own village. How're things?"

Zhang's eyes darkened. "If things were good, we would not be standing here now. We would be preparing for an attack on the Americans."

Jin nodded. "We must not despair, comrade Zhang. Our Great Leader might have died, but General Kim Jong-Il is still alive. He knows what's best for us. He will equal his father's glory."

"You're right," Zhang said while reminding himself, *A true North Korean never despairs. A North Korean does not give up.* Many years ago the schoolmaster had passed on this order from Kim Il-Sung to Zhang and his classmates. It could have been yesterday. *Thank you, Father Kim Il-Sung, for all of your wise words and your wonderful deeds.*

By now Zhang and Jin had almost reached the statue. The people took time to bow, to cry, to place flowers and to pray silently. Nobody spoke aloud. Only sacred silence was appropriate at this moment.

The wind started to blow and in the distance dark clouds were approaching. Perhaps it was going to rain. Zhang hoped that it would rain. These days of mourning deserved no sunlight.

At last Zhang and Jin stood before the statue. How many times had Zhang already stood at this place and bowed his head? Sometimes, when Jin and his friends were children, they had secretly run around the statue. Adults considered that to be disrespectful, but Father Kim Il-Sung always had the same friendly look.

They had never thought that they would pay the Great Leader their last respects here. Quite simply Kim Il-Sung could not die. If only all of the people behind him were not there. If only he could be alone to take leave of the one he considered his real father.

Zhang and Jin placed their flowers at the same time. They walked backward in military stride. Zhang made a deep bow. A salty tear found its way into his mouth. It did not matter. Nothing mattered anymore.

Zhang lifted his head and saluted. Kim Il-Sung looked straight into Zhang's eyes. He knew what the Great Leader was saying. *The country needs you, comrade Zhang.* Zhang nodded and said in his heart, *I swear that I will defend your heritage with my life.*

✪ ✪ ✪

The sound of screaming seagulls broke through the icy silence that hung over the square. The soldiers were in position behind Zhang and two other marksmen.

Zhang breathed in the cold air and quietly blew it out again. His right hand was firmly clamped to the barrel of his rifle. It was a Mosin-Nagant, a bolt-action rifle made in Russia. The magazine could hold five rounds. After that it had to be reloaded. It was Zhang's favorite rifle. Pulling the bolt across after each shot gave him the feeling of being a deadly soldier. And soon he would know what it was really like to shoot a man dead.

Once again Zhang took a deep breath. He was one of the best marksman in his company, perhaps even the best in the battalion. But this was his first execution. If he missed, he would hear about it for a long time to come. His heart was beating in his throat and he had difficulty swallowing.

This was a decisive moment in his life and he must not let his emotions distract him. If he did well today, Zhang would remain a member of the firing squad and he could specialize further as a marksman, giving him a greater chance of promotion. Perhaps Zhang could lead a group of marksmen, then an elite company and then a battalion. He would marry, have children and live in Pyongyang.

Zhang had to pay attention. This was not the time to daydream. He had a job to do that was vital if he was to realize a better life. Three months ago, when the death of Kim Il-Sung was announced, he had briefly given up this dream, but Kim Jong-Il was also a deity. Zhang was grateful that he was no longer confused. His ideals were still within reach—if he hit his target today.

From a distance a scream disrupted the cacophony of the seagulls. As the sound came closer, a lieutenant who was standing in front of Zhang, shouted, "Sergeant! Silence the condemned man!"

Just then three soldiers, armed with sticks, left the battalion and ran to two colleagues who were holding the man by his arms with considerable difficulty and pushing him forward. The traitor was trying to kick his guards and free his arms.

"Noooooooo!" screamed the man. He must have been in his early twenties, the same age as Hea-Woo. "I haven't done anything! I didn't do it! I didn't do it. Aaaah."

The soldiers with the sticks reached the man and hit him until he fell silent. Then they stuffed his mouth with gravel, placed a sack over his head and loosely tied it with a cord around his neck. They no longer had any difficulty in dragging him onto the square and tying him firmly to a pole. A hole had been dug in front of the pole, the grave for this traitor.

The man's hands were tied behind his back. A rope was placed around his forehead, another around his chest and the last around his upper legs. The sergeant checked if the ropes were firmly in place and nodded to the lieutenant. The soldiers took their place in the line.

"Lee Chin-Hwa," shouted the lieutenant, "you have been found guilty of high treason! You have put to shame the trust that the Dear Leader Kim Jong-Il placed in you. You have acted in an antirevolutionary manner by dishonoring the image of our Commander-in-Chief, Comrade Kim Jong-Il."

The lieutenant rattled on. Zhang had lost interest in the charges. In his thoughts he was aiming the first bullet into the middle of the plush sack straight through the top rope. That was the difficult shot. After that he should not allow himself to lose his concentration. The second had to hit the rope around the chest and the third shot was for the rope around the upper legs. Three marksmen had three chances to let the target fall neatly into the hole. The distance was twenty meters. There was a light breeze, not enough to affect the shot. *One, forehead. Two, chest. Three, finished. Back into position.*

"Marksmen!" shouted the lieutenant. Zhang responded immediately. "Raise your rifles!" Zhang placed the rifle against his right shoulder. "Aim!" Zhang closed his left eye and peered over the barrel to his target. "Fire!" Zhang pulled the trigger. Hit! Zhang pulled across the bolt of his Mosin-Nagant and the empty cartridge sprang out.

"Aim!" the lieutenant shouted again. Now Zhang aimed a bit lower. "Fire!" Another hit.

"Aim!" The target was now leaning far forward, which somewhat blocked the rope from Zhang's sight. "Fire!" Zhang shot for the third time. The body fell forward into the hole. Zhang brought his rifle back beside him. He had succeeded. Three hits! The barrel felt warm.

"Everybody who slanders the name of Secretary General Kim Jong-Il will suffer this fate!" The lieutenant looked sternly at his troops, but Zhang wasn't listening anymore. *Three hits!* Perhaps he should look to see whether the other two members of the firing squad had been as successful.

"Dismissed!" The soldiers behind him marched away. The three who had formed the firing squad remained in position. The lieutenant came up to them. His uniform was thicker and of a darker green color than those of the other soldiers. His medals showed that he had a considerable record of service. His cap was one size too big.

"Lee Bo-Hwa, Kim Dak-Ho, Kim Zhang. Good shots. You have proven that you can be of great value when the American invasion comes. With marksmen like you, they don't stand much of a chance. Make your rifles safe, cover that traitor with sand and report within half an hour to your commander."

"Yes, Lieutenant!" the three shouted in unison. The lieutenant marched away with giant steps as if he paraded alone for Kim Jong-Il.

Bo-Hwa and Dak-Ho slapped Zhang on the shoulders. "Good shots, man," said Bo-Hwa.

"Yeah, not bad for a newbie," added Dak-Ho. Zhang grinned shyly, enjoying the compliments of his older mates.

"Now let's see if you're just as handy with a spade," said Bo-Hwa. "You come from the province Hamgyung-nam, don't you? There are enough mines there, so you must have learned to dig."

"Best make the rifles safe," said Dak-Ho.

"Yes, comrade boss," said Bo-Hwa. Zhang pulled the magazine out of his rifle before putting on the safety catch.

Click-click, click-click. Bo-Hwa was struggling with his weapon. He cursed while pulling on the bolt. The rest of the bullets would not come out.

"Need a hand?" asked Zhang. "Looks like you're getting into a mess with that rotten weapon of yours!"

"Yeah. Yeah. Off you go to dig, peasant. Fill up that grave will you? Then at least I won't have to get my hands dirty."

Dak-Ho and Zhang walked to the hole, grabbed a spade each and started to fill up the grave with sand. Zhang looked at the dead man. The bound hands gave the body a human touch, yet they were the hands of a traitor who had taken a newspaper with a photo of the Dear Leader Kim Jong-Il on the front page and folded it up. Only sitting on the newspaper could have been worse. Whoever treated the General in such a disrespectful manner deserved nothing better. Hopefully this young man had no children. No one would want to be the child of such a criminal!

Dak-Ho shoveled quickly. He was just as tall as Zhang, but broader and more muscular. Everyone treated Dak-Ho with a lot of respect. Putting him on a pedestal, everyone was happy to do rotten jobs for him. Dak-Ho did not abuse his status. He was always friendly toward his fellow soldiers. Perhaps that was why he had not been promoted. An officer in the army must not be afraid to be hard on his men.

Zhang didn't know what to say to Dak-Ho. In the company of this veteran, Zhang was acutely aware of his inferior status—only a nineteen-year-old boy and from the insignificant village of Unsung. He wanted to break the silence and say something. The situation demanded it. "How often have you already uh . . ."

"Shot someone?" Dak-Ho finished his question. "Let's see now. I'd been in the army three years when I became a member of the firing squad. Then there were two . . . the next year . . ." Dak-Ho counted on this hand; Zhang continued to shovel sand. "Including the deserters? I guess nine. I might have forgotten one or two. Not all of them were as easy as this one, though. Once, I shot somebody who was not bound to a pole. He was a fugitive, sorry, a deserter. Ha, he'd already crossed the border into China. Now that was a fantastic shot. That guy had already crossed the river when we saw him. He zigzagged over the Chinese bank to avoid our shots. The others shot randomly and missed. I aimed quietly and pulled the trigger once. Bang. The bloke fell forward. Dead on the spot. The sergeant went nuts. 'Get him! Get him!' he kept shouting. Of course he was terrified that the Chinese soldiers would find this dead deserter."

"And then?"

"Well, we did not have a boat or anything. Fortunately, it was summertime and hot. So we took off our jackets, boots and socks and swam to the other side. There was a really strong current. Of course that fugitive had thought nobody would check there because the river is so difficult to cross at that point. We just happened to be patrolling that area."

"Was it a soldier?"

"No, a civilian."

"Fool," said Zhang.

"You can say that again," answered Dak-Ho. "Why would you flee? The entire world looks up to North Korea and the virtues of our people. The small army of our Great Leader drove the Japanese back into the sea. And when the Americans attacked us, we pushed them back at a cost of many human lives."

"No one can bear as much suffering as our people."

"Exactly. Why would you want to leave this country? There's food every day. Not only for the rich but for everybody. Everybody has work; everyone has a roof over their heads. Everyone can go to school and soon, once we have won the war against the Americans, it will be even better. Then the world shall pay tribute to us."

Immediately a picture formed in Zhang's mind. World leaders were laying flowers at the statue of Kim Il-Sung in Pyongyang. The last one to come forward was the president of South Korea. Not only did he bow but he fell to his knees and started to cry aloud.

The grave was filled. Zhang stomped down the sand a bit and walked back with Dak-Ho to Bo-Hwa, who was still struggling with his weapon. He threw his rifle to the ground and swore.

"What's wrong?" asked Dak-Ho.

"I just can't get the safety catch on. Won't budge. Useless thing!"

"Let me try," said Zhang, reaching for the weapon.

But Bo-Hwa grew even angrier. He grabbed his rifle, shaking it in the air and cursing.

"Calm down!" Zhang raised his voice.

"Look out, man!" yelled Dak-Ho.

Then a shot rang out, and Zhang felt a flaming pain in his left foot. He slumped to the ground, groaning. "Aaah! I've been hit! Ow! My foot! Idiot!"

Dak-Ho bent over Zhang. "Stay calm! Stay calm!"

"Oh no! Oh, damn it, no!" screamed Bo-Hwa.

"Calm down, Private Lee! Calm down! Take it easy! Call the medic!"

Zhang looked at the hole in his boot that was slowly turning red. It was hard to connect what he was seeing with his pain. Was this really happening? Yet the pain was real.

Dak-Ho pulled Bo-Hwa closer to him until there were just a few centimeters between their faces. "Me-dic," Dak-Ho yelled to Bo-Hwa calmly but loudly.

"Yes, corporal." Bo-Hwa turned around and went to the camp.

Dak-Ho held Zhang. "Stay calm, comrade Zhang. Everything will be okay. Everything will be okay."

Zhang closed his eyes, bit his lip and groaned. This was the end of his career as a soldier. The end of his dream.

✪ ✪ ✪

Hea-Woo leaned over the bed and tried to feed her mother some soup. Mother took a spoonful but coughed and spit it out. She looked apologetically at the smiling Hea-Woo. Zhang was watching out of the corner of his eye. Mother had not been this bad for a long time. At night she coughed so much that she nearly choked. Nobody knew what she had. The doctor no longer even came to visit her.

Finally, when Mother was able to speak again, she said, "You can stop, my dear. I've had enough. Take some yourselves. Zhang, do you want the rest of my soup? You must be hungry."

Zhang shook his head.

"And you, Father?"

"You have it, Hea-Woo," Chin-Cho said, as he put away his newspaper.

Hea-Woo walked from her parents' bedroom to the kitchen to get a clean spoon and then came to sit with her father and brother in the living room.

"Eight o'clock," Father announced, "time for the news. Zhang, can you switch on the TV? Or is that too far to walk on your sore foot?"

"Very funny, Father. You know, the more you say it, the funnier it gets!" He walked over to the TV and switched it on. "Do you want to listen with us, Mother?"

Zhang heard her say something but did not understand it. He looked to his sister. She nodded, so Zhang turned up the volume so Mother would be able to hear the news. It was just beginning.

"Comrades, it is with great sadness . . ."

Zhang leaned forward. Just once in the past had the news started with these words—when the Great Leader died.

" . . . that I must pass on this news to you. The Americans have attacked."

No! Not now! Zhang had just received his compulsory discharge from the army—too wounded to bear weapons again. They no longer needed him.

"Spies have entered our country . . ."

Only spies? Is the invasion coming later? Zhang wondered.

". . . and they have advanced across our rice fields and farmland. Once there, they spread a devastating poison on the crops. Some 85 percent of the harvest has been lost."

Eighty-five percent? How much was that exactly? What did that mean?

Hea-Woo clasped her hand over her mouth and was shaking her head "No, no, no," she whispered.

Father sat emotionless in his chair.

"The Americans shall pay dearly for this treacherous act. Unfortunately, this attack means that as of today no more food can be distributed to the people."

Recently they had received so little food, scarcely half of what they used to have. Was there going to be no more food at all now? Not even maize?

"Our Dear Leader Kim Jong-Il has expressed his confidence in the willpower of the people. He advises all citizens to go and pick grass in the mountains and to make soup from this with salt. This soup contains all the nutrients that a person needs to stay alive."

"Ridiculous!"

Hea-Woo jumped at her father's response.

Father stomped over to the TV and hit the off button. "What utter nonsense!"

"Kim Chin-Cho!" Mother called from the bedroom. "Behave yourself! The neighbors might hear you."

"And so what! It's only a matter of time. Then we'll all be dead anyway! There is no more food. The Great Leader has died and he forgot to tell his son how to grow rice."

"Father!" Zhang said sternly. "You heard it for yourself. The American spies and their poison are to blame. This is how they want to bring us to our knees."

Father sighed deeply and looked sadly at his son. "Do you really believe that? That our 'mighty' army would allow so many spies to get into our country unobstructed? No, son. This has got nothing to do with foreign powers. These are . . . our own mistakes. It is our own fault."

Zhang raised his voice. "And when you say, 'our,' do you mean Kim Jong-Il? He would sacrifice himself to protect us. You're far too shortsighted. People already doubt your loyalty. You'll have to confess one day and then we will all be . . ." He couldn't say what he was thinking: *sent to a camp.* " . . . punished."

"Shh," said Hea-Woo. "Think about Mother. She's so weak now."

Father's eyes focused on Zhang. He looked as if he were going to say something but he kept his mouth shut.

"How much food do we have left?" Mother called from the bedroom.

"Nothing," whispered Hea-Woo.

"Tomorrow I'll go up into the mountains," Zhang offered, "after the session at the research center."

"Fine," said Father. "The walk will do you good." He opened the food cupboard in the living room. There were only empty bottles and glasses and two bottles of soju, a local beer. Father took a bottle and glass and poured himself a drink. He held the glass up to Hea-Woo and Zhang. "To our Dear Leader," he said and gulped it down.

Zhang looked away.

"Aaah, just what I needed," his father sighed.

✪ ✪ ✪

"Kim Zhang!" As Zhang stepped forward, Jin whispered into his ear, "I'll finish you off." Zhang punched Jin on the shoulder and tried not to laugh. The weekly criticism session on a Saturday in the lecture room of the Kim Il-Sung Research Center was not Zhang's favorite activity but it had long ceased to be a cause for concern. Usually he agreed with Jin in advance how they would criticize each other. Today there had been no time for that.

Zhang turned around so that he could face the thirty other young men of his age. The fluorescent lamps were not on today. A little light came in through three windows to Zhang's left. The Party officer who had called Zhang forward had been his teacher at primary school. He was known as Mr. Ahn. As Zhang faced him now, an unpleasant school memory sprang into his mind. Mr. Ahn had screamed at him. "How dare you draw our Great Leader! You little reactionary! For such an offense you could face the firing squad! Even a little monster like you should know that!"

"But . . . but . . . I did it to honor him," Zhang stuttered.

"And you've got the cheek to answer back as well? You're guilty, guilty, comrade Zhang! You should know that only highly talented artists may make an image of the Great Leader, comrade Kim Il-Sung.

Anyone else deserves to be punished!" He grabbed Zhang by his ear and pulled him off his chair. "On your knees!"

Zhang had spent the rest of the afternoon in the middle of the class on his knees. And afterward he had to stay behind for detention. At the top of a white sheet of paper Zhang had written "Letter of Criticism." The longer the letter, the better, so he decided to go into great detail. "On April 6, 1981, at 1:05 p.m., during a history lesson, I found myself guilty of committing a shameful deed. Despite repeated warnings from my respected teacher, comrade Ahn Bong-Chol, I committed the crime of drawing our Great Leader Kim Il-Sung. I was not aware of the consequences of this inappropriate act..."

The following day Zhang and his classmates had to take turns criticising another classmate. Zhang got it from everybody. Only Jin chose another boy as his victim. After school Zhang and Jin sought revenge and fought with the three boys who had expressed the fiercest criticism of Zhang.

"Comrade Zhang?" Mr. Ahn was calling on him, bringing Zhang back to the present. "Go ahead."

Zhang put on his formal voice. "This week I was guilty of insulting comrade Lee Jin. Without a good reason I called him a 'donkey' because of his big ears."

Soft laughing. Mr. Ahn merely nodded. "Anything else?"

"No, comrade."

"I understand. Every week there's something about Lee Jin. Isn't it high time that you two became friends?"

"You're right, comrade. Except he looks a bit too much like a donkey." Again laughter.

"That's enough now. This is a serious meeting." Mr. Ahn turned to his audience. "Who has caught comrade Zhang this week committing an offense or behaving incorrectly?"

Jin put his hand up immediately. "Comrade Zhang called me a donkey."

"Noted. Anybody else?"

Nobody spoke. Zhang took a step forward and sat down.

"Kim Zhang stole my shoes."

Zhang's mouth fell open. *Who said that?*

Mr. Ahn walked quickly to the man who had spoken. "What did you say? Is that really true?"

"It most certainly is, comrade Ahn. I saw him running away on Friday with my shoes in his hand. He even had the nerve to wear them today."

"Comrade Zhang, what do you have to say for yourself? Are you guilty?"

No! Of course I'm not guilty, Zhang was thinking but wouldn't say. *How could I run with my wounded left foot? I may never run again!* Yesterday Zhang had been with his parents all day. Never before had Zhang been so humiliated during a criticism session. He had to defend himself. But how? If he denied it, he would certainly be punished even harder than if he admitted it. "Yes," Zhang whispered.

"What did you say?"

"Yes," Zhang said louder. "I deliberately committed this offense. I intentionally stole the shoes from comrade Kim T'an Gong."

"And what are you going to do to rectify the matter?"

"I shall give his rightful property back to him and I swear I will never succumb to this temptation again . . ."

"This is a serious offense, Kim Zhang," interrupted Mr. Ahn.

"I'm aware of that, comrade. I'm guilty."

"Okay, give the shoes back to him, and I won't report it."

Zhang took off his shoes and walked in stocking feet to T'an Gong, who avoided looking at him. T'an Gong deserved no sympathy, even if somebody could have stolen his only pair of shoes. Zhang held out the shoes to T'an Gong, and just as he was about to take them, Zhang dropped the shoes on the floor. Zhang and T'an Gong knelt down at the same time to pick them up.

"I'll get you back for this," Zhang hissed.

T'an Gong said nothing, sat down, and put on the shoes. They were a size too big.

The cold paving stones annoyed Zhang. It had been a long time since Zhang had walked barefoot in the street, but now he had to. He could not let his socks get ruined.

"It was a mean trick," Jin said, walking beside him, "but we'll have them back by this evening. That much I promise you. Even if we have to break in to get them."

Zhang nodded. *Break in? That was not enough. T'an Gong deserved to be beaten up.*

"Why don't you borrow your father's shoes and then we'll go into the mountains?" Jin continued.

Fifteen minutes later, Zhang and Jin were foraging in the hills. Autumn would soon be upon them but for now the numerous trees still had their leaves and the grass was still green. The sun gave everything a beautiful glow.

Zhang looked at the grass in a way he had never looked at grass before—as food. He and Jin both had a pair of scissors for cutting the grass.

"We'll fill your gunny sack first and then mine, okay?"

"Fine," said Zhang, getting to work. Suddenly he remembered a slogan: *We do what the Party decides.* He said it aloud.

"What did you say?" Jin asked. "You mumbled something."

"We do what the Party decides!" exclaimed Zhang.

"Correct, comrade! We do it! And let us form human bullets and bombs and with no fear of death protect our Dear Leader!"

"We unite our fatherland!"

"One hundred battles, one hundred victories!"

Zhang stood up and clenched his fists. "Every Korean is just as strong as one hundred enemies!"

Jin started to sing. "The bayonet shines, our footsteps echo through the field . . ."

Zhang joined in. "We're soldiers of the Great General! Who can hold us back? We are the army of the comrade Leader!"

"Now let's see what you can do, little soldier!" Jin shouted. He jumped on top of Zhang forcing him down into the long grass.

"Just you wait," Zhang said, pushing Jin off his back. Jin was smaller and quicker yet he was no match for Zhang's strength. For several minutes they rolled through the grass.

"Okay, okay, enough," said Jin. After the struggle, they lay on their backs in the grass, trying to catch their breath.

"I'm glad you're back from the army, Zhang. I've missed this."

"Me too." Zhang fell silent for a moment, then asked, "How was Pyongyang?"

"Oh, Pyongyang," sighed Jin. "Can you remember how often we dreamed about that city? How beautiful it looked on TV? Zhang, Pyongyang is far more beautiful than we ever imagined. Far more beautiful than the TV can possibly show. The monuments, the roads, the parks, the river . . . No city in the world can compare to it. The people have such beautiful clothes there and you see cars every day. And then the metro. That's a sort of train that goes under the ground and takes you really fast from one end of the city to the other. In the metro there's a map on the wall. The dots show the route of the metro. You can press a button for your destination and then you can see the route you have to follow. It even shows you where you have to change trains. The metro stations are just like huge chiseled arched vaults. A moving staircase takes you down to them. You don't even have to walk. At the very bottom on the platform, beautiful sculptures of soldiers have been carved out of the wall. On the other side of the wall, there are enormous paintings of Kim Il-Sung."

"I wish I could live there," said Zhang, "in a beautiful house."

"With a car," Jin added.

"With a car, yes. Shame you had to leave the Kim Il-Sung University."

Jin nodded. "My parents needed me. I couldn't let them down. And you know that if you fail to attend lectures for three months in a row, you get thrown out of the university. What about you, Zhang, what are you going to do now?"

"I'm going to work in the mines. My foot has healed enough. And I'm going to think about other options, because I don't want to live here any longer, Jin. I want to work for the Party. Then I can give my children a better future. Perhaps I can work for the Kukga Bowibu, the Ministry of National Security."

"Keep on dreaming, Zhang. Your grandparents messed up that one for you when they tried to flee with the Americans to the South during the war. Somebody with your family background will never make it far in the Party."

Zhang kept silent. Why of all people had he been shot in the foot? The army was the ultimate chance to work his way up. His best chance of showing the Party what he was capable of. Now if he wanted to make a career, it would be an uphill struggle. Jin was right. His grandfather and grandmother had fled when the Americans entered the country in 1950. They had tried to join up with the occupiers. Zhang was ashamed of his family history and then there was his father, who was no fan of the revolution. Someday his critical remarks could prove fatal for him and might pull the entire family down.

Zhang pictured himself, his father, mother and sister all standing on the platform of Hamhung, each holding a suitcase, waiting for the train that would take them to the re-education camp. That train departed once a week. On various occasions when he was in town with his mother, Zhang had seen it.

"Fools," his mother had said disdainfully. "Hopefully they'll never return."

Zhang shook his head. The shame, the humiliation—if he should ever come to stand there, he would commit suicide immediately.

"Come," Jin was standing up, "we have much more grass to collect."

We do what the Party decides. Zhang followed his friend's example. He breathed in the fresh air and once again began to cut the grass with gusto. *Was this the fate of the North Korean people? Was this the dream that Kim Il-Sung had intended for them?* Zhang closed his eyes and shook his head to rid his mind of the thought.

Jin noticed. "What's up?"

"Nothing."

Two hours later they were approaching the bare, dilapidated houses of Unsung. The sun was low in the sky and threw only a little light on the rectangular buildings, causing all the color slowly to withdraw from the town. In just a few minutes it would be completely dark.

"Wait here a minute," Jin said.

"What are you going to do?"

"Pick up your shoes, fool. Stay here. I'll be back in a moment."

Jin went around the corner, and Zhang followed at a distance. Jin knocked on the door of T'an Gong's house. It was like all the others, painted white with orange roof tiles.

T'an Gong's wife opened the door. Jin said something to her and a few seconds later T'an Gong was also standing in the doorway. He stood head and shoulders above Jin.

Zhang saw T'an Gong make wild gestures, while Jin stood with his arms folded. Suddenly his wife fell to her knees and held her hands up to Jin, who ignored her. T'an Gong disappeared inside and came back with the shoes. He bowed his head and gave them to Jin. Jin did not bow his head as he left. This shocked Zhang, as it was extremely impolite. Then T'an Gong helped his wife up and closed the door.

Triumphantly, Jin walked to Zhang with the shoes. "There you are, comrade. A fresh pair of shoes."

Zhang was flabbergasted. "How on earth did you manage that? What did you say?"

"Ah well . . . you know how convincing I can be!"

✿ ✿ ✿

Carefully Hea-Woo placed four soup bowls on the wooden table. This evening Mother sat with them at the table.

"I don't want to miss this festive meal," she said.

"I did my best," whispered Hea-Woo. "It wasn't easy."

Zhang stared out the window. He should simply have stolen some rice this afternoon—unpatriotic or not. Kim Jong-Il would have forgiven him for trying to give his sister proper food.

"Oh, dear daughter, we have received this meal from our Dear Leader," said Mother. "How could this soup fail to satisfy us now? Come, let us thank him for this meal."

Slowly she stood up and when she began to totter, Father grabbed her elbow just in time to keep her upright. She placed her hand on his shoulder to recover her balance and then stretched out both arms to the portraits of Kim Il-Sung and Kim Jong-Il.

"We thank you, Dear Leader, for this meal and all your good care of us." With Father's help, she sat down again. Her pale face revealed her vulnerability. Only her eyes still emanated some strength. She had such willpower—nothing could destroy this woman, except her illness.

"Enjoy your soup." She looked at Father. "You as well, old grumbler."

The blades of grass lay like motionless worms in the broth. Father was the first to pick up his spoon. He put it into the liquid, took a mouthful, and cursed. "Bah! Disgusting!"

Father pushed back his chair, stood up, and swiped the bowl from the table. Without saying anything, he walked to the food cupboard, poured himself a glass of soju, and downed it in a single gulp. Then he went outside.

"Now, I think it's quite tasty," said Mother, lifting another spoonful to her mouth.

Zhang took a mouthful. *How salty!* Perhaps the second mouthful would taste better. He was mistaken. *So bitter. How long would they have to eat this?*

"Yes, nice," said Hea-Woo. "We can sure keep this up for a while." Hea-Woo was a bad liar.

"What do you think, Zhang?" asked Mother.

His mother was so weak. How long could she tolerate this food? He smiled.

"Fantastic. It simply tastes nutritious."

Mother had finished her soup. "Can you help me back to bed?"

Zhang and Hea-Woo supported her. Suddenly their mother started to vomit. All the soup came up and she began to cry.

"It's okay, Mother, " Hea-Woo said. "We all have to get used to it."

Zhang clenched his fists and tensed his arms until they hurt. He had to remain calm and not show how angry he was. Why was this happening to them?

CHAPTER 2

What are we going to do now, Zhang? With Mother? She can't keep going much longer. She's so weak." Hea-Woo paused and looked at her brother. In the light of the setting autumn sun, she looked so beautiful, even though she had lost a lot of weight due to the lack of food. Zhang hoped that she would soon find a good husband and that later they would all live in the same town. Perhaps even in Pyongyang. And if that were not possible, he would at least visit her regularly and bring her goods from Pyongyang. She deserved the absolute best.

"Everything will be okay," Zhang answered. "Let's hurry. It's almost dark." He wanted to say more but he could not find the words. They continued their walk and Hea-Woo continued to talk about Mother, so Zhang remained silent.

Zhang was proud of his sister. Due to her resolute attitude, her eloquence and her ability to memorize long pieces of text from the leaders without any apparent difficulty, she had been elected as the leader of the class each year. That was most unusual for somebody with their family background. Now she taught nursery school children. More than anything else Zhang admired Hea-Woo for her boundless trust in the leaders. Since the harvest had failed, she had not complained once. Zhang had, although not aloud.

He wanted nobody to know that increasingly he asked himself

where it had all gone wrong. *Kim Jong-Il was blameless. The famine was the fault of the ministers and commanders. They should have prevented these spies from destroying the harvests. If that had not happened, they could give Mother a bit of rice occasionally, then her health would certainly be a bit better than it is now.*

"Are you listening, Zhang?" Hea-Woo poked his ribs, smiling at her brother.

"Yes, sorry. We must wait and see how things go with Mother."

"Not only with Mother."

"What do you mean?"

"There are three children in my class that I haven't seen for two weeks now."

"Are they ill?"

"They've gone. Looking for food, I think. They're not even in Unsung."

"And their parents?"

Hea-Woo swallowed. "One child has lost both parents. His sister has to take care of him and the other children."

"How old is she?"

"I think about thirteen or fourteen."

"Perhaps they've gone to see family."

"Perhaps."

"And the parents of the other two children?"

"I don't know. Perhaps those children are dead." Hea-Woo began to sob softly. Zhang put his arm around her shoulders.

"Shh. Don't cry. Everything will be fine. Everything turns out okay in the end. The Great Leader cares for us from heaven."

"I know," said Hea-Woo. She wiped away her tears. "I know he watches over us. I wish that Father would be more positive. That would help Mother."

Zhang agreed. Father and he were rarely on the same wavelength. Sometimes it seemed that they lived in completely different worlds, each with his own culture, language and view on things. Mother was completely different. She understood that Zhang could not stay in Unsung. "You are predestined to do great things for the General," she used to say.

The sun had almost set. "Shall we see who reaches the bottom first?" Hea-Woo challenged.

"Joker!" He could take this sort of joke from her. They had walked so often through these hills in the past, played tricks on each other and held deep conversations. Hea-Woo had happily dreamed with Zhang about his aspirations to be a professional soldier or a secret agent or a high-ranking member of the Party. Sometimes they talked about their parents, but more often about friends and about who liked whom in the village. They chose potential marriage partners for each other, which caused them to burst into shrieks of laughter.

Zhang wanted to make another cheerful comment or tell a joke so that his sister would laugh now, but nothing came to mind.

"The restaurant in town has closed," he said instead.

"Oh?"

"Yep. Closed for good."

Hea-Woo stared at her shoes, and Zhang realized he shouldn't have brought up the restaurant. It was not the way to cheer up his sister!

"A sort of magician lives a few villages away, I've heard," Hea-Woo said suddenly. "Apparently he sometimes comes to people's homes and heals them—with payment of course. Perhaps we should try to track him down. Perhaps he can help Mother."

"We'll certainly look into that," Zhang said, trying to sound optimistic but he knew there was no such thing as supernatural healing. "Anyway, the famine won't last much longer," Zhang added. "Next year everything will be better. Kim Jong-Il has promised that himself. Nothing will happen to us. And certainly not to you, Hea-Woo. I'll make sure of that."

Hea-Woo smiled and they walked into the village arm in arm.

"Zhang?"

"Hmm?"

"Look there." Hea-Woo pointed to a house a hundred meters away that was situated slightly higher than the other houses. Dozens of people had gathered in front of the door.

"That's Jin's house!" Zhang said as he began running, ignoring the pain in his foot. Hea-Woo followed a little way behind.

"What's going on?" Zhang yelled to the group of people. At the same moment there was a crash of glass as a stone hit the window of Jin's house. "Hey!" screamed Zhang. "Stop!"

An elderly man with a stone in his hands looked at Zhang. "Stop? Are you one of them, then? Do you also feed your pigs while we've got nothing?" The man spat in the direction of Zhang's feet and threw the stone against another window. The glass cracked. Zhang grabbed the man by the neck and squeezed hard and was ready to hit him. The man held his hands in front of his terrified eyes. "We're all hungry," Zhang said through clenched teeth.

Then Hea-Woo was beside him, grabbing his wrist with both hands. "Stop, brother! You'll only make matters worse."

Slowly Zhang released his grip on the old man, and Hea-Woo pulled him away from the crowd. Then a shower of stones hit the house.

"The car!" somebody shouted. Five men walked around the house to the black Mercedes, the only car in the village, and started to kick it. Others threw stones at it.

"There!" Zhang recognized Jin's voice and saw him come around the corner with five armed soldiers.

"Stop!" shouted one of the soldiers. He fired into the air. The people fled immediately in all directions.

Hea-Woo pulled Zhang's arm. "We must leave as well. Quick! Let's go," she pleaded. But Zhang pulled Hea-Woo toward him.

"Take it easy. It's Jin. My best friend, remember?"

"Go after them!" Jin was shouting to the soldiers.

"That's pointless, Mr. Lee. It's too dark already. But if you recognized anybody, we can always arrest them tomorrow and set an example. We do not tolerate this type of behavior."

Jin caught sight of Zhang and called to him, "Zhang, Hea-Woo, did you see it? This commotion in front of our house?"

Zhang nodded. "We were just walking past."

"Did you recognize anybody?"

Zhang knew who the old man was whom he had almost hit. He lived one street away.

Hea-Woo was pulling on his arm. "I have . . ."

"Sorry, I did not see anybody," Zhang answered Jin. "It was too dark. What about you Hea-Woo?"

"No, me neither."

Just then the door to Jin's house opened. His father, Lee Young-Nam, walked out, moving pompously as he always did. He looked as if he were searching for a dog to kick. A feeling of awe overwhelmed Zhang. Or was it fear?

Mr. Lee looked around and assessed the damage without a single trace of emotion. With a slight movement of his hand, he signaled to Jin that they all, including the soldiers, should come. Zhang knew that people came to Mr. Lee and not the other way around.

"Gentlemen." He looked at Hea-Woo but did not greet her.

"Hello, Mr. Lee," the soldiers greeted him.

"Jin, how come you were not back earlier?" Mr. Lee looked sternly at his son.

Jin stared at the ground. "No excuse, Mr. Lee."

"How many people did you recognize?"

"It was dark . . ."

"Of course, of course, that was obvious." Jin winced. Each word seemed to hit him like a bullet.

"Kim Zhang, my lad, you've got eyes like a hawk. Have you seen these rebels. I'll pay you handsomely for each name you can give me."

"I'm sorry, Mr. Lee. We were standing too far away."

"Never mind, never mind." He rolled his cigar to the left corner of his mouth. "Half of the village was involved. They must all be strung up. And that will happen. That will definitely happen. My men will take care of it. Jin, fix the windows. I don't want your mother catching a cold. It's going to be a cold night." He grinned as he spoke, then said, "Gentlemen, can I interest you in a glass of soju?"

This caused the soldiers to smile. "Certainly, Mr. Lee," they said and followed him inside.

Jin, Zhang, and Hea-Woo didn't join them.

"Jin, what happened?" asked Zhang as soon as the others were inside.

"It's my fault," Jin answered. He was walking to the shed to get the tools and wood he would need to cover up the broken window.

"What? How can this be your fault?" asked Hea-Woo.

Jin didn't answer right away. He started to hammer a plank over the window. "I was careless. Each day we have a small bit of food left from our evening meal and we give that to the pigs. They have to eat too, don't they? Usually I give it to them when it is dark but yesterday I forgot to feed them. I didn't want my father to find out and so I did it quickly this morning. Somebody saw me and got upset and told everyone what he saw."

"I'm surprised your father wasn't angrier. He seemed much calmer than I would have expected," Hea-Woo said.

Jin went for a second plank. When he got back, he said, "Take my word for it, he's furious. And he holds me responsible. He'll make that clear to me. But shouldn't you guys be getting home? It's almost dark."

"Yes, we ought to go," Zhang said and taking Hea-Woo's arm, they walked away.

✪ ✪ ✪

The next day two families had disappeared. Nobody talked about it but everybody knew where they were. "Prison camp," Mother said to her family who were all sitting on the edge of her bed.

Now her coughing spasms were hard and long. Hea-Woo placed a damp cloth on her forehead.

"That's life," Mother said. Then she closed her eyes and never opened them again.

✪ ✪ ✪

The extended family came and Mother was buried in the hills. Immediately after the ceremony, the family left. Zhang, Father and Hea-Woo followed the others at some distance. They walked silently hand in hand down the hill. "Mother's battle has come to an end. Now ours has started," said Father suddenly.

"What do you mean, Father?" asked Hea-Woo.

"Come with me." Father pulled them deeper into the woods, out of sight of all the others. He sat down, and Zhang and Hea-Woo followed his example.

"When did we last get food from the state?" Father asked.

"Oh, Father, do we have to talk about this now?" Zhang asked. "We've only just buried Mother."

"How long ago, Zhang?" Father persisted.

Zhang sighed. "About six months."

"And who is responsible for the supply of food? Who should be giving us food?"

"The state," said Hea-Woo softly. "What are you driving at?"

Father tried to smile. "China."

The word hung in the air. Then Zhang's mouth dropped open. "You're mad . . . To China? That's completely illegal! Do you want all of us to end up in the work camp?"

"They'll shoot us dead!" Hea-Woo added.

"Calm down! Calm down! Listen. Your mother would never have survived such a journey. We, however, can make it. At least now while we're still strong enough. A friend of mine travels between China and our country. He says that in China there is more food than the people can eat. He says that there are people who want to do a deal with us. Others are even willing to take you into their homes and care for you. We can work in the mines or in a factory. The conditions there are far better than here."

"But how are you going to get there?" asked Hea-Woo. "You'll never get a permit to go to China. You won't even get an exit visa to leave our district."

"We'll walk along the railway track. That's where they patrol the least. Once in a while we'll hitch a lift on the train. Then we'll go to the Tumen River, where we shall meet my friend. He knows where and how we can cross. I have put money aside. We can bribe the border guards. My friend knows some safe addresses in China. He is our only chance of survival."

"Lies," Zhang said, breathing heavily. "Lies from old fools."

"Kim Zhang!" His father's voice was stern. "Now you are going too far! How dare you speak to me like that?"

Zhang stood up and lifted his fist threateningly. "No, you're the one who's going too far! Either you're desperate or you have drunk too much soju! Don't think that you can drag us with you in your downfall. I won't allow that."

"Zhang, calm down!" Hea-Woo grabbed his arm, trying to pacify him. "They'll hear you if you carry on like that."

Zhang sat down next to his sister and looked her in the eye. "Hea-Woo, don't you understand? Mother has only just died and Father wants to run away like a scared rabbit. We'll all be sent to the work camp if he gets his way. And even if they only punish him, we will be marked for life. Everyone will view us as the children of a traitor."

"Zhang," his father's voice was calmer now, "don't you ever doubt what we're being told?"

Of course, but nobody is allowed to know that. Zhang could not help this thought passing through his brain but then he spoke quickly, "No, Father, no. Don't try to talk your way out of this." Zhang stood up. He had to get away from this conversation, because the thoughts he was having frightened him. He ran from them, thinking of only one thing—he had to stop his father.

"Zhang, wait!" Hea-Woo ran after her brother.

Her father reached out for her, calling, "Hea-Woo! Wait! Dear daughter, don't do it!"

Zhang stopped and turned toward his sister. He wanted to say, *Come, Hea-Woo. Don't let yourself be fooled. Come with me.* But Hea-Woo turned back and stood with Father. Zhang began running again. He had to hurry. If he could warn the police quickly enough, it might still be possible to save Hea-Woo. Father was already beyond redemption. Zhang quickened his pace.

A few minutes later Zhang reached the first houses in the village. Tired, he leaned against a fence. His left foot throbbed with pain. *China was madness. Didn't everybody know that the country was inferior to the People's Democratic Republic of Korea? Could there really be more food there? Probably not. That could not be true. Food or no food, a patriot did not desert his post. If Father did this, it would permanently wreck Zhang's future. Perhaps all three of them would end up in front of the firing squad. He could not allow that to happen. He had to go to the military post in the village and report Father. He had to save Hea-Woo.*

Zhang took a deep breath and ran around the corner. Suddenly he hit the ground and it took a moment to realize what had happened. A tiny stream of warm blood trickled over his cheek. As he looked around, everything seemed hazy.

Then he felt a thump on his side. "Get off me; get off me!"

Zhang rolled over and saw something—or someone—where he had been lying. Squinting and gradually regaining his focus, he was able to make out a frightened boy there on the ground with him. He had never seen the boy before. "Are you hurt?" he asked.

The boy shook his head. He quickly stood up and braced himself against the wall with his hands in front of his face, as if he expected to be hit at any moment.

"I won't harm you." Zhang said. He pushed the palm of his hand against his forehead, trying to stop the bleeding. "Who are you?"

No answer.

"What's your name?" Zhang asked impatiently.

"Hyok."

"Where do you come from?"

"I don't know."

"What do you mean, 'I don't know'? How can you not know where you live?"

"I don't live anywhere. I didn't want to hurt you. Sorry."

"It's not your fault. Where are your parents, Hyok?"

"I don't know."

Zhang sighed. "This isn't getting us anywhere and I'm in a hurry. I need to go." He tried to walk away but his foot hurt too much. It was throbbing with pain and his knees seemed to have locked. He couldn't move.

"Sir?"

Zhang turned in response to the boy's small voice. A tear left a dark trace on Hyok's dirty face, and his eyes matched the pleading in his words. "Have you got anything to eat?"

Zhang wanted to say, *I don't have the time for this,* but instead he asked, "Why don't you go to your parents?"

"They've gone."

"When did they go?"

"Two winters ago."

"But why? What happened?"

"I don't know. I was at school and when I came home, they'd gone. Only the mayor was there."

"The mayor?"

"Yes. He said that my parents had been taken away, because they read from a black book."

"A black book?"

"Yes, with a cross on it."

Missionaries. Zhang began to understand. *This boy must be the son of missionaries.* Immediately a story Zhang had often heard at school came to his mind. In the 1940s a group of children had stolen fruit from a vineyard. The owners were missionaries. They grabbed the children and wrote "thief" on their foreheads with some sort of poison. No wonder that Kim Il-Sung had done everything possible to round up this sect. Zhang hadn't realized there were still missionaries in North Korea.

Zhang focused again on the boy. "What did the mayor say to you then?"

"He thanked me."

"For what?"

"Because I had told about the black book at school."

"And then?"

"Then he said I had to go away and that I should never come back. My parents were antisocialist and therefore I am as well."

Zhang knew he should be moving on, that he couldn't lose any more time, but he had to respond to this young boy. "You're certainly not antisocialist. You are a brave soldier."

"No," Hyok said, "I betrayed my parents. I'm a coward. Everybody who betrays his parents is antisocialist."

Zhang felt a deep stabbing pain—not in his head, not in his knees, not in his foot, but in his soul. He sank to his knees, tears filling his eyes. *What am I doing? I almost reported my own father! I have to go home. Immediately!* He wasn't sure what to do. Letting Father and Hea-Woo go was not an option. He had to go home and try to talk his father out of it. And if he couldn't do it, Hea-Woo could. He had to hurry and try to prevent them from leaving before it was too late.

He stood up and his gaze fell on Hyok. He couldn't just leave him here to starve. "Come with me," he said, motioning to Hyok to follow him. The boy hesitated. "Come. I've got food."

They walked along quickly together. Zhang looked down at the boy. "Did you get hurt when I ran into you?"

"No."

"Ah, tough lad, eh? It hurt me. How old are you, Hyok?"

"Almost eleven."

When they reached Zhang's house, it was quiet. No one was there. Zhang didn't let himself think about where his father and sister might be. He forced himself to think about Hyok and his empty stomach. The family had had a bit of maize to eat and there was still a handful left. Zhang's stomach was aching with hunger but he gave the maize to Hyok. The boy grabbed the bowl and stuffed the maize into his mouth with both hands.

When he was finished, he said to Zhang, "Sorry!"

"Never mind. My sister saved it for you."

"Your sister?"

"Yes, Hea-Woo. She's a schoolteacher. You'll really like her. I think she's coming home soon. Go and sit down on the couch."

Father and Hea-Woo did not come home that evening. While Hyok lay asleep on the couch, Zhang sat in his chair staring at the front door all night, hoping for a miracle. In the food cupboard he found a quarter liter of soju. It was enough to warm him up inside for a few seconds but not enough to numb his guilt. With each tick of the clock, he knew that the distance between him and his family became greater.

✪ ✪ ✪

The sound of the front door opening woke him up. He jumped from the chair where he had fallen asleep, expecting to see Hea-Woo and his father, but it was Hyok's back that he saw.

"Where are you going, kid?" Zhang tried to walk to him, but his foot and his right knee were hurting, slowing him down.

"I didn't want to wake you up," Hyok said.

"But where were you going to go?"

"I don't know."

"If you don't know, then you might as well stay here. It's cold outside."

Hyok looked at Zhang with wide eyes, "Can I?"

Zhang nodded and Hyok came back into the living room and then asked hesitantly, "Have you got anything else to eat?"

"No, sorry. You'll have to wait for a day. Or we'll have to go and look for plants outside Unsung."

"What is Unsung?"

"Our village, of course!"

"Oh. Are there rats here as well?"

"Sure. Of course!"

"We can also eat a rat," Hyok offered.

"Eat rat? Is that possible? And do you know how to catch one?"

Hyok felt around in his coat pocket and finally produced a small steel hook on the end of a piece of string. "With this. I learned it from my father."

Zhang had eaten everything the past six months—grass soup, bark porridge, locusts, dragonflies, worms, and a variety of insects. Together with Jin, he had even stolen a chicken from another village. Catching a rat was something new.

"Perhaps we'll find a rat with rice in its burrow."

"Pardon?"

"Clever rats collect grains of rice and store them."

"Oh, okay, perhaps we'll be lucky!" Zhang tried not to betray his astonishment at Hyok's knowledge. "Now, comrade Hyok, let me see your trick."

"Are your parents coming home today?"

"Uh . . . I don't know, Hyok."

"I hope not. Then we won't have to share. Do you have a spade?"

They went up into the hills in silence, the little man in front. Now Zhang knew that Father and Hea-Woo must have left for China immediately. Zhang had searched through the house last night and had become even more confused as a result. It appeared that Father had organized the escape in advance. Two sets of clothing were gone from his closet and from Hea-Woo's. All Zhang's clothes were still there.

Zhang found Father's gold watch on Zhang's bedside table. That was Father's treasured possession. A relative had given it to him years ago and he had worn it ever since. It was his most valuable material possession. *How could he have left without that watch?*

"Good morning, comrade Zhang!"

Zhang was startled out of his thoughts as Mr. Ahn approached, calling to him. Ahn was not tall but he was broad. Previously he had even had a small pot belly. For as long as Zhang could remember, Ahn always had a walking stick with him. He could turn his hand to anything—Party official, schoolteacher and chair of Zhang's neighborhood unit. "Never say anything to Mr. Ahn," Father always said.

"You can't trust him."

I didn't clean the portraits this morning, Zhang realized all of a sudden. *And I didn't bow. Has Ahn seen something?*

"How do you do?" Zhang responded.

As soon as Hyok had heard Mr. Ahn's voice, he had stopped and moved back a few steps to stand directly behind Zhang, as if hiding behind his big brother.

"Very well, thank you," Mr. Ahn was saying. "My condolences on the loss of your mother, Zhang. Unfortunately, I could not attend the funeral due to Party commitments."

"Thank you."

"I've heard that your father and sister did not come home last night. Nothing serious I hope."

"Thank you for your concern, but indeed nothing serious has happened. Father and Hea-Woo are accompanying my grandmother on her journey home. She is most distraught following the death of my mother."

"Quite understandable. Coming to terms with the death of a child is not easy. Yet regrettably I fear we will see more deaths in the near future. Those devilish Americans . . . Ah well, I'm glad to hear that everything is okay with your father and sister, at least as good as one could expect under the circumstances." Then leaning to one side to get a look at Hyok, Ahn asked, "And who is this little lad?"

"Kim Hyok," answered Zhang, "a nephew. He is staying with us for a few days."

"Pleased to meet you," said Ahn. "I hope that you enjoy your time here."

Hyok stayed where he was behind Zhang's back and said nothing.

"Fine then. I wish you a pleasant day."

"You as well. Good-bye."

Ahn walked a few steps away and then turned and said, "Zhang, keep an eye on your father. Make sure he does nothing stupid. We all know how impulsive he is."

Zhang raised his hand in reply, and Ahn walked back toward the village.

As Zhang watched him go, he thought, *Ahn probably knows Father better than anybody else…Father Kim Il-Sung, please let my father and Hea-Woo come to their senses. Please let them turn back before it is too late.*

✪ ✪ ✪

For a half hour, Hyok had been searching the ground without saying a word. Zhang was becoming impatient. "What are you looking for?" he asked.

"Shh," Hyok whispered. "Look. There's straw. They put that in front of their burrows."

"And now?"

"Fire."

"Fire?"

"Shh. Just watch."

Hyok gathered a few sticks, placed them in a pile in front of the entrance to the burrow, and started to skillfully twist a somewhat bigger stick between his two hands. After a few minutes, a small flame appeared. The smoke drifted upwards.

"Blow the smoke into the hole," said Hyok.

"Yes, comrade boss."

Zhang squatted down, took a deep breath, and blew several times. Hyok moved to the side of the entrance. Suddenly the rat jumped out as if he wanted to grasp Zhang by the throat. Zhang fell backwards in the grass.

The rat was squealing. Hyok had literally hooked it. The animal thrashed about.

Zhang took a deep breath. His legs felt weak from the shock. "Finish off that rotten animal," he growled.

"Not yet. First, open up his burrow."

Zhang could hardly believe what he was hearing and was about to protest but then decided to do what Hyok said. He began to dig but couldn't help asking, "Why am I doing this?"

"You'll see."

After a few minutes of digging in the hard soil, he reached the end of the underground network. "Look there," said Zhang, "a storage room." He bent closer for a better look at the rat's booty. Under a layer of dead leaves were grains of wheat, maize and rice.

"How much is there?" asked Hyok.

"A handful. Half each?"

Zhang carefully plucked the grains and half grains from under the leaves, not missing a single one, and divided the plunder into almost equal-sized portions, taking the larger pile for himself and handing the other to Hyok. They ground the grains between their teeth and then Zhang asked, "And now how do we prepare that rat?"

"Not yet." Hyok took a long, thin piece of string from his coat pocket and tied this around the neck of the rat, which was still thrashing about with pain. Zhang wondered what else this lad kept in his pockets.

"He has another hiding place."

Hyok let go of the rat, which ran for his freedom. It was not difficult to keep up with the wounded rat. He crept into another burrow. Hyok pulled him back out immediately and said to Zhang, "Finish him off now. He has not got long to live anyway."

Zhang hit the rat on its head three times with the spade, until it lay motionless. Then he dug open another underground system. Again they found a bit of food, but less than in the first tunnel.

"Shame," said Zhang.

Hyok shrugged his shoulders. "Food is food." He pulled an old knife out of his coat pocket and skinned the rat. Zhang looked for a stick for a spit, and then while Hyok threaded the rat on the spit and grilled it, Zhang lay stretched out in the grass.

The hunger overwhelmed Zhang. He felt like a wild animal. The handful of food that he had just eaten only aroused his hunger. The smell of the meat on the spit made his mouth water.

He pictured himself sitting at the table with his parents and Hea-Woo. *When Mother took the lid off the pan, he saw large pieces of meat in it—rabbit, chicken, pork. With his chopsticks he quickly put some meat in his bowl already full of rice. He started to eat.*

Zhang shook his head to get rid of the thought and sat up. The outside of the rat was getting quite black. The rat was not ready to eat by far, but just the smell gave Zhang stomach cramps. He could not bear this. He had to get away.

Yet what if Hyok made off with the rat? He couldn't let that happen. He had to wait until the rat was ready. He had to. He had to. Zhang stood up. His stomach felt as if something were eating him up from the inside. Nervously he began walking from tree to tree.

"That will only make you more hungry," said Hyok.

He was right. Zhang sat down on a rock and stared at the ground. *Then he heard his father's voice:* "A friend of mine travels between our country and China. He says that in China there is more food than people can eat." *No. What Father said could not be true. That was a lie. Treachery. Whoever left his country, deserted Kim Jong-Il. Surely Kim Jong-Il knew what hunger was. Of course. He would do everything for his people. When he was young, he had received a brand new pair of boots, but his friends were walking on bare feet. He had taken his boots back to his mother, because the young Kim Jong-Il wanted to be like his comrades.*

But Kim Jong-Il was the leader. He would be taken care of. Perhaps nobody told him about how much his subjects were suffering. If only I could go to Pyongyang and inform the Dear Leader in person about just how bad the situation is. Kim Jong-Il would travel to Unsung and say what has to be done. Who knows, he might even offer a true patriot like me a job in Pyongyang.

It would never happen. Without the right papers Zhang could not get anywhere near Pyongyang, and the chance of his obtaining such permits was zero. His family was too unimportant. And now Father was on his way to China with Hea-Woo. *How far away would they be? They had only been gone for a day. They must still be in the area. Perhaps I should go after them. But then what about Kim Jong-Il? Would the Great Leader understand that I had to break the law to prevent my father and sister from making a big mistake? Mr. Ahn had probably figured out that they were fleeing. How long would it be before he informed the local party of the disappearance? And what will happen to me then?* He looked over at Hyok whose eyes were on the roasting rat. *And what about young Hyok? What will happen to him? The orphanage? Nobody survived long in the orphanages.*

"It's ready!" said Hyok triumphantly.

"At last!" said Zhang.

Hyok took the spit from the fire and scraped the black crust from the meat. After that, with some difficulty, he cut the meat into pieces with his blunt knife and gave half to Zhang. The meat was too hot to hold with bare hands. Zhang used the outside of his sleeves so that he could take a bite straight away. He burned his tongue and the roof of his mouth, but the feeling of food moving slowly down his throat and into his stomach was fantastic. At last his stomach was satisfied, even though the amount of hot meat he had eaten so quickly made it hurt a bit.

In a few minutes, with the meat consumed, they lay next to each other in the grass and stared at the sky. Zhang felt tired and full. If only he could keep this satisfied feeling forever. If only he could share it with Hea-Woo. Then he realized he must make a difficult decision.

"We're going to China soon," said Zhang.

"What's China?"

"A country on the other side of the river."

"Is it far?"

"Yes, it's pretty far."

"Okay."

✪ ✪ ✪

With a thud Zhang dropped the stolen fruit on the table in his living room. *I can't believe I have stolen from the state! Going in the middle of the night to steal apples from a state owned farm! I never imagined I would do something like this.* Zhang's thoughts were suddenly interrupted, "May I have an apple?" asked Hyok, looking hopefully at Zhang and Jin.

"Just one. We need to sell the rest of the fruit. Then perhaps we can buy some bread on the black market."

Zhang offered Jin an apple, but he shook his head. "We'll sell that apple. I'd rather have bread."

Hyok had already finished the apple. "I'm going to bed," he said, as he headed into Hea-Woo's bedroom, closing the door behind him.

Outside it was starting to get light. They had gotten home just in time.

"Want a glass of soju?" asked Jin.

"Sure." Zhang lit a candle and placed the glasses on the table.

"My father's got plenty of it!" Jin poured a drink and lifted up his glass. "To the future!"

Zhang smiled and raised his glass as well.

They sat in silence for a while. Then Zhang looked at his friend and asked, "Jin, I can trust you, can't I?"

Jin looked up in surprise. "Of course! You're my best friend. Have I ever let you down?"

"My father has fled," Zhang said quickly and then watched for Jin's reaction.

Jin stared at the empty glass in his hands. Finally he said, "I know."

"How do you know?"

"Mr. Ahn visited my father this afternoon. I heard them talking."

"What did they say?" Zhang felt his stomach tightening.

"That your father and sister were away visiting family . . . but I knew they must have left."

"Do you think your father knows?"

"My father's not stupid." Jin reached for more soju.

Zhang shook his head. "What now?"

Jin raised one eyebrow and looked at Zhang. "What do you mean, 'What now?' They've gone. Final. I don't really know how to say this, Zhang . . ."

"Say what you've got to say." Zhang looked intently at his friend.

"If they escape, you'll never see them again. And if they get arrested, you won't see them either. You have no choice. You must simply forget about them and carry on with your life, however hard that might sound."

"How on earth can I do that?" Zhang raised his voice. "It's my family you know!"

"Calm down. It's not my fault. Listen, I'm your friend. We're on the same side. I'm your family."

Zhang walked to the window and gazed at the empty street outside his door. Finally he said, "I can't stay here. They'll come and get me, simply a matter of time."

Jin shook his head. "I don't believe that. My father knows you're a good guy. I wish he thought about me the same way he thinks about you. He'll make sure that the secret service doesn't pick you up just because your father left. The camp is only for people who really need to be reeducated."

"I already made up my mind yesterday, Jin. I'm going to China."

"What?" Jin jumped up from the chair where he was sitting and rushed toward Zhang, waving his arms in the air. "Are you out of your mind! Don't be so stupid. How desperate are you to die?"

"It's only for a while. I'll come back as quickly as possible."

Jin was shaking his head. "Think about it, man. You've no money and no permit to travel."

Zhang looked down at his father's gold watch on the table. "I've got this," he said, picking up the watch. Then he leaned toward Jin, looking him in the eye. "Are you really my friend?"

"You know I am."

"Will you go with me then?"

"My father would kill me."

Zhang nodded and then asked, "Are you going to report me?"

Jin put his hand over his heart. "No!"

"You won't say anything to your father?"

Jin looked down at the floor. "I could get a lot of hassle about this."

"I know."

Putting his hand on Zhang's shoulder and looking him in the eye again, Jin said, "I'll keep my mouth shut." He looked away again and then asked, "When are you going?"

Zhang didn't hesitate to tell his friend his plans. "The day after tomorrow at sunrise."

Hugging Zhang and patting him on his back, Jin said, "Be careful, comrade."

"Are you going home already?"

"Yes, Jin nodded, "you've given me a lot to think about."

Then as he was about to leave, Jin turned back and said to Zhang, "I hope you will change your mind."

The stolen fruit had not sold for much on the market, just enough for two loaves of bread, which he and Hyok would finish this morning. Zhang had hoped he would make enough money to buy maize for their journey. He hurried home, staving off the temptation to eat both loaves on the way.

"Good morning, Zhang! Have your father and sister returned yet?"

Zhang recognized the voice and hid the bread in his jacket. "Morning, Mr. Ahn. I expect them in three days time."

Ahn looked as if he wanted to ask another question, but Zhang walked along quickly. He spent the rest of the day trying to think how they could best escape. As soon as it was twilight, they had to walk to Hamhung. With a bit of luck there would be a train that would leave the town tomorrow. If that were not the case, they would walk farther. The chance that Zhang's disappearance would be noticed quickly in Unsung was considerable. They had to get out of the district as quickly as possible.

And then the real adventure would begin. If they were asked for their papers and travel documents at a control post, they would be exposed straightaway. Hyok would be sent to the orphanage and Zhang would be sentenced to hard labor. He had no illusions about that. He remembered his father's plan—walk along the railway track and whenever possible hitch a ride on the train, if necessary on the roof, even though he was not certain if Hyok could do that. They would try to do what his father had suggested.

The commentator on the radio announced that the new slogan for North Korea was: "Today we do not live for today. Today we live for tomorrow." Zhang thought about the meaning of the slogan. *When would it be tomorrow in North Korea? Would it already have been tomorrow if Kim Il-Sung had not died? A pointless question*, he decided.

A useful question would be how he could discover where Father and Hea-Woo were. Perhaps China was just as big as North Korea. They did not have any family living in that country, so that was not a lead. However, he knew there were many ethnic Koreans living in Northeast China. Zhang would have to ask around in their villages and towns and hope that he found them.

After finding his father and sister, the next step would probably be even more difficult still. He would have to convince them to return with him to North Korea. Even if there were more food in China, it was better to live under the leadership of Kim Jong-Il, their only hope. Zhang began to think about what life would be like if Kim Jong-Il were no longer alive. The factories would no longer receive any direction, the agricultural companies would not survive without his instructions and they could certainly not win the imminent war with America without his strategic insight.

In the evening, Zhang became aware that he was doing everything in the house for the last time before what he assumed would be a long absence. He cleaned the portraits of Kim Il-Sung and Kim Jong-Il for the last time, he folded his clothes for the last time and he washed himself in the small bathroom for the last time.

The silence in the house troubled him. Never before had he felt so lonely. Mother was dead. Father and Hea-Woo could already be in China—or perhaps they had been arrested. He switched on the TV and turned up the volume.

Zhang went through all of the cupboards and drawers to see what he could take with him. They should not give the impression that they were traveling. Taking a bag with extra clothes was a stupid idea. Perhaps he could wear an extra pair of underpants and a shirt.

On his mother's bedside table was a sketched drawing of the family that Hea-Woo had done two years ago. He took the drawing from the frame and gently rubbed the four faces with his thumb, lingering on Hea-Woo's face. Zhang folded the paper in half and put it in his trouser pocket. What a pity they had never been able to have a photo taken of the four of them. It was just too expensive. Now it was too late.

Hyok had come into the living room when he heard the TV. Now he sat watching a film about Kim Jong-Il. Zhang flopped down next to him and they watched the images in silence. A woman in her early twenties was clearly distressed by something that had happened.

"Don't worry about us, sister," said her little brother, who looked about Hyok's age. "Our father cares for us."

The woman sighed, and all of the actors looked at the portrait of Kim Jong-Il. The camera zoomed in quickly and a golden glow enveloped the head of the broadly smiling leader. The woman threw an arm around the two younger children. A moving piece of music started to play. Together the actors fell to their knees in front of the portrait. One of the children picked up an accordion and they sang:

We open our hearts, without reserve, full of hope.
We live trusting in the General as our god,
Only in our General for always.

The music became livelier; a choir joined in the singing. Now on the screen there was a large group of people running with torches and a large campfire.

Our entire nation trusts in him.
The whole world depends on him.
We live trusting in the General as our god,
Only in our General for always.

Poof. The TV and light went out. The power had gone off.
"Bedtime, says the General," Hyok said grinning.
Zhang laughed. "Where did you get that from?"
"That's what my father used to say."
"Okay then, let's do what the General said. We've got tough days ahead of us."

✿ ✿ ✿

The alarm went off at five o'clock. Zhang woke up Hyok. They got dressed and a few minutes later they were ready to go. But first Zhang took leave of all of the rooms. *Bye bed. Bye table. Bye cupboard. Bye book. Bye TV. Bye radio. Farewell home.*

He looked up at the images of Kim Il-Sung and Kim Jong-Il. He bowed. *Father Kim Il-Sung, please may I see Father and Hea-Woo again? I'm sorry that they could not say farewell to our home.* Should Zhang see his sister again, he would give her the drawing of the family. He solemnly promised that.

"Come," he said to Hyok. He opened the front door but then immediately closed it again. Hyok bumped into him.

"What's up?" asked Hyok.

"Shh. Mr. Ahn and Mr. Lee are standing outside on the street."

"Who?"

Zhang signaled that Hyok must be silent. His heart was beating heavily. *What on earth were they doing on the street at this time of day? Had they worked it out? Would Zhang and Hyok have to find a different means of escape? Was it too late already? Had they been betrayed?*

Then there was a soft knock on the door. Zhang held his breath.

"Psst. Zhang, it's me. Open up."

Jin! Zhang opened the door carefully, and Jin slipped inside.

"What are you doing here?" whispered Zhang, as he quickly closed the door behind Jin.

"I'm going with you."

"What? You can't be serious!"

"I've made up my mind. I'm going with you. I can't let you go alone, can I? You'll never make it."

"And what about your father?"

"He knows nothing about it. I told him that I am going to visit an uncle for a while."

Zhang shook his head. "You're mad. You've got a good life at home."

"Not as good as people think."

Zhang studied Jin's face and then asked, "But how are we going to get away from here? Mr. Ahn and your father are walking on the street."

"They do that sometimes. Father points out the people who

attacked our house. Mr. Ahn makes sure that they disappear for a while."

"But your father didn't see anybody."

Jin shrugged his shoulders. "I think they're gone now, Zhang. It's starting to get light. Father's always home by sunrise. We can leave now."

Zhang opened the door a crack and peered outside again. The coast was clear. He motioned to Hyok, who walked to the door while buttoning his worn-out jacket. Hyok stepped outside and told his two older friends to follow him, as if he were the leader of the group.

Zhang called to him in a quiet voice. "We need to go the other way."

Hyok turned and followed Zhang.

"Do you know the way, Zhang?" Jin asked.

"We follow the railway track north," Zhang answered. "Then we can't fail to reach the border."

"Makes sense," Jin said and fell in behind him.

✪ ✪ ✪

An old lady took a bag out of her ragged brown jacket, opened it and took out a few grains of rice. Bending over a man lying on the bench, she said, "Come, son, eat something. You need to eat. Mummy will make you better again. Eat something. Eat something, please."

The man remained motionless. His face was swollen. The woman tried to push the rice between his cracked lips, but she couldn't.

"He's dead," Jin said to Zhang, but Zhang was in a daze. He had been at the train station in Hamhung before yet he had not previously experienced this chaos. To reach the platform, the three companions had to squirm, squeeze and push their way through a stationary mass of people.

Because he was taller and could see which way to go, Zhang led the way. He pushed people aside to his left and right, making room for Hyok and Jin to follow. Suddenly Zhang's foot became caught in a piece of clothing. Zhang grabbed the shoulders of a man in front of him to keep from falling.

"Look out, man!"

"Sorry," Zhang said, irritated. Angrily he looked around to see what had grabbed his foot. On the ground lay a middle-aged woman, her mouth gaping, her eyes staring wide open, her hands next to her body. She had to be dead.

Jin pushed Zhang forward. "Walk, Zhang. Don't look around too much."

When they reached the platform, they found that it too was packed. Loud talking and screaming filled the air. "What are all these people doing here?" asked Zhang.

"What?" screamed Jin.

"What are all these people doing here?" Zhang yelled in Jin's ear.

"What does it matter? When's the next train due?"

Zhang shrugged, and then tapped a woman on the back. "When's the next train leaving, madam?" he asked.

She scowled. "How should I know? I've been waiting here four days."

"So I guess we wait," Jin yelled to Zhang.

From the corner of his eye, Zhang saw several police officers talking with a man and a woman in their late twenties. A little girl with a large pink ribbon in her hair held on tightly to the legs of the woman. The man took his identity papers out of a rucksack and handed them over. Zhang was starting to feel nauseous. *We've got to get away from here.*

Then to Jin he said, "We're going to walk. We are still too close to Unsung. They'll soon realize that we've gone. They might not look for you but they will for me."

Zhang could not stop watching the young family. The senior police officer gave a condescending glance at the papers. Then without looking up from the documents, he gave an order and the other officers raised their weapons. The parents were handcuffed, and the little girl screamed and then began to cry. She tried to climb up her mother's leg. One of the agents took her hand and carefully pulled her off. He placed his other hand on the mother's back and pushed her gently forward.

Zhang turned around and walked with Jin and Hyok in the opposite direction toward another exit. They left the station and began following the railway track north. On the way they came across various people walking along the track. It made Zhang nervous. He felt as though he was being watched, as if everybody knew what he was doing—committing treason.

✪ ✪ ✪

Zhang sat down with a groan. He massaged his stiff upper legs. Today they had walked thirty kilometres, and yesterday at least twenty-five. And in total this week? No idea. Hyok took off his shoes and rubbed the soles of his feet. He had not complained once, despite the considerable distances that the three of them had walked each day, sometimes through fields, sometimes over the railway track, and on the odd occasion over the road. Once they had managed to hitch a ride for fifty kilometres on a truck.

Surprisingly they had not come across any patrols. However, they had passed people who Zhang suspected were also on their way to the border. These people avoided eye contact and conversations, just as he did.

Now they were going to spend the night in another crowded train station. Zhang did not even know which town they were in.

He studied the people surrounding him. Most of them were unwashed, unshaven and clothed in rags. The politeness and discipline that so characterized the North Korean people did not exist here. In front of him two men were in a heated argument. It was only a matter of time before they would start hitting each other, but nobody made an effort to intervene. Since guards were nowhere to be seen, the law of the jungle prevailed.

Zhang was tired, wet from the rain and hungry. They had last eaten three days ago when Jin had stolen food from an old lady while she slept. Zhang felt ashamed about this but he had been too hungry not to eat it. He tried to think about something other than his hunger and he let his thoughts wander in search of a pleasant memory. His favorite memories were of summer days when Hea-Woo and he went swimming in the lake at Unsung. That was a fantastic time. Zhang rested his head against a wall and closed his eyes.

But Jin interrupted his pleasant thoughts. "We can't keep this up much longer, Zhang."

Couldn't Jin stop complaining for a change? Zhang kept his eyes closed and said, "We must keep going. We can't give up."

Jin poked him in his side. "We must travel farther with the train. My feet are taking a beating with all this walking."

Irritated, Zhang looked at Jin. "How do we know when the train will come? It might be another week."

Jin crossed his arms in front of him. "Then we must wait—for as long as it takes the train to come," he said resolutely.

Zhang shook his head. "No. Too dangerous."

Hyok, who was listening to their conversation, added, "My feet are hurting too."

Zhang sighed. Walking was causing him pain as well. "Okay. We'll go by train."

Jin jumped up.

"What are you going to do?" Zhang asked.

"Pick up some food."

"And where do you think you'll find food?"

As Jin was moving away from them, he said, "I'll think of something. You guys can go to sleep but take care of our stuff."

"What stuff?" Hyok was confused.

Jin grinned and walked away. Zhang closed his eyes again and sank into a deep sleep, not waking until it started to get light. Even then he didn't want to wake up. The station was just as busy and noisy as yesterday evening. Hyok lay next to him with his coat pulled over his head. Zhang pulled down the coat.

Hyok took a bite from an apple and quickly hid it under his coat again. Zhang pulled the coat down a bit.

"Don't. They'll see the apple."

"How did you get it?" asked Zhang.

"Comrade Jin."

Jin poked Zhang and pulled another apple from a bag and handed it to him.

"Huh?" Zhang couldn't believe it. "Where did you get these apples?"

Jin smiled. "What shall I say? I'm a swindler, comrade. Eat up. I've already eaten. We'll save the rest for the journey."

Suddenly it became noisier and the mass of people started moving.

"What's going on?" asked Zhang.

"The train!" shouted Jin. "Get up! Let's go to the platform!"

Zhang and Jin pushed people aside as they made their way to the platform. Hyok held firmly to Zhang's jacket and wiggled his way through behind them. Slowly the train approached. Everyone was pressing, jostling, getting into position so they could board the train. Somebody shoved Zhang and he nearly fell onto the tracks.

"Hey! Hey! Look out!" he yelled.

As the train came to a stop, the brakes screeched and the pushing got worse. Men shouted, women cried and children screamed. Zhang picked Hyok up and made his way to the doors, which were slowly opening.

There was mass confusion as the people who wanted to get into the train pushed the passengers who wanted to get out back in again. One man, trying to get out, flailed his arms to create space. Zhang grabbed him by his arm and pulled him outside. Then, still holding Hyok, he took hold of the pole at the door and pulled himself in. Jin followed. There were still two seats facing each other next to the window, and Zhang and Jin flopped into them, breathing heavily. There was no room for Hyok on the seats so he sat on the floor between them. Next to Jin sat a young, armed soldier, and next to Zhang was an older man who was completely out of breath. He wiped the sweat from his forehead with a handkerchief.

The doors closed. They'd been lucky. Those who had not managed to get into the train would certainly have to wait several more days, perhaps even weeks. But that didn't matter to Zhang now. He looked around him, expecting to see police officers appear to check the passengers' papers, but the train departed without any policemen or guards appearing. It gave Zhang a sense of hope. Perhaps they would not come at all. "Thank you father Kim Il-Sung," he whispered.

✪ ✪ ✪

The skinny soldier opposite Zhang was probably no older than nineteen. His uniform was dirty, and his eyes seemed dull as if he were drunk or drugged. Zhang pointed to the sack of apples that Jin held firmly and then pointed to the soldier. Jin shook his head.

"What's your name?" Zhang asked suddenly, surprising himself.

The soldier did not look up as he answered. "Private Kim."

"On your way to the barracks?" continued Zhang.

"No. Home," he murmured. "Sick."

"How old are you?"

"Eighteen." The man next to Zhang held his chin up high, as though feeling superior, but he was following the conversation. Jin kicked Zhang's leg and Zhang understood the signal. It was better not to be too curious. Keep your mouth shut and don't attract attention.

✪ ✪ ✪

The brakes of the train screeched so loudly that it seemed as if the train would fall apart at any moment. The soldier had fallen asleep. There was a good chance that he had missed his station. The same man still sat next to Zhang. They were only twenty kilometers away

63

from China. So close and yet so far. Exactly what sort of world lay ahead of them?

Zhang began to have second thoughts. Perhaps they should turn back. He could always say that he had been with Jin visiting family. But he knew he could not go back. The authorities must have realized by now that Father and Hea-Woo had fled. As the only member of the family remaining, Zhang would certainly be punished. So he had no choice. It was all or nothing. The only hope left was to reach China alive. If he could find Father and Hea-Woo there, then in the future they could return and ask forgiveness. At least that is what he hoped.

The old man next to Zhang stood up. He had not exchanged a single word with his fellow passengers throughout the entire journey.

"Follow me," he said.

"Pardon?" Zhang was confused.

The man took a good look at the soldier. The poor chap sat dazed in the seat and was completely unaware that the train had stopped. Without looking at Zhang, the man spoke again. "If you want to survive this, then follow me—at a distance. At my home we'll talk further." Without looking up or around, he left the train.

Zhang gave Jin a questioning look and shrugged his shoulders.

"Do you think he realizes we're going to desert?" whispered Jin.

"Can we trust him?" asked Hyok.

Zhang had his doubts. Perhaps this man was a spy and trained to trap fugitives. At the same time Zhang did not have a clue how they should proceed further from here. Obviously they had to cross the river. But after that what? They needed a guide. "There's only one way to find out," he said. "Quick. Let's follow him."

The town they were in was very similar to Hamhung. Except that people were better dressed and fed. Clearly some people wore clothes that came from China, where there was better material for clothing. Those wearing Chinese clothes had to be highly placed people from the Party. They were the only ones who occasionally went abroad.

Ten minutes later they reached the house. As the man was about to go inside, he gestured to the three comrades that they should follow quickly. When they were all inside, the man closed the door. They walked through a bedroom and into the living room.

The house looked like most of the other houses in North Korea—it was long and narrow, with one floor. The rooms were small and there was a simple kitchen. On the wall were portraits of Kim Il-Sung and Kim Jong-Il and a radio. The TV was the biggest that Zhang had ever seen. Next to the TV was an odd-looking box.

"What's that?" Zhang asked.

"A video recorder. Have you heard about them?"

"Yes. I know you can use it to watch films."

The man hung up his jacket and pointed out to Zhang, Jin and Hyok where they should sit. Coming out of the kitchen, a young woman greeted them with a brief nod but did not bow. Her long, black hair was tied in a ponytail. She was slender but not thin and she wore a pair of black trousers and a pink jacket made in China. She also wore a Kim Il-Sung badge on her lapel.

There was a table set for two, and the man sat there. "Another three plates please, dear daughter," he said. He turned to his three guests, while lighting a cigar. "Around here they call me Uncle Sung. That's what you must call me as well. My daughter's name is Young-Soon."

Young-Soon placed three plates and chopsticks on the table.

"Our names are . . ." Zhang began but Uncle Sung interrupted.

"There's no point in saying your names." He took a deep puff from his cigar and blew the smoke toward the ceiling.

"Did you think you could really make it on your own?" he asked without looking at them. "What was your plan?"

"What do you mean?" asked Zhang.

"You are on your way to the border, are you not? That's pretty obvious. Three lads, not brothers, who look like tramps, making their way north. It's a miracle that you were not arrested. But you won't get across the border, not without help."

Young-Soon placed five full bowls of rice on the table. Zhang, Jin and Hyok stared wide-eyed at the food. Hunger had yet to reach this house. Yet the food made Zhang cautious. He could not remember the last time he had been offered a bowl of rice.

"Eat first," said Uncle Sung.

They ate in silence. The rice tasted as if it had been delivered directly from the kitchen of Kim Jong-Il. Zhang wished he could spend the rest of his life at this table, filling his stomach with rice. A few minutes later the rice was finished, and Zhang used his chopsticks to scrape the last grains from the bowl and with his finger wiped up the bit of liquid that remained, then he licked his finger.

Uncle Sung got up from the dinner table and went to a comfortable armchair. Zhang, Jin and Hyok moved to the couch opposite him, while Young-Soon began to clean up. She had not yet spoken a single word. Zhang tried to watch her from the corner of his eye as she moved gracefully between the living room and kitchen. He estimated that she was slightly older than he.

"Let's talk," Uncle Sung began as he relit his cigar. "You're not the first to have tried to cross the Tumen River. It used to be a lot easier, certainly when the water was frozen. Kim Jong-Il treats his people like rats . . ."

Zhang began to feel warm inside.

". . . yet these rats may not leave the sinking ship. Each rat that tries to save itself must be killed. Orders from the Great General. The best soldiers in the country serve at the border. They are armed and shoot to kill. You cannot escape and you cannot go back. In effect, you are already dead."

Uncle Sung sank into his chair and crossed his legs. He looked at the threesome and smiled.

"Unless we reach the other side," said Jin.

"As I said, you won't succeed without help."

"And who is going to help us then?" asked Jin.

Uncle Sung leaned forward again. "Tomorrow evening Young-Soon will cross the border. We need rice and clothes. She knows the way and knows most of the border guards. You can go with her—but not for free."

"What's your price?" asked Zhang.

"Five hundred yuan per person."

"Fifteen hundred yuan?" exclaimed Zhang. "We don't have that much."

Uncle Sung frowned. "That's going to make things difficult. How much do you have?"

Zhang looked at Jin. He shook his head. Zhang emptied his pockets and took out three hundred yuan.

"You certainly have more than that," Uncle Sung grumbled.

Zhang had no more money. He had no extra clothes or shoes to offer. The only thing he still had was the gold watch his father had left behind. He took it off his wrist. "Is this enough?"

Uncle Sung took the watch, checked the weight, and looked at it carefully. Then he smiled and nodded. "At this time tomorrow you'll be in China."

✪ ✪ ✪

They had already been lying in the damp grass for an hour, with their coats and shoes off, and Zhang wondered if the promised light signal would still come. Young-Soon had forbidden her "clients" to talk. Hyok did not make a single sound. He was probably sleeping. Jin's face was tense.

Zhang gazed almost continuously at the other side of the river. The moonlight illuminated part of the water and the wood. Zhang felt a cramp developing in his left leg and rolled on to his right side. A twig snapped. In a flash Young-Soon turned her head. *Even when she looked angry, she looked beautiful* thought Zhang. Yet he still felt ashamed.

Then there were footsteps. Zhang tried to determine which direction the sound was coming from. Jin was breathing heavily. It sounded as though they were coming from the riverbank. A light went on and off—the signal from the bribed border guards. Young-Soon stuck up two fingers at Zhang and Jin. Two more minutes. Zhang poked Hyok gently. The boy looked surprised, and Zhang quickly placed his forefinger in front of his mouth. Hyok did not make a sound.

Suddenly Zhang became aware of his heartbeat. It seemed so loud that he feared the border guards would be able to hear it.

Young-Soon glanced at her watch and got up without looking around. Zhang followed her; then came Hyok and Jin. Young-Soon quickened her pace and ran to the water. Zhang sprinted after her, clinging to the bag that held his clothes. *The moon is too bright. Everybody can see us running,* he thought.

Just before they entered the water, Young-Soon slowed down. With small but resolute steps, she entered the water. Zhang followed. The cold water encircled his ankles. He held his clothes and shoes above his head and waded farther into the river. Halfway across he looked back at his beloved fatherland. *I'll come back,* he said to himself. *I'll come back and fight against the imperialists. They have caused Father and Hea-Woo to flee. It's their fault that I have to betray my country.*

The river was about forty meters wide. Now the water was up to Zhang's waist and he realized that it would probably come over Hyok's head. He went back a few steps and whispered to Hyok to climb on his back. Young-Soon had already reached the other side. Jin came alongside him, and Zhang walked carefully so as not to slip on the smooth pebbles. Slowly they drew closer to the Chinese side.

It was a relief to get out of the cold water. Hyok slid off his back, and Zhang looked around, realizing that he was on foreign soil for the first time in his life.

Hyok and Zhang walked toward Jin and Young-Soon, who were already pulling their dry clothes over their wet shirts in the shrubs. As Zhang put on his clothes, he gazed across the river at his fatherland. A few minutes ago he had still been there. Now the country seemed to be impossibly far away. *The next time I'm here, I'll be going the other way and I will have at least Hea-Woo with me. Perhaps Father as well.*

Then Young-Soon motioned that they had to move on quickly. With her fast pace she showed that she had walked through these dark woods often. The moonlight scarcely shone through the densely growing trees, yet she maneuvered as though she knew the way by heart. Zhang, Jin and Hyok followed her silhouette.

Suddenly a male voice screamed in Chinese. Young-Soon gave a short scream. This was not good.

"Stop!" said a voice in Korean.

"Run!" shouted Young-Soon.

Zhang ran, trying to keep up with Young-Soon. Then he heard a shot. Jin shouted, but he was running so fast that he could not have been hit. Zhang's shoulder hit a small tree. He fell on the ground and cursed.

Another scream from the woods. This time the voice was that of a terrified boy. "Hyok!" called Zhang. Then he yelled to the others, "Stop! We have to go back!"

"Too late, Zhang!" called Jin. "You have to save yourself."

But Zhang stood facing in the direction of the boy's scream. He realized the Chinese had stopped the pursuit. Then he heard a man shout and a boy cry.

Zhang sneaked toward the sounds. From behind a thick tree he saw two Chinese border guards with their weapons over their shoulders. A third guard hit Hyok with the palm of his hand and he fell to the ground. The others kept shouting in Chinese.

Zhang had to do something. He searched the ground and saw a thick branch, which he grabbed and then ran shouting toward the guards. Two of them took fright and each fled in a different direction. The man holding Hyok got the branch straight in his face. He sank to his knees but did not let Hyok go. Zhang kicked the guard's forearm. Now the man hit the ground and cried out in pain.

Zhang grabbed Hyok's hand, but before they could run, they

heard, "Hands up" in Korean. One of the guards had returned and was pointing his rifle at Zhang. It was finished. He would never see Hea-Woo again.

But then suddenly there was a thud. The soldier sank to his knees without a sound and then fell forward onto the ground. Behind him stood Young-Soon with a club. The other soldier tried to crawl away, but Young-Soon also knocked him unconscious with a single blow.

"Thanks," said Zhang.

"That was brave, Zhang . . . and stupid. Never try that one again," she whispered angrily. "If I say, 'Run,' then you run until I say you can stop. Clear?"

Zhang nodded.

"I don't want to be the victim of your stupidity. What if they had caught you as well? Would you have betrayed my father and me?"

Zhang remained silent.

"Now get a move on. They'll come looking for these two soon." Taking large steps, Young-Soon walked away.

Hyok looked up at Zhang. "Thanks," he whispered in a scarcely audible tone.

Zhang nodded and smiled.

A hundred meters farther along, Jin was waiting. He said nothing when they caught up to him.

✪ ✪ ✪

Zhang stood atop a hill and looked down on the awakening Chinese town in the valley. Never before in his life had he seen so many cars at one time. In Unsung only Jin's father had a car. Sometimes a civil servant from Pyongyang came to the village by car and occasionally a truck passed through the town.

As Zhang watched the Chinese in the town below, they seemed like people from a different planet. They wore clothes in all colors of the rainbow. He could see men in suits and some women in glittery jeans.

Schoolchildren in blue uniforms (the girls with skirts to just below the knee!) walked laughing to a waiting bus. And the bus looked new—there was no rust on it. A young couple—he wearing sunglasses and she in a fashionable cap—were kissing as though no one else were around.

Zhang looked at the colorless outfit he was wearing. His trousers were still damp from crossing the river and his shirt was clammy with sweat.

Young-Soon lit a cigarette.

"A woman who smokes?" Jin frowned.

Young-Soon exhaled the smoke toward him and said, "We go our separate ways here."

"What? That wasn't the agreement," Zhang said. "You were to bring us to a contact address."

She moved her head in the direction of the town.

"You'll find enough contact addresses out there. A whole town full."

"Wait a minute!" said Zhang. "We've paid to be dropped off safely."

"And to whom exactly are you going to report me, my friend? The police perhaps?" She laughed as she pulled her rucksack onto her back.

"How do we know who to trust?" Zhang called after her.

Young-Soon took a final long draw on her cigarette and blew out the smoke before answering. "Look for a house with a cross on it. If nobody helps you there, then nobody will help you." Then she turned and went back into the woods.

"What do we do now?" Jin asked. He looked around nervously. "We could also go back. I still know the way, I think. It's not good that we're here."

"You can go back if you want, Jin. I'm not going. I must find my father and Hea-Woo. If I come back with them, the state will forgive us for having been in China. We must find a house with a cross."

"That's not difficult," said Hyok. "There are buildings with crosses all over the place. What sort of people live there?"

"I don't know," said Zhang.

"I don't trust it," Jin said. "Perhaps Young-Soon has lied to us. What if they ask who we are?"

"Don't worry, Jin. We've come this far. We'll soon be safe."

Hyok looked up at Zhang. "Really?" he asked.

Zhang tried to sound confident. "Yes, really," he said and gave Hyok a pat on the back. He doubted that his words had convinced Hyok and Jin. He wasn't even certain himself that they would have a safe place to sleep that night. He was afraid that the chance was greater that they would be spending the night in a cell.

"Let's go," Zhang said as he started down the hill. Jin and Hyok followed and five minutes later they were walking on the streets of the town. "Stand straight and look bored," Zhang told the others. "Then we will look as inconspicuous as possible."

"There!" shouted Hyok. "A cross!"

"Shh!" Jin said. "Don't point and don't talk."

Zhang's heart beat in his throat as if it were trying to leave his body. The three comrades crossed the street and came to stand in front of the cast-iron gate of the building that was further separated from the street by a hedge. An old man with a large bald patch on the back of his head was cutting the grass and did not notice as they opened the gate.

Zhang tapped him on the shoulder. The man glanced in their direction, stopped the lawnmower and smiled. He looked from Zhang to Jin to Hyok and suddenly held his breath.

Then he began to shout in Korean, "Go away! Go away, please!" As fast as his old legs could carry him, he ran into the house.

"Wait, wait!" Zhang shouted, following the man. "Stop! We don't mean any harm. We've . . ."

But the man paid no attention to him. He disappeared through a doorway and the door closed in Zhang's face. Zhang looked up at the cross as if to be sure he had not made a mistake. *If they can't help you there, then nobody will help you.*

Jin followed Zhang's gaze and seemed to read his mind. "Let's go back," he said, breathing hard as though he had just run a marathon. "They'll kill us here."

Zhang scowled at Jin. "You go back."

"Hey, Zhang. Take it easy. I won't let you down. You know that. Friends forever. We'll look for another building with a cross."

They walked along in silence. Zhang noticed that many citizens in this town were ethnic Koreans. And a lot of Korean was spoken on the street, but this did not reassure Zhang. He had the feeling that everybody looked straight through him, that everybody knew who he was and, most important of all, where he came from.

They walked past a produce stall laden with fruit and vegetables.

"Tasty apples, sir! They're on sale today!" shouted the vendor.

Zhang did not respond. In the distance he saw a wooden cross on the roof of a building and did his best to walk calmly toward it. When they reached the building, Zhang knocked at the door, which was opened by a small Chinese lady. She looked briefly at the three North Koreans and immediately closed the door again. Zhang closed his eyes tightly and clenched his fists. Inside he cursed and wanted to pound on the door but he kept his hands down at his side and turned to leave.

Just then the door opened again. Now a Korean man stood before them. He was almost as tall as Zhang. He had a friendly face and a long, gray goatee.

"Quick," he said, "come inside." The man grabbed Zhang's hand and pulled him toward him, while urgently signaling to Hyok and Jin to come inside as well.

Through the door they came into the main room of the house, which was full of white plastic chairs, all placed neatly in rows. Beyond the chairs was a podium with a sort of pulpit. On the wall hung a cross with a half-naked man on it. Zhang sneered. *These people worship somebody who is dead!*

They followed the man into a smaller room behind the podium. His wife was already busy pouring tea. The man took a chair and motioned to his guests to sit. He cleared his throat. "I'm brother Lim.

My wife is called Mei. Would you give us the pleasure of sharing your names with us?"

Zhang and Jin gave each other a questioning look.

"You can trust us," Lim assured them. "With the help of our Lord, we can assist you."

Which Lord? Zhang wondered but said, "My name is Zhang. These are Jin and Hyok."

"Three brave men," Lim said smiling at them. "Unfortunately you are not the only people to have come here from your country. You're not safe here."

"I thought you said you would help us," Jin said.

"Yes, we will help you. In a little while my wife will phone friends of ours. Once it is dark this evening, they can take you to their house. You will be safer with them than you are here. Drink your tea first. Soon we will talk more about it."

"Are you hungry as well?" Mei smiled at her husband.

Lim started to laugh. "Ah, dear wife, of course! These men want to eat something. Just let them see how well a Chinese woman can cook."

They drank their tea in silence while their thoughts were racing. *Would friends of the man really come? Or were they somehow already alerting the police?* Zhang looked to see if there were other exits. As far as he could see, this house had just one door. The windows were high up on the walls. They could not get through those.

The most appetizing smells reached them from the kitchen. Zhang's mouth began to water. He smelled rice and meat. The first dish that Mei brought was full of rice. This was followed by pork. Then she put down a plate of cucumber and carrots. Next came a basket with apples, bananas, and pears, along with a jug of water, plates and chopsticks.

Never before had Zhang set his eyes on such a bountiful meal.

CHAPTER 3

I n the beginning God created the heavens and the earth. Now the earth was formless and empty, darkness was over the surface of the deep, and the Spirit of God was hovering over the waters. And God said, 'Let there be light,' and there was light. God saw that the light was good, and he separated the light from the darkness. God called the light 'day,' and the darkness he called 'night.' And there was evening, and there was morning—the first day." Zhang closed the Bible again. During his four months in China, he had already tried to wrestle through the book twenty times. Not because he wanted to but at the insistence of his host and hostess, brother Lee and sister Ping. They called themselves Christians, and Zhang knew that Christians were bad, dangerous people. He was afraid they would hand him over to the Chinese police but that had not happened yet. There was something strange about them. They were so nice, especially to Hyok, who at first felt very uncomfortable with all the cuddles he received from the lady of the house. Yet now he was used to it and even seemed to enjoy it, despite Zhang's warnings. "Don't get too close to them, Hyok. You do not know if you can really trust them."

Brother Lee and sister Ping were in their sixties and had no children. They lived in a small house just outside the town. Zhang, Jin and Hyok slept in a cellar, which had one small window that could not be opened. Lee worked as a watchmaker, not a well-paid job.

However, he had a lot of contacts and arranged a job for Jin in the mines. Zhang had become a waiter in a Korean restaurant. On Lee's advice, Hyok went to a hotel each day where a lot of South Korean businessmen came. He received more money per day begging there than Zhang could earn in a day.

Each day the couple and their "guests" got up at 5:30. First they studied the Bible together and then Lee and Ping prayed. After this was breakfast. In the evening after dinner there was once again Bible study and prayer. Sometimes other Christians stopped by. Every Sunday they went to the church. Zhang had to admit that there was a friendly atmosphere there and some of the songs had a beautiful melody. However, some of the words of the songs were very confusing, such as "Come back, Lord Jesus," "Your blood cleanses us," and "Your offering gives us eternal life." *How could a murdered man save people from death?* Zhang wondered.

Despite the many police officers in the town, Zhang, Jin and Hyok had not yet been caught, but they remained continually on their guard. Lee and Ping's house was in the church building. There were few places to hide within the residence, but there was a carpet-covered trapdoor in the podium of the church. If somebody knocked at the door, they could hide there within thirty seconds. They practiced that each week.

Zhang put the Bible back on his bedside table, next to an empty beer bottle that had fallen over, and closed his eyes. China was so different from what he had imagined. There were more inequalities than in North Korea, yet it seemed that even the poor were better off than the average citizen in his country. And to put it mildly, boys and girls were free to have relationships with each other. Each day he saw young people kissing on the street. In clubs the Chinese danced close together. Cafes with affordable beer and shops with more products than they could ever sell were all over the place.

If Zhang had not been so stupid, he would have already found Father and Hea-Woo. They could have regained strength together and then returned to their fatherland. But where were his father and sister? Hopefully he would find them soon. Once he had saved enough money, he would be able to go and search. Lee had already asked his contacts to look out for them, but so far without result. Nobody had heard of them.

Crashing down the stairs, Hyok came jumping into the room. Zhang opened his eyes slowly. He felt so tired.

"What's up with you, little brother?" he asked, his voice sounding hoarse.

Hyok gave a broad smile, as though he would burst from joy. "I belong to Jesus!" he shouted.

"What did you say?"

"I belong to Jesus! Mrs. Ping said that I can belong to Jesus!" Hyok jumped onto his bed. "I belong to Jesus!" he shouted again.

Zhang threw his pillow at Hyok's head, who tipped over onto the mattress as though mortally wounded.

"Quiet down, kid, and tell me what happened," Zhang urged his young friend.

Hyok sat up and his expression became very serious. "I prayed with Mrs. Ping," he said quietly.

"You did? Tell me about it. Tell me the whole story."

Hyok eagerly told his story. "I said to Mrs. Ping that I had betrayed my parents and that I really regretted that. Then she said that I had to pray and that I must ask Jesus for forgiveness. So I did. Then she said that from now on I must always trust Jesus, and that He would help me if I asked Him."

"Nice for you." Zhang was already feeling a bit envious. "Have you already asked Him for something?"

"Yes, that He will take good care of Mom and Dad and that you will see your father and sister again."

"That's kind of you."

"He can make it happen," Hyok's voice rose with his intensity. "Honestly! He loves all of us. Mrs. Ping said so. He can make everything good. Perhaps you should pray to Him as well, comrade Zhang."

Zhang sat up straight and looked away. "No" was all he said.

"Why not?"

He couldn't control the hostility he felt from coming through. "Because it doesn't make the slightest bit of difference. That man's been dead for two thousand years."

"Not true!" Hyok was wide-eyed with the joy of what he had learned. "He has risen again!"

"Yes, yes. And now He's in heaven and 'watches' over us. I know the stories, Hyok. If you want to believe in Him that's fine, but I've never seen a dead guy come back to life. If Jesus were still alive, then there would be no famine in North Korea, my mother would not have become ill, and your parents would not be in a camp."

"But . . ." Hyok's huge smile was fading quickly.

"Sorry, Hyok. I don't want to hear any more. I'm going to sleep." Zhang lay down on his bed and turned onto his side, facing the wall.

"Are you angry?" asked Hyok.

Zhang shook his head.

Hyok walked to Zhang's bed and stood looking down at his friend's back for a moment before turning silently and walking back upstairs. He closed the door with a click.

As soon as Hyok was gone, Zhang buried his face in his pillow; then he wiped moisture from the corners of his eyes. He thought about Hea-Woo and his father, imagining that they too were in a cellar, lying in bed, talking about the past, about Mother's bossy nature, about the headstrong and stupid Zhang.

Hea-Woo looked upset. Father tried to comfort her. Suddenly, Zhang saw fear in Hea-Woo's eyes. The windows in their home had disappeared. They had become bars. Soldiers—not Chinese, Korean. They came closer. Father got a smack with the butt of a rifle. Hea-Woo screamed. Two men grabbed her by her arms and pulled her outside. Hea-Woo called for Zhang. They bound her to a pole. Zhang aimed the rifle. Head. Chest. Legs. "Zhang! It's me!" A shot rang out.

Zhang jumped up with a start. His clothes were drenched with sweat. He gasped for air. *That nightmare once again. Breathe deeply. In through the nose and out through the mouth.* He fell back onto his pillow and placed his left arm over his eyes. He had to find Hea-Woo. Even if it was the last thing he did. She had to forgive him. She just had to.

Then he heard heavy footsteps on the stairs. Even before Zhang saw Jin, he could smell the alcohol. Jin, still holding onto the banister, took a good look around the room.

"Comrade Zhang." He carelessly saluted and then threw a bottle of beer to his friend.

"Stand to attention," he bawled. "Tonight we celebrate."

Zhang couldn't help smiling but he remained lying down. "Sure, general. And what do we have to celebrate?"

"What do we have to celebrate? What do we have to celebrate? Comrade Zhang, you antirevolutionary! Don't you know what day it is today?"

Zhang shrugged his shoulders. With large gestures Jin started to explain. "Today in the year Juche 31 a large monster rose off the coast of Pyongyang from the depths of the sea and sang a song of praise. On that same day, in the middle of the winter, flowers spontaneously began to flower. On the holy mountain Paektu the ice opened up and a double rainbow shot into the sky. Cranes announced the birth of a son of the gods and a new star appeared in the sky."

Then Zhang jumped up and started to sing with Jin.

Let morning shine on the silver and gold of this land,
Three thousand leagues packed with natural wealth.
My beautiful fatherland.
The glory of a wise people
Brought up in a culture brilliant
With a history five millennia long.

Let us devote our bodies and minds
To supporting this Korea forever.

The firm will, bonded with truth,
Nest for the spirit of labor,
Embracing the atmosphere of Mount Paektu,
Will go forth to all the world.
The country established by the will of the people,
Breasting the raging waves with soaring strength.
Let us glorify forever this Korea,
Limitlessly rich and strong.

The song had changed Zhang's mood. "Let's drink to that!" he shouted, raising the bottle of beer.

Jin made the toast: "To the Dear Leader, secretary-general of the Worker's Party, chair of the National Security Council, supreme commander of the army, General Kim Jong-Il. May he have a long and prosperous life."

"And death to the Americans," Zhang added.

"Cheers, comrade."

They screwed the caps off the bottles and both took a large swig. Zhang let the beer slip down his throat and enjoyed every millisecond of it. Jin said something about imperialists and South Korean marionettes. Zhang scarcely heard him. He concentrated solely on the beer that warmed up his body from the inside.

"Are you coming to eat, boys?" Sister Ping's friendly voice brought Zhang back to reality. Zhang and Jin quickly took a few more large gulps to empty the bottles. Then Jin put them in a brown paper bag, which he then placed under his bed.

Zhang walked with some effort up the stairs. He was tired and his head felt heavy. This evening there was a Bible study with other members of the church. He was not looking forward to that.

Brother Lee and Hyok were already sitting at the table. Hyok had been putting together a jigsaw puzzle and was clearing it away. Sister Ping put a steaming dish of rice and chicken on the table. Once everybody had sat down, Lee prayed. He thanked God profusely for the food and especially for the conversion of Hyok. He also prayed for the body and soul of Zhang, Jin, his wife and himself. As always when Lee prayed, Zhang felt confused by the words he said, and especially today. *What did "the conversion of Hyok" mean?*

After the prayer, they started to eat dinner in silence.

"What was that beautiful song you two were singing just now?" Lee looked from Jin to Zhang.

"Our national anthem," Jin responded quickly.

"And is there a special reason you were singing it today?"

Zhang looked at Jin, who remained silent, so Zhang answered, "It's the Gen . . . I mean . . . Kim Jong-Il's birthday today."

"Ah," Lee said and stopped eating his rice. "The Leader's birthday. You must be missing your fatherland today."

Zhang shrugged his shoulders. Jin kept his eyes on his bowl.

"Tell us about the special occasions in your country, Zhang. What happens today?"

Zhang was happy to talk about his country. "It used to be far more beautiful than now. Then there were parades throughout the entire country. At school we always received new uniforms and usually some sweets as well. The birthday of Kim Il-Sung is usually celebrated on a bigger scale, yet Kim Jong-Il has always been my hero. I could look into the night sky for ages searching for the star that appeared when he was born. Then I felt there was nothing more beautiful than to serve him. And now I'm sitting here . . ." His voice trailed off as he became lost in thought.

"Now you're sitting here," Lee repeated. "And how do you feel about that? Do you get homesick?"

"I don't want to talk about it," Zhang said and started eating again.

Lee continued, "Talk about it with God sometime. That'll do you good. Zhang, Jin and Hyok," he looked at each of them, "you've been through a lot, far more than you can ever tell Ping and me. But God already knows about it. He was there. He has brought you here so that you can meet Him. He wants to forgive you."

"Who says we need forgiveness?" asked Jin fiercely.

"My dear boy, we all need forgiveness, each and every day," answered Lee.

"If that's the case, then His forgiveness is never enough. Then you can never be really forgiven."

"So it's better to console yourself with drink then?" asked Ping. "You know that we don't like your drinking here in the house, Jin. And that applies to you as well, Zhang."

Lee motioned to his wife not to continue with the subject of their drinking.

"Why don't you tell them where Kim Jong-Il was really born?" said Ping to her husband.

This caught Zhang's attention. "What do you mean?" he asked quickly.

"I don't think now is the time to . . ." Lee began.

"I want to know what Mrs. Ping is hinting at," Jin interrupted.

Lee sighed and looked away for a few seconds. Then he gazed intently at Zhang and Jin. "You've been here for four months now. We've talked a lot about North Korea. I've tried to understand you and I ask your forgiveness if I've failed to at times. I'm a simple watchmaker and an ignorant person. Now I think you know that the reality is sometimes different from what you have learned."

"What are you driving at?" Jin asked.

"I will tell you what I know, but please remain calm."

Zhang nodded and Jin just stared at Lee.

"You've always learned that during the Second World War Kim Il-Sung defeated the Japanese with his small army and liberated Korea. Also they told you that Kim Jong-Il was born on the holy mountain Paektu in North Korea. The truth is that Kim Il-Sung did indeed fight against the Japanese. However, during most of the war he lived in the Soviet Union. That is where Kim Jong-Il was born, in 1941. In other words the year Juche 30."

"What?" exclaimed Jin, jumping up from his chair. He pointed his forefinger defiantly at Lee. "That's a lie! How dare you claim that? Everybody knows that the Dear Leader was born in Juche 31 on the holy mountain Paektu! And that from there the Great Leader Kim Il-Sung drove the Japanese into the sea and liberated our nation!"

Zhang tried to speak calmly. "What you say is impossible."

With both hands Lee motioned to Jin to sit down and be calm, and Jin slowly sank back down in his chair. "I understand that this is really upsetting for you. It's a perfectly understandable reaction," Lee said, "but you've been here for four months now. It's about time that somebody tells you this. Kim Il-Sung lived in the Soviet Union in 1941. That's where his son was born as well. There are documents that prove this." No one spoke. Then Lee asked, "How old were you in 1981?"

"I was eight," stammered Zhang.

"Probably too young to remember," continued Lee. "In that year your country celebrated the fortieth birthday of Kim Jong-Il. Yet in 1982 he celebrated his fortieth birthday again. Then he said he was born in the year Juche 31, in 1942. I'm sorry to have to tell you this, more sorry than I can say. Kim Jong-Il is not the man that he claims to be."

"Why...?" Zhang wasn't sure what to ask.

"Kim Jong-Il was appointed as the successor of Kim Il-Sung in that period, yet he did not have the same godly status," said Ping. "So to give himself that status, he seriously exaggerated the story of his birth."

Zhang slouched in his chair and stared at the ceiling. *Could it really be true?*

Jin had no such doubts. "I don't believe a word of it," he mumbled.

An icy silence filled the room. Everyone stared at the half-empty bowls. Suddenly Jin cursed and then jumped up. "Come with me, Zhang."

"There's Bible study tonight," Ping protested.

"Shh," Lee said to his wife. "Let them go."

Zhang and Jin walked outside in silence. A few minutes later they were in the park. Jin cursed again. His anger made his whole body tense. He walked around in circles, then kicked a tree. Zhang let his friend be.

Finally Jin announced, "We must get away from here."

"Where do you want to go to?"

"Home. I'm going mad here—mad from all the lies. They can fool everybody, but not me, not me. Do you hear me, Zhang? They can't fool me!"

"I hear you, comrade." Neither of them spoke for a moment and then Zhang added, "You know that I can't leave."

Jin grabbed his friend's arm. "Zhang, listen. The longer we stay away, the heavier the punishment when we return."

Zhang pulled his arm away. "I'm not going back without Hea-Woo. My sister has her whole life ahead of her. I must take her back home. Perhaps I can talk my father into returning as well. I'm not going back without them."

Jin leaned against a tree. "Comrade, be honest with yourself. You know how we've asked around. None of the Chinese and Koreans who help defectors have seen them. Perhaps they never even reached China. Perhaps they are waiting for you at home."

"Oh," responded Zhang, "so we're defectors now, are we?"

"In the strictest sense of the word, yes. We've abandoned our country. We must go back; we must do it for our families."

"But I no longer have any family."

Jin looked troubled. "If you stay here, it'll be your downfall."

"We shall see."

"How can you be so indifferent? Have you heard what happened in the mines today?"

Zhang shook his head.

"No? I thought as much." Jin sank down beside the tree he had

84

been leaning on. "The police appeared all of a sudden. They've taken our comrades Chin-Mae, Dong-Yul and Eunji. We won't be seeing them down at the bar anytime soon."

This time it was Zhang who cursed. "How did you escape?"

"By sheer luck I was on the toilet."

Zhang sat next to Jin and threw his arm over his shoulders. "We still have each other. Friends forever. You remember?"

"Yes," said Jin without enthusiasm. "Friends forever. That's the whole problem."

"What do you mean?"

"I promised never to abandon you but I've made up my mind. I'm going back home—with or without you."

"I can't leave, Jin. Not without my sister. But I understand if you want to go back. Yet at the same time I'm scared about what might happen to you. Everybody knows that you've been away for months."

My father will save me from all of that," Jin said with confidence. "If I'm not caught at the border, then everything will be fine."

"When are you going?"

"At sunrise."

✪ ✪ ✪

Jin left before dawn. As he headed for the door, he and Zhang reaffirmed their bond with a strong hug—friends forever.

"I hate abandoning you like this, Zhang," Jin whispered.

Zhang gave Jin's shoulder a reassuring squeeze. "Comrade, you can never abandon me. A man's got to do what a man's got to do. For you, that means going home. For me, it means finding my father and sister."

Later at breakfast, when Lee heard that Jin was on his way to North Korea, he began frantically searching for him. About midday he returned—without Jin. "The first time in twenty-seven years," he murmured, staring out of the window.

"What do you mean?" asked Hyok.

"For the first time in twenty-seven years, my shop has remained closed on a Wednesday morning." He shook his head. "What on earth will my clients think about me?"

"But it's never that busy in your shop," Hyok said.

Lee looked at the boy absentmindedly. "Every soul counts," he said while walking away, "every soul."

When Jin had been gone for three days, he was no longer spoken about in Lee's house and that irritated Zhang. Yet worse still, he wondered if his friend had made it. *Is he at home with his parents or is he languishing in a prison cell? Who knows, perhaps Jin's father had lost his protected status due to Jin's flight. After all, every single member of Jin's family had all of a sudden become family members of a deserter—simply because Jin had crossed a river.*

Zhang sat in the living room with Lee, Ping and Hyok, ready for the daily Bible study. He had to pay attention, because Lee asked questions to see whether his audience had understood the message. By now Zhang knew the facts of the Bible. He knew that God had needed seven days to make the earth. The first people were Adam and Eve, who ate from the forbidden fruit. The people became many in number yet they made stupid mistakes. God allowed all of them to be destroyed in the great flood (*what sort of god would do such a thing?* he wondered). Only Noah's family and some of the animals survived. Later there was Abraham, the forefather of the people of Israel. Israel committed offenses and was repeatedly punished for these. Eventually God remained silent for hundreds of years until Jesus arrived in the world in an unlikely manner—born of a virgin (*where on earth did they get that from?*). Over a period of three years He made many disciples, despite His confusing stories (*how could anybody ever make sense of those?*). Eventually the Man was sentenced to death for being a troublemaker. In this way He paid the price for people's sins. He also rose again from the dead.

The story simply made no sense. If with His death this Jesus had ensured that God granted forgiveness to everybody, then why did people still go to hell? What sort of god condemns simple people to such a terrible place anyway? And that was not by far the most incomprehensible part. What Zhang could not grasp to save His life was that, after His resurrection, Jesus returned to heaven and left His disciples behind. Okay, they wrote letters full of beautiful—yet empty—words, but each of them died a martyr's death. Had they really given up their lives for this Man? That was simply beyond belief.

Nevertheless, Lee, Ping and Hyok believed that this "Bible" was true, that this Man really had lived and that He still cared for them. Yet in reality nobody had seen Him during the past two thousand years.

With a firm "Amen" Lee ended his opening prayer. "Today I'm speaking to you with a glad heart," he said with a broad gesture. "Last night, the Lord Jesus gave me a dream. I saw a darkened room with nothing on the wall. In the middle of the room I saw a group of people kneeling. There were three of them. I did not recognize their faces. One tall, dignified man broke an orange into pieces. First he squeezed some juice out of each piece into three glasses and then each of them drank from a glass. Next he gave each of them a piece of the orange. I heard him say, 'The Lord has said, "Take, eat. This is my body."' Then I saw the face of the one who distributed the orange."

Lee looked at Zhang. "Who then?" asked Ping.

Lee was silent until Zhang said, "Who was it?"

"You, Zhang," Lee answered.

"Impossible."

Lee smiled. "I'm only telling you what the Lord has shown me."

"If He's got something to tell me, then why doesn't He come to me?" Zhang asked in disbelief.

"I think the Lord's got big plans for you, Zhang. This is what He wants to tell you today."

Though Zhang couldn't believe what Lee was saying, he couldn't resist asking, "In North Korea?"

Lee hesitated for a moment. "I think so," he finally said.

"As a representative of your faith? A Christian? How can that be? I still don't understand a thing about your beliefs."

Lee smiled. "All in good time, Zhang. You must be patient. God has a plan for your life. He didn't bring you out of North Korea for nothing. It's not mere chance that you're living with us now. The Lord foresaw all of this. One day you'll get to know Him as He is. From that moment on everything will become clear to you, and God will show you what you have to do one step at a time."

"Can He show me where I can find my sister Hea-Woo?"

Lee remained silent.

"I thought as much," said Zhang abruptly.

Then Lee spoke softly, undeterred by Zhang's attitude. "Do you know why the Lord God only shows you one step at a time? Because if you knew the entire path, you would probably not dare to take a single step."

"So if Jesus knew He would end up on the cross, He might never have started out in the first place?"

"There's no need to be so disrespectful," said Ping. "Jesus was not a person like we are. He's God's Son."

"And am I not God's son as well?" asked Zhang. "You read it yourself yesterday evening: 'Children, I write this to you so that you will not sin.' Who was it again who said that?"

"The apostle John. You have a good memory, Zhang."

"You're always saying that we are God's children, that God leads us like a shepherd. Then why doesn't He lead me to Hea-Woo? Then perhaps I could go home. Then I could continue with my life. Or doesn't He know where she is at the moment? Has He perhaps murdered her already?"

"God doesn't murder people, Zhang," Ping answered.

"Oh, no? When I read the Old Testament, the blood almost splatters from the pages. Last week you talked about Samson who killed a thousand men with the jawbone of a donkey after God's Spirit had taken control of him. Now that's what I call mass murder."

Ping shook her head and then responded patiently, "The essence of the story is that when God's Spirit comes upon you, you are capable of doing unimaginable things. One day you'll experience that."

"I don't even want to! Before, I wanted to achieve everything in life. I wanted to become a general and defeat the Americans to show the world that my people are not to be made fun of. I wanted Kim Jong-Il to be proud of me. But not any more. Now I want only one thing."

No one spoke and then Hyok asked softly, "What then, comrade Zhang?"

Zhang looked into the boy's innocent eyes. He felt tears welling up but fought against them. "I want my life back," mumbled Zhang.

Lee moved next to Zhang and put his arm around his shoulders. "I've often asked you about your past, Zhang. Yet you didn't want to talk about it. I respected that. I think that the time has now come for you to tell us about it."

Zhang continued to fight back the tears but he couldn't help it. He began to cry. Nevertheless, in a broken voice, he started to tell his story. He talked about his mother, who had taught Zhang to be a true patriot, about his authoritarian and rebellious father, about the dreams that he and Hea-Woo had had, about the death of Kim Il-Sung, his mother's illness and her death. He told about the conversation with his father and Hea-Woo in the woods. He even talked about how he had wanted to betray his father and about the watch that his father had apparently left behind on purpose. Finally he sobbed, "It's my fault that they're dead." Finally, resting his head on Lee's shoulder, he gave into his tears.

"You don't know if they're dead, son," Lee said.

"But we haven't been able to find them. For months you've been inquiring about them through the Christian networks. Nobody has seen them."

"There are many networks. God is great. There is always hope."

Zhang shook his head. "It's impossible to find them. I shall never see them again.

But Lee responded, "Nothing is impossible for God, Zhang."

After that Zhang went to his room, where he continued to sob. He felt ashamed but could not stop crying.

"*You're a man now,*" his mother had said, "*a soldier. You may not cry. Your country needs you.*"

It was too late. Zhang had let everybody down—his mother, his father, Hea-Woo, Jin, his country, his god Kim Il-Sung. It was almost a year ago that Zhang had stood in front of the statue in Unsung and had said, "I swear to you, father Kim Il-Sung, that I shall defend your heritage with my life."

Zhang became aware that Hyok had nestled up against him on the bed. "You're my big brother, comrade Zhang."

Zhang tried to smile and pressed Hyok against him. "I have to go to work," he said.

✪ ✪ ✪

"There you go! Hope you enjoy it." Zhang put two cups of cappuccino and two cakes on the table for two Korean businessmen.

"Thank you, waiter," one of them said.

"My pleasure," Zhang responded as he walked away, lifting his tray high in the air so that he could pass his colleagues easily.

"You're in a cheerful mood today," his boss observed.

"It's a beautiful day," Zhang answered, unable to suppress a smile. Strangely he realized he hadn't felt so happy since arriving in China. It had done him good to get things off his chest this morning. It was as if a weight had fallen from his shoulders. Zhang reported to the bar, where Fen was washing up glasses. She was by far the prettiest girl who worked there. Zhang leaned against the counter. "Hello, beautiful," he whispered.

"Pardon?" Fen responded, while looking at him out of the corner of one eye.

"Got any plans for this evening?"

"The word boredom does not exist in my vocabulary."

"Wanna go with me to the Green Dragon cafe?"

"With you and your friend Jin? No thanks. That'll only be another disaster."

"No, no. Jin's gone."

Fen stopped her work and looked at Zhang. "Gone? How do you mean gone?"

"He's gone back home," Zhang whispered.

"Oh—voluntarily?" she whispered back.

Zhang nodded.

"Thank goodness—that he went voluntarily, I mean. He wasn't my type but I would not wish anybody to . . . Not that it matters now. He's no longer here. Didn't you have to go with him?"

Zhang shook his head and stared at Fen.

"Why not?"

"Because of you," he said, still gazing at her.

Fen's cheeks turned red. "What do you mean by that? You can never say anything serious." She picked up another glass to wash.

"Well listen. How can I go back home if I've not even been out with you once?"

She stopped washing and took a long look at Zhang; then she said, "You must promise me one thing."

"I promise you everything."

"If you ever go back, you must take a letter from my mother. She still has an aunt living in . . . ah . . . your country, by chance near Unsung. You came from Unsung didn't you?"

"Shh. Not so loud."

"Sorry."

"Never mind. Okay. I'll take the letter with me. On one condition."

"And that is?"

"That you go out with me tonight."

"Ha! Okay then. After work I'll get changed and we'll go to the Green Dragon. But I can't promise you that I'll stay for long."

"Fantastic. See you later!" Zhang turned and walked away to take another order.

"Zhang?" she called to him.

He turned back and was instantly swiped with a wet sponge.

"Hey!" said Zhang pretending to be angry. "What have I done now?"

"No getting drunk tonight, okay?" She was not smiling.

"Don't you worry about that," he said.

❂ ❂ ❂

Zhang ran—faster than he had ever run before. His feet scarcely seemed to touch the cobblestones. His chest was heaving, but he continued to run, forcing himself to keep running, despite the pain in his left foot. He pushed people aside, fell once, and then grazed his arm on the wall when he took the corner too tightly. He didn't care.

"Poor little devils," one Korean customer had said to his colleague. "I gave them some money each day."

"It's sad. This is a sad country," another responded.

"Very sad," said the third man. "What will happen to them now?"

Zhang wondered if he could not go faster. *Steal a bike perhaps? No, that was pointless.* He was almost there. He had to see it for himself. With his own eyes. He had to know for certain that...

"What will happen to them? You don't need to have illusions about that," the first man had said.

"Sent back. Even at their young age . . ." added the second man.

"And it happened in front of our hotel—in broad daylight."

"Which hotel? Not the Rainbow Hotel?" Zhang had asked.

The men had been surprised by Zhang's question. "Yes, the Rainbow Hotel."

Zhang had flung down his tray and dashed out.

"They've probably taken them already!" one of them had called after him.

Jumping onto the sidewalk, Zhang just managed to avoid being hit by the truck. But the truck stopped, and the driver, a Chinese soldier with large, black sunglasses, leaned out the window and subjected Zhang to a volley of abuse. He acted as though he wanted to hit Zhang, but his colleague pulled him back into the vehicle. Then the truck slowly started off again. Onlookers watched it move down the street.

It was a fluorescent green military truck, one with an open back, used to transport soldiers. At the tailgate sat two young, slender soldiers quietly talking to each other. Zhang could not see clearly who else was in the truck. He jumped onto the hotel steps to be high enough to look into the rear of the truck. He saw a group of Korean children. Most of them were crying. Suddenly, one of the boys stood up and raised his hand.

No . . . it could not be true . . .

Zhang looked into the mournful eyes of Hyok. He wanted to run behind the truck, but his legs did not move. Hyok placed his right hand on his heart and waved with his other hand. Zhang looked away. The truck went around the corner.

The doorkeeper of the hotel glanced sideways at Zhang. "You aren't one of them are you?"

Zhang's heart raced. "No!" he nearly shouted.

✪ ✪ ✪

Zhang stepped inside a cafe. Alone, he had walked through the town for hours. The bright winter sun had given him a stabbing headache, and the memory of that truck disappearing out of sight hurt even more. One hundred times per minute he saw Hyok with his puppy eyes standing in that truck. He waved to Zhang as if he wanted to thank him for everything Zhang had done for him, and Zhang had looked away.

Another scenario ran through his head. In this one Zhang ran after the truck, and Hyok jumped out. Together they fled from the soldiers and laughed later that evening at their miraculous escape, while drinking cups of tea.

Over and over he heard the voices: *"Poor little devils . . . Sad . . . What will happen to them now? . . . You don't need to have any illusions about that . . . You aren't one of them are you?"*

"What can I get you, mate?"

"Eh . . . what?"

"What do you want? Or have you just come to the bar to hang out perhaps?"

"Oh . . . ah . . . beer, draft beer."

"Had a hard day?" asked the bartender, while he poured a large glass of beer. Zhang mumbled something, drank the glass down and ordered a second. After the fifth glass, the alcohol started to have some effect.

Zhang took a good look around the cafe. It was nowhere near as busy as the Green Dragon, where he had usually gone with Jin. At least there were young trendy girls at the Green Dragon. Here, except for Zhang, there were just three old men. On one wall hung a huge antique painting portraying a fist knocking on a considerably aged wooden door. Zhang could not read the Chinese text.

"What does it say?" Zhang asked, pointing to the painting.

"'A clear conscience need not fear if there is a knock on the door during the night.' Don't you speak Chinese?" the bartender asked.

"Not that good."

"Where do you come from? South Korea? Seoul? Business trip?" The bartender continued, though Zhang had not answered a word. "Yes, I can see that. Do all Korean businessmen wear waiters' clothes these days? Is that the latest fashion in Seoul?"

Zhang shrugged his shoulders. The bartender laughed so hard

that his beer belly scraped against the bar. "You needn't be scared of me. I won't betray you," he said. "I don't want that on my conscience."

"Do you have a clear conscience?" Zhang asked.

The man laughed again. "Me? At least as clear as yours!"

"Are you sure? Have you also betrayed your father and sister? And dragged two friends with you to a certain death? I've let everybody down. I've failed them big time. I hope that there will be a knock on the door tonight and that they take me and finish me off. I've had enough of life. Another beer please."

The bartender filled up the glass again. "This one's on the house," he said.

"Xie xie," Zhang said—thanks in Chinese.

The men did not speak to each other again. Zhang finished his beer and got off his stool, staggering a bit. He felt in his left jacket pocket. No money. And none in the right side. The barman stood with his back turned to Zhang. Quietly Zhang slipped out the door.

Suddenly the bartender was calling after him. "Where are you off to?"

Zhang started to run. He was lightheaded but managed to stay upright. The barman began to chase after him but stopped not far from his establishment. Zhang quickly crossed the street.

"They should arrest the lot of you and send you back!" the man shouted after him from the door of the bar.

It was already midnight when Zhang arrived at the house of Lee and Ping. They were sitting at the kitchen table. From the look of their folded hands, they had just been praying. Zhang remained standing in the doorway.

"Zhang!" said Ping. "Oh, thank goodness for that, you're home. Is Hyok with you? He should have been home long ago."

"We've already phoned everyone, but nobody knows where he is," added Lee.

"He wasn't . . .There was a raid this afternoon somewhere. Oh dear Lord, he hasn't . . ." Ping couldn't finish what she was going to say.

"I saw him," said Zhang.

"And?" said Ping. "Where is he?"

"Hyok isn't coming back again." He turned around, walked down the stairs to his room and flopped face forward onto his bed. In the distance Ping screamed in anguish. Zhang grabbed Hyok's pillow and pulled it over his head.

CHAPTER 4

od, if you exist, then please let Hyok escape. Let him return to us safely. He's still so . . . little, so young. God, please help him, wherever he is. Please give him food and make sure he isn't scared. Above all I ask you to rescue him. Amen."

Zhang had been praying the same prayer for eight months. Every morning, afternoon and evening.

"Nothing is impossible for the Lord," Lee said almost every day. "Only He can bring deliverance."

"Only He?" asked Zhang the day after Hyok's arrest.

"Only He," Lee repeated resolutely. "In Isaiah God says of Himself: 'I, even I, am the LORD, and apart from me there is no savior.'"

Zhang was reading the Bible with increasing regularity, even though the words still meant little to him. He prayed twice a day, mainly for Hyok, sometimes also for himself, his father and Hea-Woo. Occasionally he prayed for Jin, brother Lee and sister Ping. He still drank regularly, but less heavily than before. He also flirted less with Fen. Everything seemed so pointless. He picked up his diary, which on Lee's advice he had written in regularly since the disappearance of Hyok.

"Prayed again today. God remained silent. Lee said that Christians may never stop praying, hoping and believing. Outside, the winter is setting in. God remains silent. It's eight months since Hyok was taken away. Does God exist? Perhaps He only exists in the heads of the Chinese and the Americans. Perhaps He is only their God. Otherwise, surely He would have said something by now. After all, this is the ideal chance for Him to demonstrate that He really does exist. Each morning I look at Hyok's bed and expect to see him lying there. Each morning there's disappointment. Yet I keep on praying. It's all I can still do. Only I don't have the feeling that my prayers reach heaven. God remains silent. Yet why? I don't think He exists."

"Zhang, time for Bible study!" Ping called from the top of the stairs. Zhang put his diary away, got up from his bed and walked to the living room. The people from the Tuesday evening Bible study were already sitting there. Zhang still did not know most of their names.

There was a slender man with a thin moustache. In his mind Zhang called him "Moustache man." Next to Moustache man there was "Goatee man," an old fellow with a long gray goatee. The couple "Farmer and Farmer's wife" were there as well. Farmer's wife was clearly the boss, as Zhang had noticed earlier. Farmer did not usually say a lot and, if he did say something, he always agreed with his wife. Zhang had yet to come up with a nickname for the second couple. They were in their twenties, slightly older than Zhang. The rest were easily fifty-five years or older. Brother Lim who had helped Zhang, Jin and Hyok to this safe house was there as well.

Zhang greeted them politely, and they immediately stopped talking. "You don't have to be scared of me," he said. "Or was it me you were talking about?"

"No, son. You needn't worry about that," said Farmer's wife. Then there was another brief silence.

Finally Goatee man said, "We were talking about your country."

Farmer's wife let out an agitated sigh. "Do we really have to talk about it now?"

"Zhang is twenty, an adult. He's entitled to information. Or would you rather not know about it, Zhang?" asked Goatee man.

Zhang leaned forward with interest. "I'd like to know everything, sir."

"Brother Lim found a compatriot of yours yesterday," said Lee.

"Oh?" Zhang looked at Lim.

"We can thank God for that," Lim began. "He was more dead than alive. I found him during my daily walk in the woods. All of a sudden I saw a figure standing in the distance. 'Hello!' I shouted. He disappeared immediately. I had the feeling God wanted me to go after him but I can no longer run at my age. You've got the same problem haven't you, brother Woo?"

Goatee man smiled broadly and nodded.

"Then I heard a shout," Lim continued. "The man had fallen flat on his face. Soon I caught up and turned him over. He was as light as a toddler. When the man saw me, he started screaming. I was so shocked that I fell over backwards. The man just wouldn't stop crying out. I tried to calm him down. From his clothes I could see he was a North Korean. "Friend!" I called. "Friend!" He did not respond and kept on shouting while lying there on the ground. I was scared that the wrong type of people would hear him. All of a sudden he stopped. He had lost consciousness. I am ashamed that I did not pray for him while he lay there screaming."

"What did he look like?" asked Zhang.

"Terrible, emaciated, clothes dirty and worn out, big scratches on his face, his nails broken. He looked as if he'd escaped from a concentration camp."

"How do you know what people from a concentration camp look like?" Zhang asked.

"My dear Zhang, I spent seven and a half years in re-education camp number 20. What I saw there, I pray that you never have to experience it. I have experienced hunger. I've seen friends die from sickness and hunger. But . . . I have also seen God's love there as never before."

"In the camp? How can that be?" asked Zhang.

"That's something I can't explain. Something you can only experience."

"We're getting off the subject," said Farmer's wife. "Come now, brother Lim. Please finish your story."

"I dragged the man to the lake. That wasn't far from where we were. I threw some water over his face and got washed myself. He awoke in a drowsy state, and I started to talk to him slowly and quietly in Korean. He was calmer then. I promised to bring him some food, if he would wait. I quickly went home to get some rice. When I came back, I didn't see him at first. Fortunately, he appeared shortly afterward. He greedily ate the rice. It was now dark and I took him home with me."

"And had he said anything?" asked Lee.

"No, not even a single word. From his eyes I could see, however, that he had understood me but he said nothing. He didn't speak when we got to my home, and we once again gave him something to eat. Occasionally I asked a question. What his name was, where he came from, how he felt, if he liked the food. Yet he did not utter a single sound, just looked out of the window."

Lim sighed deeply. For a few moments he stared at the floor before resuming his story. "In the end I gave up. I gave him a spot in the living room where he could lie down. I didn't dare take him to the cellar to sleep. I had no idea how he might respond to such a small room. My wife and I went upstairs, but I couldn't sleep. I heard him walking about in the room. Suddenly, a door creaked. We only have one door that makes such a sound—the front door. Quickly I put on my sandals and sprinted downstairs, although sprinted isn't quite the right word . . ."

"Had he left?" asked Farmer's wife.

"He wasn't in the living room. The front door was still open. I went outside and saw him straightaway. He stood there looking at the stars. I placed my hand on his shoulder. He had not heard me and was startled. I was scared that he would start shouting again in his panic. That would have given us away. I do not know where it came from, but just before he was about to shout—his mouth was already open—I said, 'Comrade! It's okay!' I took hold of his hand and gently pulled him inside again. 'Couldn't you sleep?' I asked. He didn't answer. So I continued talking. 'Me neither. I'm far too restless. But you must not go outside. Otherwise you'll soon freeze to death.' I made some tea. 'Sung-il,' he said all of a sudden. The mugs almost fell out of my hands. 'What did you say?' I asked. 'Sung-il,' he repeated. He muttered more than he talked. 'Is that your name? Sung-il?' He nodded. For a moment all was silent."

"And then?" asked Zhang.

"He sat down, took a sip of tea, and fixed his eyes on me. And he started to tell his story. At first hesitatingly. He asked if I had ever heard of North Korea. I answered that I knew something about North Korea. 'You know nothing,' he said bluntly. And to my shame, he's right. What I heard pierced deep into my soul. He spent the entire night telling me what is going on in North Korea."

"Tell us, please, Lim. Then we can pray about it this evening," said Lee.

"The famine has gotten worse. People are lying dead in the street. Throughout the country groups of orphans are wandering about."

"Gotchabees," offered Zhang. "That means 'parasites.' That's how people refer to orphans in my country. Hyok was a gotchabee."

"There are thousands of Hyoks now," said Lim. "Perhaps even tens of thousands. When captured, they are locked up in orphanages, where they experience a slow, lonely, loveless death. Sung-il said that the fathers usually die first. The mothers keep going for longer. And once they're dead, there is not usually any safety net left. Countless people are wandering around through the country in search of food. Terrible!" Lim swallowed before he could go on.

"And in Pyongyang the Dear Leader is building a super expensive hotel! What a world!" Ping exclaimed.

"And no normal hotel, either! A huge pyramid," exclaimed Farmer's wife.

"How can people possibly wander about the country? They don't all have permits, do they?" Zhang asked. "Something's not quite right about Sung-il's story."

"The guards are less strict than when you lived there. Everybody needs food, including the guards and soldiers. And if they are at their posts at all, they're easily bribed."

"And how do people get it?" Zhang asked. "Private trade is forbidden. The state distributes the food."

"If I understood Sung-il correctly, there are markets everywhere. One moment here and one moment there. Sometimes legal, sometimes illegal, sometimes tolerated. I'm not exactly sure how it works."

"Why did Sung-il flee?" Zhang probed further.

"His wife is very pregnant with their first child. He is looking for food. He wanted to go back tonight. Fortunately, I managed to convince him otherwise. At least I hope so. He must get stronger first. If he doesn't, he won't survive the journey back. During our church service on Sunday, I would like to hold a collection for him."

"A collection?" asked Farmer's wife. "How on earth will that help him?"

"If Sung-il is arrested at the border, he might be able to bribe the border guards. I would rather he lost his money than the food. Otherwise his trip will have been for nothing," Lim explained.

"I think we have heard enough now," Lee said. "Let us go to our heavenly Father and plead with Him for Sung-il, Zhang and their compatriots."

"And let us also remember our brothers and sisters there," added Ping.

Zhang gave her a perplexed look. "Do you mean Christians?"

"Yes, Christians, Zhang. Even in your country, there are some," Ping answered.

Zhang couldn't believe it. "I've never seen a single one of them."

"They're Christians in hiding," Lee explained. "Come, let's pray."

Christians in North Korea? Tens of thousands of people roaming about? No checkpoints? It was all so surreal to Zhang.

Lee started with a long prayer for the North Korean people, and then Lim, Moustache man, Goatee man, Farmer's wife, Farmer and the young couple prayed. Ping closed the prayers and asked God to touch the heart of Kim Jong-Il. Zhang said nothing. In his heart he prayed for Hyok, Jin and Hea-Woo but he felt it was pointless. There was no God to hear his prayer.

✪ ✪ ✪

Sung-il had returned to North Korea within a week. Zhang would have liked to have met him, but brother Lim would not allow it. "Too dangerous. If he is arrested, he could betray you as well."

"And what about you?" Zhang had said. "He knows exactly where you live."

"Oh, well, if they find out what will they do with me? Put an old man in prison? Then let them. If my cell door opens, the Lord is waiting there for me. Sometimes . . . I long for that."

"I don't understand that. How can you long to go to prison? Zhang asked. "Why do you take the risks you do?"

"God's love compels us, Zhang. One day you'll experience this. Remember this: if you have trusted in people who have let you down, then carry on believing in people. If you have hoped for a miracle that has not happened, then continue to hope. If you wanted to leave a trace of love and somebody else trampled it underfoot, then keep on loving."

"I still don't get it," Zhang admitted.

"Think about what I've just told you, Zhang. Think about it."

Later Zhang wrote in his diary:

"I have memorized brother Lim's text about faith, hope and love, and for the past five days I've been thinking about it but I still don't get it. I have believed in Kim Il-Sung and Kim Jong-Il. They did not let me down, but I have let them down. I want to continue hoping in the miracle that one day I will see Hea-Woo again, but that's just like hoping that Mother will come back from the dead or that Hyok will once again stand at the door. And as for leaving a trace of love behind? So incomprehensible. Loving is something I can do, I think. But how do you bequeath love? I don't know. Brother Lee says that I must nevertheless keep on praying. So that is what I do, even though it is costing me more and more effort. Is somebody listening? And if there is, He had better answer quickly."

Zhang put the diary back on his bedside table and picked up the family portrait that Hea-Woo had drawn. With his index finger he moved across the faces. He breathed deeply. His alarm went off. Time to go to the restaurant.

"Hello," he said a little while later to his first customer. "What would you like?" The woman ordered a cup of coffee.

When he passed Fen on the way to the coffee pot, she said, "Your Chinese is improving, Zhang."

"Thank you. And may I say, dear lady, that you once again look stunning today?" Zhang said in Chinese.

"No, you may not," she said, pretending to be indignant. "I'm engaged now, you know."

"Oh that's a pity," Zhang continued in jest. "Never mind. I'll just have to ask the boss if he can take on a few more beautiful single girls."

"I've heard that he plans to take on another ten waitresses."

"Really?"

"Yep, otherwise there would be no chance of finding somebody who will like you."

"You rascal," said Zhang, and Fen burst out laughing.

Five soldiers came into the restaurant and sat down in the corner. Zhang looked at Fen.

"I'll serve them," she whispered. Go and wait in the kitchen until they've gone."

A few minutes later, Fen came into the kitchen. "Have they left already?" asked Zhang.

She shook her head and then pointed behind her. "This lady would like to speak to you." And Zhang saw that Ping was following her. Fen went back into the restaurant.

"Sister Ping? Is something wrong?" asked Zhang.

"There's news. About Hyok."

"What sort of news?"

"A girl is at our home. Can you come now?"

"If you tell Fen. There are soldiers in the restaurant. I'll take the back exit."

Zhang grabbed his jacket from the coat hook and hurried outside into the freezing cold. He waited around the corner for Ping and they hurried home together. The strong wind seemed to cut straight through his jacket. He pressed his chin onto his chest to let through as little cold as possible. *News about Hyok? Was he still alive? Had he fled again?* The cold and the wind made it impossible to talk.

In his heart Zhang hoped that there was no girl sitting waiting for them but that it was Hyok who was sitting there. He imagined how that small boy would describe his miraculous escape. Hope grew in Zhang's heart. *If you have hoped for a miracle that has not happened, then keep on hoping.* Had he hoped enough after all that this miracle would take place? After everything that Zhang had experienced, after all of the prayers to the invisible God, Zhang believed he had earned a miracle.

Ping opened the door and Zhang followed her inside. Immediately his eye caught sight of the young girl and a strange man who had apparently come with her. They were drinking tea at the table in the living room. Zhang guessed she was about fourteen years old. Lee was sitting next to her. He looked tense.

"And?" Zhang asked immediately. "What's the news?"

"This is Hyon-hi," said Lee. "Do you recognize her?"

Zhang shook his head.

"I recognize you, though," she said.

He sat down and looked at her perplexed. "I saw you at the hotel, when the police came to take us. Hyok said later that you were his best friend."

"Did they arrest you then as well?"

She took another sip of tea and nodded while still holding the metal mug against her mouth. A trickle of tea ran down over her chin.

"Dear girl," said Ping, "we are so thankful to God that you are here. Will you tell us what happened?"

Hyon-hi placed her mug carefully on the table and nodded again. Then she began her story. "The six of us arrived at the hotel where we came each day. The police were already hiding everywhere, in the hotel and on the street. When they saw us, they came out. We had to get into the truck. They brought us to the police station. They asked us who we were, who our parents were, and whether we had papers. Then they put us into a single cell. They took good care of us and were not very strict. After a few days we were put on a train. We had to take the laces out of our shoes and use these to tie each other's hands together. We traveled for a few hours and when the train doors opened, I saw North Korean soldiers."

"Were they also friendly?" asked Ping.

"Yes at first. Until the Chinese had left. Then they started hitting us." Hyon-hi's voice started to shake. "I was so scared."

"Ah, poor girl," said Ping. "Did they take you to the police station?"

Hyon-hi shook her head slightly. "To the prison," she said.

Ping put her arm around the thin girl. "Oh, my child."

"We were all put in a single cell again. This cell was already occupied by two men and a woman. They were very dirty and insects were crawling over them. They caused us to itch. And there were only four beds. One of the men was the leader of the cell. He did not allow us to talk all day. We were all given a saucer of water. Then for a while nothing happened. It seemed like they'd forgotten us. Someone asked if they brought us food and the cell leader hit him."

"Oh, my child," Ping said again. "Poor child," she held Hyon-hi against her. The girl did not resist and carried on with her story.

"We could only leave the cell after three days. Then we were all summoned. The prison director asked us questions. I was so hungry and thirsty but I was not allowed to have anything. Only if I gave an honest answer. They asked how we had got to China, where we had been and who had helped us. Sometimes somebody was kicked or hit—really hard."

"How did Hyok respond?" Zhang asked.

"He was really calm. He scarcely said a word and never complained."

That was the Hyok Zhang knew! "So how is he?" Zhang asked. "Where is he now? Is he still in prison?"

Hyon-hi stared at the table. Now she was almost crying. "Then the director asked if we were hungry or thirsty. He sent away a guard to get a present. The guard came back with an iron bowl. The director took off the lid. The rice smelt so delicious. I was so hungry. I could scarcely stand on my legs any longer."

Zhang didn't want to hear all of this. "Is Hyok still alive?" he asked loudly.

But Hyon-hi continued with her story. "The director walked in front of us taking small mouthfuls. He said, 'If one of you gives the right answer to my next question, then he or she may have the rice. The rest of you will go to bed without an evening meal.' I was so hungry I almost fainted."

Then Zhang interrupted again. "I'm not interested in that. Please tell me about Hyok."

Now Hyon-hi looked directly at him. "The director asked, 'Which of you has had contact with Christians in China?' A boy stepped forward."

"Hyok?" Zhang asked anxiously.

She shook her head. "Pom-su, a boy of fifteen. The director asked him if he had met Christians. He said no. Then the director asked, 'But you know who has seen Christians?' Pom-su nodded."

"What happened to Hyok?" Zhang asked angrily.

Hyon-hi continued, "He then pointed to Hyok."

No! "Is he still alive? Girl! Tell me he's still alive!" shouted Zhang.

The girl buried herself in Ping's arms, and Lee tried to quiet Zhang. "Calm down, calm down, Zhang. Let her tell her story. What happened next, Hyon-hi?"

Zhang sank back in his chair. He was sweating profusely.

The girl remained silent as Ping held her close. "You're safe here, Hyon-hi. It's good that you've come to us. Tell us what you have to tell."

"Go on," said the strange man. "Hyok meant a lot to these people. You don't need to be scared."

Finally Hyon-hi continued. "I feel so guilty," she said. "They put us in an orphanage, and I escaped again. I don't want to go back."

Please be coherent, thought Zhang. He squirmed about restlessly on his chair.

Then Lee asked, "What did they do to Hyok?"

Once again Hyon-hi turned her worried face toward Zhang. She resumed her story. "The director put the bowl on the desk and picked up a stick. He walked to Hyok and asked him if he had met Christians. Hyok looked scared but then said, 'Yes.' The director only nodded. 'Are you a Christian?' he asked. 'Yes,' said Hyok so softly that we could scarcely hear him. Then he got a blow in his stomach with the stick and fell to the ground. 'Are you a Christian?' the director asked him again. He cried. 'Yes,' he said, and he received another blow with the stick. 'And now?' asked the director. Hyok lay on the ground. I could see he was angry. And sad. Yet he still said, 'I love Jesus and I shall always be with Him.' They started to kick him. The men were so cruel. And we had to look. I had to look at how my best friend was beaten."

Zhang held his head in his hands. "No, no, no! Tell me it's not true! Tell me that he is still alive!"

Hyon-hi cried. "He screamed so loudly. He called out to Jesus. At the end he said, 'I love You . . .'"

"And then?" asked Zhang. He felt like pulling the hair out of his head.

"It was over. We had to go back to our cell."

"And Hyok?"

"He no longer moved."

Zhang felt a deep pain in his chest, as if somebody had driven a knife into his heart. He cried like he'd never cried before. Lee pulled him to him and tried to calm him down. "It's all over now. Shh, Zhang. It's okay."

Zhang's sobs filled the room.

"Calm down, son. Hyok is in a better place now. He's with Jesus now."

The sobs stopped almost as quickly as they started. Slowly Zhang lifted up his head. "What?" he said. "With Jesus?" Then he pushed Lee away so hard that he fell onto the floor. Zhang stood up. "With Jesus?" he screamed. "Without Jesus, Hyok would still be alive! Then he would be sitting here instead of this girl! Didn't you teach Hyok that he was never allowed to betray Jesus? It's your fault! You've murdered Hyok! You and . . . this Jesus!"

Zhang pulled a wooden cross that hung on the wall and hurled it at Lee who just managed to duck in time. Hyon-hi screamed. Then Zhang swung around and swept a vase from a side table. He stormed off to the cellar and threw his belongings into his bag. His chest was heaving and his head felt as though it would burst.

Lee followed him down the stairs. "Zhang, what are you doing? You're not leaving are you?"

"I've got no reason to stay here."

"Please don't do anything stupid," Lee pleaded.

Zhang took his savings from under the mattress. He counted the money. Two hundred yuan. Far too little for a year's work in China! He cursed.

"Zhang, if you don't want to live with us, then perhaps we can find you accommodations elsewhere."

"I'm getting out of here." He had finished packing his stuff.

"Where are you going?"

"Beijing and then . . ."

"South Korea," Lee added.

Zhang did not consider Lee worthy of a glance as he flew up the stairs. He also ignored Ping, the man and Hyon-hi. A few seconds later he was outside. The cold air pricked his face like needles.

Mother and Hyok were dead. Hea-Woo, Father and Jin probably also. He had never found happiness in North Korea and equally not in China. In a mere two years he had lost everything that was dear to him. He would go to the capital and once in Beijing he would report to the South Korean embassy. South Korea was a different world. Perhaps in that other world he would find ultimate happiness and forget that North Korea even existed.

The wind picked up again and it started to snow softly. The moon and stars were not to be seen.

✪ ✪ ✪

The train raced through the darkness. Sleet flew against the windows, changing immediately into streams of water. Zhang felt in his left trouser pocket. A 100 yuan note and a train ticket. In his lap was half a bottle of drinking water and between his legs he held his rucksack with a set of extra clothes. The only other things he had were the clothes he was wearing and of course Hea-Woo's drawing of their family. This was all he possessed.

Zhang took a sip of water to moisten his dry throat. The journey would take at least another three hours but Zhang had made up his mind to spend no more money until he arrived in the Chinese capital. With 100 yuan he could buy at most a bit of food and some water.

On the seat opposite Zhang a pair of lovers were sleeping, hand-in-hand, their punk haircuts seemed interwoven as their heads touched. The girl next to Zhang was listening to music on her portable CD player. Occasionally she hummed along to an English or Chinese song.

Zhang's heart was still beating violently, as though he were about to present a performance on stage. His plan was to go to the South Korean embassy in Beijing. He imagined himself pushing the Chinese agents aside. Would it then be long before they would take him to the South Korean ambassador? *Surely that man must consider himself a winner.* Zhang begrudged the ambassador that. He felt like a traitor—dirty, filthy, unreliable.

But what options did he have left? Returning to North Korea meant in the most favorable case a stay in one of the camps. When he was twelve years old, he had almost seen such a camp during a family outing. The rocks were steep and smooth. Mother and Hea-Woo had stayed behind. Zhang climbed far easier than his father and was quite some distance ahead of him. Suddenly he stood still.

"Zhang!" called Father. "What is it, son?"

Zhang stared at the sign on the fence in front of him.

DANGEROUS!
THIS FENCE IS ELECTRIFIED
NO ENTRY

Zhang walked up to the fence to see if he could see something or somebody. All of a sudden his father grabbed him firmly from behind by his wrists. "Careful! That's dangerous. You can read, can't you? Come, we're going!"

"What is that, Father?"

"I think it's a camp. That's where they put people who don't obey. Come on. Let's go."

Zhang walked behind his father. "Could I end up in such a camp, Father?"

"Not if I can help it, son."

Perhaps Father was in such a camp right now. Zhang would

never know. And Hea-Woo? He didn't want to think about that at all. He closed his eyes so tight that it almost made him dizzy. And he felt as if somebody had drilled a hole in his heart. Zhang laughed at himself—*a hole in my heart. Where on earth did that idea come from?*

The girl next to Zhang tapped rhythmically on her knees and sang softly in Chinese. Zhang could understand the words. "Give me something for the pain. Give me something for the blues. Give me something for the pain. I feel I've been dangling from the hangman's noose."

Zhang longed for whisky.

✪ ✪ ✪

Chaos. Zhang could use no other word to describe the main station in Beijing. Businessmen, families, young people, older people, people with large suitcases and packages, people with rucksacks, train guards, police agents, soldiers. Everyone was in a hurry and seemed to know exactly where they were heading.

Zhang could not see any signs pointing to the exit, only people crisscrossing past each other. Zhang swore inside. Why weren't they as disciplined here as in North Korea where the train guard blew on a whistle and everyone stood orderly in a row? Zhang heard Korean being spoken behind him. Perhaps those people knew which direction Zhang had to go. Perhaps they could even tell him how he could reach the South Korean embassy.

The Koreans were standing with their backs to Zhang and were busy getting their suitcases out of the train. Zhang tapped the shoulder of a man who was putting on his jacket.

"Excuse me, sir? May I ask you something?" Zhang asked in Korean.

The man turned around and looked at Zhang with a disapproving stare. He gave a brief nod.

"Do you know which way I should head for the center of Beijing?"

"Go right here." The man pointed ahead of him. "Follow the people."

Zhang looked to where the man was pointing. "Thank you. And do you happen to know how I can reach . . ." Zhang's words stuck in his throat for he had just noticed that on the businessman's jacket was a Kim Il-Sung badge. Zhang shrank back and stumbled over a suitcase, falling to the pavement.

"Sorry! Sorry!" said another Korean. "I shouldn't have left a suitcase there." He stuck out his hand to help Zhang back up. Zhang pushed the hand away. Again he saw a Kim Il-Sung badge. Then five Koreans bent over Zhang at once. All of them wore the image of Kim Il-Sung on their chest.

"It sounds as if you come from our country as well, right?" asked one of them. "Do you need to go somewhere? Could we drop you off perhaps?"

"Sorry! No." stammered Zhang. He scrambled to get up, ignoring the outstretched hands, and squirmed away into the crowd. He headed for where he thought the exit was. He had to get away, away from this mass of people, away from the station, away from this country.

✪ ✪ ✪

The lights were still on inside the South Korean embassy. They contrasted so strongly with the dark sky outside that Zhang felt he was staring at a painting. From the alley he took a good look at the building. A green cast-iron fence protected the South Korean territory from the Chinese. The building was a yellow-white color. Behind the windows hung large net curtains. Three luxury cars were parked on the square. *Were these Mercedes or BMWs?* What difference did it make anyway? The only important question was how Zhang could get inside without the police officers seeing him. They were not Korean. They were Chinese. They would arrest him if Zhang reported at the gate. There was no doubt about that.

The fence was not particularly high. Zhang would only have to stretch out his arms to be able to grab the top of it. He could sprint across the road, pull himself up the fence, and then sling himself over the top. By the time the agents saw him, Zhang would already be on the other side. But would he be safe then? Or would he have to be inside the building to be safe? It was just too big a risk to try that out now.

The streetlights came on. Just to be safe, Zhang took a step backward so that the officers could not see him. He would have to return tomorrow. Then it would be Wednesday and Zhang could closely observe the activities of the day. In particular it would be good to know when the police officers relieved each other and how they did that. He would also need to observe the visitors. What did they look like? How did they behave? How carefully were they checked? Who was allowed through and who was not? Yes, it would be wiser to investigate these things properly before attempting to get inside.

Zhang turned around and walked past a hotel. He was freezing. It had been sleeting for some time and he was drenched. A Western businesswoman with a thick fur coat and high heels passed Zhang quickly and walked into the hotel. He stared after her. A bit of warm air escaped from the building and warmed up Zhang's face. If only he could book a room and observe the embassy from the hotel. Through the glass door he could see the reception and a price list. The cheapest room cost 420 yuan per night.

Zhang walked farther. He had to find a place to sleep. In North Korea Zhang would have gone to the station, as a lot of people sleep there at night. Yet Zhang did not know for certain if that were the case here. After his encounter this afternoon, he did not want to run the risk of accidentally meeting North Koreans again. His only option was to look for a dry place on the street for the night.

Turning onto a side street, Zhang found a sheltered doorway and sat down. He was shivering from the cold and was annoyed that he had lost his bag of clothes at the station during that fuss with his countrymen. And they were his decent clothes. Those were the ones he had wanted to put on when he went to the embassy.

Gradually the sleet turned into snow. Zhang fell asleep. He dreamt that Father and Hea-Woo were waiting for him inside the embassy.

❂ ❂ ❂

"Hey you! Dirty tramp! Get away from my shop!"

A kick to Zhang's thigh woke him up. He rubbed the aching spot, and the man kicked him again.

"Stop it! I'm going." Zhang struggled to get up. Sleeping in the doorway in the cold had made his muscles stiff.

The shopkeeper glared at him. "Are you Korean?" he demanded. Only then did Zhang realize he had spoken Korean. "I ought to turn you in!"

"Go on then," Zhang said defiantly in Chinese.

But the shopkeeper turned to go into his shop. "Get out of here! And never let me see you again."

Zhang walked away rubbing his arms and chest, trying to warm up a bit. It was cold, but at least the sun was shining. At a supermarket, Zhang bought water and a roll for 25 yuan and ate half the roll immediately.

When he reached the embassy, he settled down in the alley in a sunny spot. From here he could see enough, and if he did not get any closer, it seemed unlikely that he would attract any attention.

As the hours passed, Zhang saw various luxury cars drive inside through the big gate. He could not see if the ambassador was in one of them. He would not recognize him anyway. The Chinese guards in their green uniforms looked more like soldiers than policemen. They stood the entire time in their sentry box until visitors reported.

It was mostly businessmen who wanted to get into the embassy. Sometimes entire families as well. Zhang paid particular attention to the children. They played with a ball, sauntered listlessly behind their parents or pulled the hair of a younger brother or sister.

How could they look so happy? Before Zhang had fled to China, he had seen photos of demonstrations in the South Korean capital, Seoul. People with banners were protesting against their government. That was quite unthinkable in North Korea, and Zhang had considered himself fortunate to be part of a far more disciplined people.

Zhang forced his thoughts back to the present. The image of the playing South Korean children stayed with him. *So fortunate, so carefree. Had they ever seen a friend die of hunger?* According to the North Korea newspapers, they had. Yet their expression was far happier than that of their North Korean contemporaries.

By late afternoon the sun was gone and a shadow hung over the alley. For some time now, no new people had gone into the embassy. Occasionally cars drove off.

Zhang closed his eyes to think. He had seen policemen change guard on three occasions. It happened without a lot of pomp and ceremony. However, it was a moment when the guards were distracted, as they appeared to be chatting to each other about their duty so far. If Zhang wanted to try to climb over the fence, then that would be his best opportunity. On the other hand, there were twice as many policemen around then.

"Who are you?"

Zhang was wrenched out of his thoughts and looked up into the eyes of a tall man. Zhang jumped up quickly. His legs were stiff from the hours of sitting. The man had a South Korean appearance and a stern face that reminded Zhang of Mr. Ahn from Unsung. His eyes were squinting behind the lenses of his large glasses as he watched Zhang, waiting for an answer.

"I . . . uh . . ."

"Come with me," said the man. Together they walked fifteen meters farther down the alley, away from the embassy. "This is far enough." The man paused and looked at Zhang. "I've seen you from my window. You have been sitting in this alley all day."

"Do you work in the emba . . .?" Zhang began. "Are you the ambassador?"

The man laughed. "No, no. I'm not the ambassador. But I work there. Now that's enough about me. Something tells me that you'd like to get inside."

"How do you know that?"

The man smiled. "You hardly need to be Sherlock Holmes to figure that out."

"Who?"

The man laughed again. "You've just given me more evidence of why you're here. The entire world knows who Sherlock Holmes is, except for our northern neighbors, of course. Never mind. Take a look at yourself. Your clothes are threadbare. You've been waiting the whole day in front of the embassy but you've not gone inside. And then there's that beautiful accent, the fact I frightened you and . . ."

"Can you help me get inside?" Zhang interrupted

But the man continued his train of thought. ". . . and the fact that you probably don't read the newspapers. You don't know that China and my country are embroiled in a political storm at the moment. No? I thought that much. You know, uh . . . what's your name by the way?"

Zhang remained silent.

"Fine. You know what, son, you're not the only North Korean who comes knocking at our door asking for asylum. That gives us a mountain of hassle and paperwork. That's not so bad, though. I've worked at the embassy for fifteen years and embassies are good at doing paperwork. Seems as if they were made for it. Yet the paperwork is not the worst. China doesn't like North Koreans coming to visit us. That's what we're talking about with them right now. China wants to repatriate economic refugees like you. In other words they want to send them back. And China is an important country to us—trade relations and money—you know the story."

"I asked if you could help me get inside," Zhang was impatient with the man's complaints.

"If I help you get in, it'll cost me my job. If you succeed in reporting to the embassy, we're obliged to help you. Our constitution states that we're not allowed to refuse asylum seekers from the North."

"So you're not going to help me?" Zhang felt instantly deflated.

"I've got a family."

"I've got nothing," Zhang stated matter-of-factly.

The man lit a cigar.

"Okay then," Zhang said. "What must I do to get into the embassy safely? Should I climb over the fence?"

"Climb over the fence?" The man was surprised by this idea. "That's a new one. You can try it. Officially you're then on South Korean territory and the Chinese policemen can't do a thing to you. But in practice it doesn't work that way. Within half a minute they'll pick you up and drag you back onto the street again. Half an hour later you'll find yourself in a cell. A week later you'll be back in your home country. Of course the South Korean Republic will make an official protest and you'll be the subject of the next political discussion. Perhaps the newspapers will even write about you." He took a deep puff on his cigar and exhaled the smoke. "That means a week full of work and hassle for us. After that you're nothing more than a name in a file in this part of the world, whereas in your own country you'll be fighting for your life."

Zhang leaned back against the wall and took a deep breath. "What's your advice then?"

"To get into the embassy?"

Zhang nodded.

"Try to convince the policemen that you need a visa or that you lost your passport. If they let you through, you'll walk to your freedom."

"And if not?"

"Then you'll go the opposite way."
Into the prison camp.

Zhang could have kicked himself. Although the man did not want to help him get inside the embassy, he might have been prepared to give him some money. If only Zhang had asked him! Now he had run out of money.

For the fifth day in a row, Zhang stood across the street in front of the embassy. Twice he had almost walked up to the gate. Once, at the end of the afternoon just before closing time, he dared to cross the street to the fence. He was given a warning and fled immediately. Climbing over the fence at night was not an option. The embassy was closed then. They would arrest him for attempted burglary.

Now, without money, without food, without clean clothes, he had to do something. Zhang realized he had already waited too long. He walked back to a nearby hotel and looked at his reflection in the window. *A tramp*, thought Zhang. *I look like a tramp.*

There was no possibility of shaving, maybe he could wash himself. He could slip into the hotel and find a toilet. No, that could lead to a commotion. That was the last thing that he needed now. He remembered a park nearby and went there.

Zhang shivered from the cold. The sun had just disappeared behind the clouds and it felt as if the temperature had instantly dropped by ten degrees. Perhaps it was even freezing now. Zhang found a drinking fountain and repeatedly threw small quantities of ice-cold water over his face. He dried it with his sleeve.

Zhang's heart beat frantically in his chest. *This was the moment. It was now or never. Freedom or prison camp.* Zhang squatted down. Was it really that simple? Just walk to the embassy and ask if they would let him inside? It had to work. He was a young man of almost twenty-one, in the prime of his life. It had to be possible for him to make something of his life. He had to survive this. If this went wrong, he would fight for his life. Whatever happened, they would not catch him—better dead than repatriated.

He stood up, smoothed down his dusty jacket and said to himself, *Off we go. Freedom here I come.* With a firm stride he walked back to the embassy. *Concentrate now. This is important.* He was close to the embassy and he found his pace beginning to slow down. The embassy was now in sight. No more doubting. *Walk through confidently so as not to look suspicious.*

He crossed the street and walked directly up to the gate. The two policemen looked up briefly, said something to each other and waited until Zhang reached them before they came out of their sentry box.

"Good afternoon," said Zhang in Chinese.

"Good afternoon," answered one of the policemen. He was broader and taller than Zhang. His colleague was a lot smaller but had broad shoulders. Zhang felt weak. In a fight he would not beat them.

"I'm visiting Beijing but I've lost my passport." Zhang's hands were wet from sweating but he tried to act as nonchalant as possible.

"That's not good news, sir," the agent said. "What's your name?"

"Choi. Choi Zhang," he lied.

"And how long have you been in Beijing?"

"Ten days."

"Where did you lose your passport?"

"Close to my hotel, I think."

"Which hotel are you staying in?"

"The New Beijing Hotel."

"Oh, then you have a good view of the lake?"

"My room's on the other side."

"Facing the park?"

"I've not had much time to look out of the window."

"Right. Please wait here while my colleague phones the embassy reception." The man nodded to his colleague, who was once again in his sentry box. While he phoned, he kept on looking at Zhang. Zhang diverted his eyes to the ground and took a deep breath.

"Is it just as cold as this in Seoul at this time of year?" the tall guard asked Zhang.

"Sometimes even colder." He tried to look past him to the guard in the sentry box, who had now finished his phone call. From the corner of his eye, Zhang saw a police car stop and three policemen get out.

"And in Pyongyang?" the guard opposite him grinned.

"Never been there," said Zhang and he kicked the man in his groin. The small agent at the gate had already taken his baton off his belt and his colleagues were running toward him. The chance to get into the embassy had gone. *Go. Go. Go!*

Zhang ran. He felt light, as if he were running in a dream. There was no hunger, no thirst and no tiredness. The policemen behind him moved in slow motion. Yet they were getting closer.

Zhang turned left onto a narrow street. He tipped over two trash barrels, but these scarcely slowed down the policemen. Zhang heard his pursuers ranting and screaming in the distance.

Suddenly screeching tires jerked Zhang back into reality. He jumped out of the way of a car driving directly toward him. Then behind him he heard a loud crash. When he turned around, he saw that a black BMW had stopped sideways across the street. The police-men had run into the car.

The driver jumped out of his car. It was the embassy worker who had talked with Zhang.

"Kamsahamnida," shouted Zhang, though he was completely out of breath. *Thank you.*

The man looked at him and said nothing.

The first policeman was already climbing over the hood of the car. Zhang started running again. He ducked into an alley. Several hundred meters farther he stopped running, gasping for breath. The policemen were no longer to be seen or heard.

✪ ✪ ✪

Night had fallen. Zhang was bitterly cold. He rubbed his arms to keep warm. His shoulder hurt. When he fled from the police he must have crashed into something but he could not remember what it was. The hunger started to become unbearable. Zhang did not dare steal any food for fear of being arrested. Everything was better than getting arrested and repatriated. It would even be better to die from hunger and cold. That could indeed happen tonight.

Zhang coughed so hard he had to stand still a minute to catch his breath. He shivered and continued walking. He had to keep moving, but walking took a lot of energy. Occasionally he let his eyes close but then shook his head to drive the sleep away. The night was just a few hours old. Zhang could not keep this up.

He had to try to keep his thoughts in the here and now. But he would drift off and see himself playing with Jin in the green hills of Unsung. He laughed with Hea-Woo and cuddled with Mother and Father. He stood in front of the statue of Kim Il-Sung and promised to be loyal to him forever. Mother was buried. Father and Hea-Woo had fled. Zhang tripped over Hyok. Together with Jin they crossed the border. Jin went back home. Hyok died in prison. Zhang was at the embassy, fleeing, caught.

He woke abruptly from his sleep and realized with relief that he had not been arrested and he was still alive. "I'm still here!" he said aloud. "I'm still here!" He staggered but he knew he had to fight, fight against the exhaustion and cold.

Supporting himself with one arm against the building, he began to walk again.

After a while, he mumbled, "Rest. Rest. Please. Rest. Not here. There. At the street. Lamppost. Warmer." Half walking, half stumbling forward, he managed to get across the street and sank down onto the sidewalk and leaned against a building. The light of the lamppost was not as warm as he had hoped. He felt his body drawing him into sleep. He resisted. *I must not lose consciousness. I must not freeze to death.*

Zhang looked up at the building. It was not like the others on the street. On the large door hung a wooden cross. It was a church. He began to cough, causing shudders to travel through his whole body. He wished Hea-Woo were with him to hold his hand.

Once again the cross attracted Zhang's attention. How often had he prayed for Hyok, Jin, Hea-Woo and Father? It had made no difference. God did not listen. That cross, the symbol of the Christians, was the cause of Hyok's death. And weren't the Americans—the source of all misery—Christians as well? Zhang coughed again and felt his strength ebbing away. Sleep was coming over him. He shook his head. He did not want to die. He wanted to live. His eyes closed.

Whoever has the Son has life.

Zhang jumped. The words had entered his mind so forcefully that for a moment he thought that brother Lee was speaking to him. Zhang had the feeling that the cross was looking down at him.

Whoever has the Son . . .

"It's not true," groaned Zhang. "You don't bring life, only misery and death." He pulled his knees closer against his chest. He could no longer stop shivering. "Can you really give life?" he suddenly called out to the cross. "Can you give food? Can you make me warm?" He put his forehead on his knees. If only he could stop shivering. The cold, the hunger, sleep, the cross . . .

"Then do it!" he screamed at the cross. "Give me life!" Then his anger switched to sorrow. "Give me one more chance, God," he whispered. "One chance to make something of my life. Give me life. Give me freedom. Give me a chance. Give me one more chance to make something of my life." He sobbed. His resistance was broken. Sleep crept upon him like an assassin. He let himself sink away.

CHAPTER 5

Warmth. Light.

"I think he's waking up. Let's see. He has not really opened his eyes yet."

"Perhaps he can hear us, though. Friend, hello? Hello? Hmm, he's not responding. Make some tea just in case."

"I already have. Do you think he understands Chinese?"

"No idea. He looks North Korean. What should we do? "

"Phone the pastor."

Darkness.

✪ ✪ ✪

Warmth. Flowing over the lips and through the throat. Small drops of warmth. Darkness. Too strong.

✪ ✪ ✪

Light. People. Can't tell them apart. Voices.

"Lord Jesus, please watch over this brother. Bring him back to us."

Darkness.

✪ ✪ ✪

Pain. Left arm. Light again. Voices once again.

" . . . injection with antibiotics. That's all we can do for now."

"And pray, doctor. And pray."

"Indeed. His life is in God's hands."

✪ ✪ ✪

Zhang opened his eyes. Slowly the images came into focus. He lay on a leather couch under three thick blankets. His muscles felt stiff and painful. In the kitchen he could see a small, young woman. She saw that Zhang was trying to sit up.

"Let me help you," she said in Chinese hurrying to his side. She carefully pulled him up straight and rearranged his cushions so that he could stay sitting upright. "Would you like some tea?"

"Thank you," Zhang said.

She poured him tea then said, "I'll be back in a moment."

Zhang nodded. A little while later she came back with a much older man, who reminded Zhang of Goatee man. "I think he understands Chinese," she said.

"I can also speak it reasonably well," Zhang said in a hoarse voice.

"Oh, thank goodness." The man smiled broadly. "My Korean has never been that good. My name is Wong Manchu and this is sister Lee Mei Ling."

"Zhang."

"Welcome, Zhang. How do you feel?"

"I'm hungry."

"That's a good sign." He laughed. "Mei Ling is already cooking rice. We can eat lunch soon."

"Where am I?"

"In Beijing, in the parsonage of the church. You fell asleep on the pavement. It's a miracle you survived in this freezing cold. You can thank God that you did. He has given you a second chance."

Alive. I'm still alive! "Yes, I think He did."

Manchu looked at him in surprise. "Are you a Christian?"

Zhang shook his head. "I . . . don't know God. I have . . . underestimated Him."

"Would you like to get to know God?"

"Perhaps . . ."

Manchu drew a chair up near the couch and sat down. He leaned toward Zhang. "What do you know about Jesus Christ?"

"That He lived and died two thousand years ago."

"Died for who?"

"For me . . . my sins." *Am I really saying that?*

"Hallelujah," Manchu said softly and smiled. "That's all you need to know for now. As long as you believe it."

"Is that all? Is it that simple?"

"That simple and yet so difficult. Only by God's grace can you say that Jesus Christ is Lord over your life."

"But He isn't."

Do you want Him to be?"

"Yes, but it can't be."

"Nothing is impossible for God."

Zhang closed his eyes tightly. "I've done terrible things."

"God loves you."

Zhang shook his head violently. "I've betrayed my father and sister."

"God loves you."

"I've shot somebody dead."

"God loves you."

"I've caused the death of two friends."

"God loves you."

"I don't deserve it."

Manchu put his hand on Zhang's shoulder. "Zhang, look at me."

Zhang opened his eyes and looked into those of Manchu. "Do you regret the wrong you've done?"

Zhang closed his eyes again and cried. He had betrayed everybody. Manchu put his arm around him and repeated with a tremor in his voice: "Do you regret the wrong you've done?"

"Yes."

"Then listen carefully to what I have to say now. Jesus has heard you. He looks straight into your heart. He was there during everything you've gone through. He saw you. He carried you through the difficult moments. He brought you here and has kept you safe. Jesus came to earth so that I can say this to you now: your sins are forgiven."

"No . . ." Zhang shook his head.

"Jesus has forgiven you for the wrong things you've done. You can make a clean start."

"That's not possible."

"Believe it. It is true. Jesus says, 'I am the way, the truth and the life. No one can come to the Father but through me. I did not come into the world to condemn the world, but to save it. I am the resurrection and the life. He who believes in me will live, even though he dies; and whoever lives and believes in me will never die.' Do you believe this?"

"Yes," said Zhang through his tears. "I believe that . . . Jesus really can forgive me?"

"Have you listened to what I just told you?"

"Nobody is as guilty as me."

"He has already done it, brother Zhang! Come, let's go and eat."

Zhang shook his head.

Manchu looked at him in surprise. "No? Aren't you hungry anymore?"

"I want to pray first. I would like to . . . offer God my apologies."

"Okay, go ahead."

Zhang folded his hands and started to speak. "God, I have often prayed in the past but I always thought that you did not listen. Now I know how wrong I was. You were always there. I do not know You, I do not know who You are but I want to know You. I just want to know that You love me and that You forgive me. God . . ."

"You can call him Father," Manchu suggested.

"Father, please forgive me. I am sorry that I have betrayed Hea-Woo and my father, that I shot a man dead, that it's my fault Hyok is dead and perhaps Jin as well. Father, wherever they are, will you look after them? Forgive me that I've been so ungrateful. Thank You that You have given me another chance."

No one spoke for several seconds.

Finally Zhang looked at Manchu, "And now?" he asked.

Manchu looked at him with a wide grin. "Amen and hallelujah," he said. "Welcome. Yes, welcome into the Kingdom of the Lord."

✪ ✪ ✪

Zhang ran with large strides up the green hill, ignoring the stitch in his side. With the arrival of spring (his second in China) Zhang's energy had also returned. He had had pneumonia but it was gone and the good food, along with the prayers of his brothers and sisters at the church, had strengthened him.

Manchu had taken him to his home outside the city. He was the pastor of a church in Beijing and a church in a village some distance from the Chinese capital. Zhang felt at home in the house church in the countryside. The people were warm and involved. They were interested in his past, but also did not press him if Zhang did not want to tell them something. Their love appeared to be unconditional.

However, brother Lee, sister Ping and the other Christians in the border area had treated Zhang just as lovingly. He could see that clearly now and realized that he, not the Christians, had changed and he thanked Jesus each day for this change.

Here, running, with the wind in his face, Zhang felt more free than ever before. He had reached the top, and looked up to the sky and shouted aloud: "Thank you, Lord!" He was gasping. "Take a brief rest," he said aloud. "Sit down for a moment."

He looked out over the valley. The grass was green once again and the leaves on the trees were also coming out. In the distance farmers were working on the land. Several clouds moved slowly across the sky. Today was a beautiful day. "Thank you for the day that You have given, Lord."

He took a small Bible out of his inside pocket. After his conversion—that was still such a strange word—Zhang had read the entire Bible in a month. He had been amazed by God's rescue plan. He was surprised that God had given people a free will and yet still used them. Zhang felt sorry for the Israelites in the Old Testament. They were like Zhang—the truth had always been in front of their eyes, yet they were misled and did the wrong things. There was still a lot that Zhang did not understand about the Bible and, in particular, about Jesus. Yet he tried to overcome that. He read that Jesus was loving and noted that He mainly gave attention to simple fishermen and sinners. That gave Zhang a warm feeling. If somebody was simple and if somebody needed forgiveness and healing, it was he.

Jesus could also be strict, especially with people who acted as if they loved God but in their hearts did not really believe. Yet His disciples also got reprimanded sometimes. That was strange; after all, they could not help it that they knew less than Jesus.

In Acts he read about the coming of the Holy Spirit. The letters of the Apostles were complex but often beautiful. The letters of John attracted him most. So loving, so full of mercy, that is how Jesus must have meant it. After reading the last two chapters of the Bible, Revelation 21 and 22, he had to cry. If only things were like that already. If only the new heaven and new earth were already a reality. He prayed that he would meet Father, Mother, Hea-Woo, Jin and Hyok there.

Now Zhang opened his Bible to another of his favorite books, Isaiah. The past few weeks he had had a feeling that God wanted to tell him something through this prophet. It almost seemed as if this book had been written in North Korea. The hopelessness, idol worship and the refusal of people to follow God the book described were so applicable to Zhang's fatherland. He started to read in chapter 42: "Here is my servant, whom I uphold, my chosen one in whom I delight; I will put my Spirit on him, and he will bring justice to the nations. He will not shout or cry out, or raise his voice in the streets. A bruised reed he will not break . . ."

Zhang stopped reading. *A bruised reed he will not break.* It seemed so pure, so beautiful, so loving. He read on. He paused again in chapter 43. "Before me no god was formed, nor will there be one after me. I, even I, am the LORD, and apart from me there is no savior. I have revealed and saved and proclaimed—I, and not some foreign god among you."

"Yes, Lord, You are the Lord. Apart from You there is no one who saves," Zhang said and then underlined the verse. He read the two chapters again. Now his eye was caught by Isaiah 42:8. "I am the LORD; that is my name! I will not yield my glory to another or my praise to idols."

Again Zhang spoke aloud about what he had read. "Yes, Lord, You do not share Your majesty with another. Nor do You share Your praise with an idol. Like in my country. But Lord, the people there do not know it. They do not know it!"

Suddenly, it was clear what God desired of him. "They do not know it," he said more to himself now. "No, Father, no. That cannot be. That's impossible." Zhang stood up and walked down the hill. His head was bowed and he was deep in thought. "You . . . You cannot be serious," he said aloud. "It's too dangerous. It cannot be done. Surely You know that! They'll put me in a camp. They'll finish me off."

I will not yield my glory to another or my praise to idols.

"There are others, Lord Jesus. Why me? What can I do?"

A bruised reed he will not break.

"Stop, Father. Give me time to think about it. I'm so happy. I'm free, as free as somebody from North Korea can be. Why this then? Why risk everything?"

Zhang started to walk more slowly. Suddenly he had to think

about Jesus, who was with God before He descended to earth. In his thoughts he heard Manchu saying, "Jesus had the choice of staying with the Father but He left the heavenly throne room and descended to a world that did not know Him, a world that despised Him. For our sakes He became a lost Son to bring us back to the Father. You are a lost son as well, Zhang. And so am I. And from the moment that a lost son comes to his senses, it is his duty to point others toward the Father."

The door to Manchu's farmhouse was open and Zhang walked straight into the living room. The old man appeared to be busy preparing his sermon. When he looked up from his Bible and his notes, he felt concern for his young friend. "You look so pale, Zhang."

"Jesus wants me to go back."

"What do you mean? Back where?"

"Back home. God does not yield His glory to another or His praise to idols." Then Zhang walked around the table and disappeared into his room. Manchu followed him and sat down on Zhang's bed. Zhang paced up and down the small room.

Finally Manchu asked, "Why does that mean that you must go back?"

"Well, who is going to tell my countrymen? How can they know that they must worship the true God? You yourself have said that a lost son must lead people to the Father."

"What have you said to God?"

"That it cannot be. That it's impossible. They will murder me there. I do not want that. I'm happy and free—more or less. You are like a family to me. Why should I go back?"

Manchu laughed and slapped his knee.

"Why are you laughing?"

"Oh, sorry! This is a most serious matter, of course. It's just that if God asks you to do something, you had better not refuse. Otherwise you'll end up in a fish."

"You mean just like Jonah?"

"Yes. I'll tell you exactly what I mean in a moment. First of all let's pray that God will confirm whether this is the path you should take and if He will give you peace and rest concerning it."

Zhang knelt on the floor, and Manchu asked God to reveal His plans. After the prayer he said, "Now read the story of Jonah and see if God speaks to you through that story as well. Seek confirmation. And whatever your decision, consider this: He who is in us is greater than he that is in the world."

"Why Jonah?"

"You'll see that when you read the story from start to finish, Jonah went even though he didn't really want to."

By evening Zhang felt a bit calmer. He knew God was in charge of everything. He was stronger than the devil, even stronger than Kim Jong-Il. Who could harm Zhang if God was with him? One man plus God was a majority. Even in the prison camp God reigned supreme. But what all this might mean in practice was a mystery to Zhang. There were many (tens of thousands? hundreds of thousands?) Christians in the camps. Manchu had told Zhang that. Why didn't God get them out of there? It was beyond Zhang. Yet he still believed that somehow God was protecting them.

Zhang opened his Bible to the book of Jonah. He read how Jonah got into problems because he refused to go where God sent him. Zhang smiled. He identified strongly with the pigheaded Jonah. In his heart Zhang rejoiced when he read how Jonah eventually submitted to God's command and at the effect that his words had: the city repented immediately.

Zhang closed the Bible with a smack. "You really want me to go, don't you?" He said out loud. "You want me to go. Okay, Lord, You win. Please don't send any fish to get me. Here I am, Lord. I will go. But I need Your guidance. Amen."

He got up and walked into the living room. Manchu was reading a book and did not notice Zhang until he cleared his throat to attract attention. Then Manchu took off his reading glasses and looked at him.

"I'm going back home."

Manchu laughed, stood up and hugged Zhang. "It's about time. I've been praying for this moment for months!"

"What?" Zhang shouted and then, suppressing a smile, he said. "So this is all your fault?" He grabbed Manchu by the throat and pretended to strangle him.

Manchu laughed. "Of course it's my fault! You don't think I explained the gospel to you each day so that you could keep it for yourself, do you?" Then Manchu's tone became serious and he placed his hands on Zhang's shoulders. "I shall prepare you for your return. Now your life is about to begin for real, comrade Zhang."

"Brother Zhang."

"Yes, indeed. Brother Zhang." Manchu kept his hands on Zhang's shoulders for a long moment. Then he dropped them to his side and returned to his desk.

✪ ✪ ✪

The moonlight bathed the Tumen in a silver glow. The river bordering between China and North Korea was 30 meters wide at this point. On a hill hidden between thin trees, Manchu and Zhang sat looking into the dark North Korea. Behind them shone the neon advertisements of Chinese shops and casinos. This evening in the Chinese town, people would become drunk, gamble, argue and fight—the downside to freedom. Yet behind Manchu and Zhang there were also Christians who could meet in relative freedom.

In the country in front of Manchu and Zhang, that was impossible. In Zhang's fatherland only "the sons of gods who the heavens had sent" were honored, Kim Il-Sung and Kim Jong-Il. The first was no longer alive but was still officially the president. How could Zhang ever have believed that? The sons of the gods had kept a stifling stranglehold on North Korea for the past fifty years. How much longer could these people survive without oxygen?

Every time Zhang thought about Kim Il-Sung and Kim Jong-Il, he had to try really hard not to hate the pair of them. Every day he asked God not to let hate gain a foothold in him but instead to fill him completely with heavenly love. Yet regularly he caught himself harboring feelings of bitterness. Without Kim Jong-Il, Mother might still be alive and he would never have been separated from Father and Hea-Woo.

There, on the other side of the water, Father and Hea-Woo were not waiting for him. What was waiting for him then? Hunger? Disease? Death? The camp? Or perhaps a large group of people who yearned for the liberating message of God's mercy? Zhang clearly felt the heaviness of God's call on his life. Hopefully He would intervene soon. Hopefully the regime of Kim Jong-Il would be converted, or otherwise quickly fall, so that there would be more room for the gospel. Hadn't the people suffered long enough?

Zhang had to think of Psalm 13:

How long, LORD?
Will you forget me forever?
How long will you hide your face from me?
How long must I wrestle with my thoughts
and day after day have sorrow in my heart?
How long will my enemy triumph over me?

How long would Zhang have to risk his life for Christ? For just a little while? Or from this day onward for the rest of his life?

It was a month since God had made it clear to Zhang that he had to return. Now that he could see North Korea for the first time in almost two years, covered in darkness, a flood of memories entered Zhang's mind.

In his thoughts he was once again walking the hills around Unsung with Hea-Woo, and together they were dreaming about the future. And Jin and he were wandering through the streets of Unsung to throw stones against Mr. Ahn's windows. Together they ran down the hill to chase away imaginary Americans. Jin brought back Zhang's shoes after he had had to give them to Kim T'an Gong during the criticism session in the village. Perhaps Jin was waiting for Zhang in Unsung. *Don't think about it. Not now. Remain focused.*

Are you sure you want to do it? Once again the question came from deep inside. Zhang tried to ignore it. He was convinced that God wanted him to return but still he was scared to death.

It was as if Manchu could guess his thoughts. "Zhang," he whispered. "Whatever might happen across that river and whomever you might meet, remember you have just three enemies. I've told you before. The traitor on the inside, that voice that goes against the will of God, which even uses Bible texts to hold you back, is the first. How do you combat that?

"Jesus says, 'What good will it be for you to gain the whole world, yet forfeit your soul?'"

"Very good. Quote the Bible. The second enemy is the world, people's thoughts. The world says, love yourself. And the Bible?"

"Love the Lord your God with all your heart and with all your soul and with all your mind and love your neighbor as yourself."

"The world says, gather your treasures here on earth."

"The Bible says it is better to store treasure in heaven."

"The world says that you are a slave."

"In Christ I am free."

"The world says that you shall not live without bread."

"I live from every word that comes out of the mouth of God."

Manchu was satisfied. He gave Zhang a fatherly clap on the shoulder. "Who is the third and last enemy?"

"The devil. He will attack me at my weakest points. He will use the traitor from within and the world to fight against me. He will bring me into problems and cause me to suffer. Then he will say to me that I am a child of God and should therefore not suffer. He is a big liar who cannot speak the truth."

"And how do you fight against him?"

"I will humble myself and resist the devil and then he will flee from me. I fight him with the truth, with God's Word."

Manchu squeezed his shoulder. "Good, son. Very good. In times of trouble always think about what the Lord Jesus Christ has done for you."

Zhang inhaled deeply the warm spring evening air, trying to relax. But it did not help. "How many people have you helped cross over the river again?" he whispered.

"Back to their country? Five. One man and four women."

"How did it turn out for them?"

Manchu shook his head. "I've not heard anything from them since."

Zhang pulled his knees up and rested his chin on them. Finally he said, "I'm scared, Manchu."

"You know, Zhang, you've always had contact only with me and a few others, because that was safer. But worldwide there are tens of thousands of people who support us. Perhaps even more. There are people who pray each day for you and your country, even though they do not know you. They know that God is at work in North Korea, that He calls people to establish His Kingdom and they pray for those people."

"Really? So many people? That's fantastic. But how do they know that they must pray for me?"

"They do not know you personally, of course, but God uses their prayers to give you strength and to protect you. Believe me. God is good. He knows what He is doing."

"So what do you think will happen when I cross that river in a little while, Manchu?"

"I've already told you. For a while we must avoid every form of contact. Perhaps even for one or two years. After that I will send people to find you in Unsung. Perhaps then we can see if we can help you."

"So I am on my own now?"

"Not on your own, brother Zhang, not on your own. Do you

know why I think the earth revolves, Zhang? Because then there is always somebody who is awake to pray for you!"

Zhang smiled. Old Manchu knew how to give a positive twist to everything.

"I'm serious, Zhang. In the end you need only one person: the risen Jesus Christ, the Man who said, 'I have been given all authority in heaven and on earth. I am with you, all days, until the end of this world.' Isn't that fantastic? God's Son, who has been given all authority in heaven and on earth, says to you that He will be with you, all the days of your life. And I know I can add to that: in all of your circumstances."

Zhang looked up toward the night sky and spread his arms out wide. "Thank you, Father."

Then Manchu was standing up. "Time to go. Get yourself ready, Zhang."

This was the moment. His heart skipped a beat. Now his search for Hea-Woo and Father had come to an end. Here at the river it stopped. A miracle would be needed if he were ever to see his father and dear sister again. He had fervently prayed for this and would continue to do so. But now he had to obey and return to the largest open-air prison in the world.

Quickly Zhang checked his rucksack. It contained a Bible, clothing and food. He stood up, stretched and pulled at the sleeve of his jacket that was too short. The clothes he had on were from another refugee. The material was far rougher than the Chinese clothing he was used to.

Manchu stood right in front of Zhang, took hold of him by both shoulders and looked him in the eye. "Pray and read your Bible, Zhang. Realize that every page of the Bible can give you comfort, courage and persistence."

"Every page?"

"Every page of the Bible contains enough wisdom, comfort and love to help a human life endure."

Zhang sighed. "Manchu, what will I do without you?"

Manchu sat down again and had a serious look on his face. "You know, Zhang, the Bible was written by persecuted Christians for persecuted Christians. All of the writers of the New Testament were persecuted, including the twelve apostles of Jesus. Despite persecution they were full of joy. Do you know why? Because in addition to the gift of faith, they had also received the gift of suffering. They got to know a side of God that remains hidden to other Christians. You are going to discover this other side."

He paused briefly. "What will you do without me? Soon you will be able to trust only in Jesus. He will help you. I have taught you on His behalf from the Bible, but He will reveal to you whom you can trust. Perhaps you will be taken prisoner. Perhaps you'll not even survive your journey. In the light of eternity, what difference does that make? This earthly life is but a passing stage. Jesus has already prepared a room for you in His Father's house. Come, let's pray."

Zhang knelt down beside Manchu. While they were praying, he felt Manchu's two strong hands on his shoulders. Manchu prayed for God's guidance, blessing and protection.

After they had finished praying, Manchu asked, "What do you think, Zhang?"

"I feel more at peace now. I think that it's time."

"Me too," said Manchu.

A cloud had half covered the moon. They walked as quietly as possible to the river. Zhang's heart began to beat wildly again. He felt warm. He had to go to the water. It had to happen now. He had to take off his coat and other clothes. No waiting. It had to be now.

Manchu tugged on Zhang's arm. Zhang turned around. What could Manchu want now? Manchu placed his hand on Zhang's head. Manchu said nothing, but Zhang knew that Manchu was blessing him in Jesus' name.

Zhang wished that Manchu would let him go. His heart was beating in his throat. He had to cross the river. This was too dangerous. The seconds were ticking away. Or was it minutes? Slowly Zhang's heart rate slowed. His breathing became quieter.

Manchu bent forward and whispered in Zhang's ear. "So says the Lord, who created you, who formed you. Zhang, I have called you by name, you are mine. If you must go through the water, I am with you; or through rivers, the current will not carry you away. If you must pass through fire, it shall not consume you, the flames will not scorch you. Because I the Lord am your God, the holy one of Israel, your Savior." Manchu kissed Zhang on his forehead. Never before had Zhang been kissed so lovingly. It was as if God Himself kissed him.

Zhang cried without a sound. He shook Manchu's hand awkwardly and then hugged him. Would he ever see Manchu again? Or would they only meet again in heaven? He took a deep breath as he watched Manchu walk away. The old man waved once more and disappeared into the darkness. Zhang was alone. The moon had disappeared. It was pitch black around him. The sound of the lapping water was the only thing he could hear.

Zhang took off his outer clothes and put them in the rucksack. He checked to see that his Bible was still in the bag; then he closed it tightly. He took one more look at the land behind him.

Cautiously Zhang walked with the bag above his head toward the water. Suddenly his feet felt cold and wet. *Here we go.* The doubts returned. If Zhang wanted to stay—in the "safe" China—this was his last chance. He only had to turn around. He could say to Manchu that he had heard North Korean soldiers, that crossing was impossible, that going back was not the smartest idea after all.

Zhang took a step forward. The water, colder than expected, enveloped his ankles. *Entertain no doubts. Take the next step.* He took a second step and a third and waded farther. Seconds later the water was up to his middle. There was a light breeze. Zhang moved on. He had to get across to the other side as quickly as possible and set foot on North Korean soil. Yet he still walked cautiously to make as little sound as possible. The water had already reached his shoulders. Hopefully he would not have to swim.

A ray of moonlight penetrated through the cloud cover and revealed a bit of the woods ahead of him. He had to wade through only another ten meters of water. The last few meters were difficult. The pebbles under Zhang's feet were smooth and slippery, and the current made keeping his balance tricky. But quickly the river became shallow and a moment later he was out of the water.

He shivered from the cold. In the woods he took off his wet underwear, cleaned his feet with them and put on dry clothes. He put the wet underwear in a side pocket of his bag. After that he unzipped the other side pocket to feel for his Bible—it was still there. And then he thought, *I'm back, Hea-Woo. Hopefully you'll return as well.*

Strangely reassured he threw the bag over his shoulder and started to walk. He imagined how he would like it to be when he arrived in Unsung again.

It would be a beautiful summer day. The hills and trees are green, the sky so clear, blue and beautiful as it could only be above Unsung. The afternoon sun casts an orange glow over the houses. Jin comes running to meet Zhang and embraces him. Together they walk to his parents' home. Father opens the door and laughs heartily. He gives Zhang a firm handshake and pulls him inside. As usual Hea-Woo is sitting in the living room, reading. Zhang places a hand on her shoulder. She turns around and can scarcely believe her eyes. After that she kisses Zhang on his cheek and hugs him. Zhang tells them about his adventures in China and his meeting with Jesus. Hea-Woo and Father nod. They understand and ask Zhang how they can become Christians as well.

Zhang shook his head. He had to stop daydreaming. Otherwise he would not be alert for danger. Still, he hoped that he really would be reunited with his father and Hea-Woo. If they had reached China, perhaps they had also become Christians. Then they would be capable of forgiving Zhang. Ah, there were so many people to ask forgiveness from—Father, Hea-Woo, Jin, Hyok, brother Lee, sister Ping. Yes, certainly brother Lee and sister Ping. Before leaving China, he had wanted to visit them again to thank them for their good care and patience. However, Manchu had convinced him that it was not wise to do so. He explained why.

"Not long after your departure, the police discovered them," said Manchu. "Brother Lee spent a month in prison. They are still watched closely. It is better if they avoid every contact with North Koreans."

"How long?" Zhang had asked.

"Perhaps forever."

"I would still like to visit them."

"No, Zhang. I will visit them shortly and I will tell them that everything is well with you and that you belong to Jesus now."

"Will you tell them that I am sorry?"

"I shall tell them that as well, comrade."

"Brother."

Zhang had already been walking for three hours when it started to get light. He heard rustling in the bushes and darted behind a tree. His breathing quickened again. Zhang pressed his sleeves against his nose and mouth. He should not make a sound. Minutes passed. Zhang still heard the rustling of leaves. It had to be an animal, a small animal. Cautiously Zhang began to walk. He stepped on a twig, and the cracking sound scared three squirrels away. In the dim light he saw the little animals hopping away from him. A little farther away all three of them made a big jump forward and then ran on with their characteristic trot.

Zhang walked to the spot where they had all jumped. Under a few twigs he saw a hole, a big hole. Zhang could have easily fallen into it. He pushed the twigs to one side. "Oh dear Lord," he said, putting his hand over his mouth. "Oh, God . . ." He walked around the hole and started to run. "Oh God . . ." That could so easily have been him . . . him who had fallen into the hole . . . onto those . . . bamboo stakes. They had been stained a deep red, the color of dried blood. On one of the stakes there was a piece of clothing. Blue. Probably a trouser leg. On another one was a lady's shoe.

Suddenly he stopped running. He had to be careful. Perhaps there were more traps. He closed his eyes for a moment and took a deep breath. *Be calm now. Be confident. Stay alert.*

✪ ✪ ✪

The shaking of the truck woke Zhang up. It had stopped suddenly. Zhang stretched and tried not to hit the heads of his fellow passengers. He thanked God that he had been able to hitch a ride on this crowded truck. They had not been checked at all on the way. He had not yet reached Unsung but they had stopped at a nearby village. Ten kilometers farther up lay his beloved home village.

Zhang's stomach was growling. In China he had prepared himself for his journey back home by not eating much over the past few weeks, but this was his first day in North Korea, his first morning without breakfast. He had a little food with him but needed to eat it sparingly, not knowing when or how he would be able to get more. The men around him ate an apple or a handful of maize. Nobody offered Zhang anything. He had forgotten—a North Korean does not share his food.

Zhang felt for his Bible in his rucksack. *It was still there.* Just imagine if somebody discovered it. That would mean a one-way ticket to a prison camp. He threw the bag over his shoulder, thanked the driver and jumped down. Without looking up or around, he headed toward Unsung. He walked at a good pace out of the town and into the green hills.

On the way he came across a lot of people walking to or from Unsung. Zhang did not recognize any of them. He tried not to look at them. It was too painful. Their bodies were emaciated, their gazes dull and they wore colorless, unwashed rags. Zhang had prepared himself for this in prayer, but actually seeing his countrymen in such a state cut into his soul. Without looking at them, he prayed for the people he met on the way. To be honest he wanted to give them some food or tell them that they must go to China. But he had to keep his food to himself and telling others about his visit to China was effectively suicide.

The village came into view—just a short way to go. Zhang picked up his pace, despite the pain in his legs and feet. The outline of the village was becoming clearer. Initially the houses seemed unchanged. The orange tiles were a bit duller than Zhang remembered. Also some of the white walls were damaged on the outside. Here and there were holes in the roofs and some of the windows had been replaced by wooden boards.

Zhang walked into the village. A group of men, all dressed in plain black, were squatting on the corner of the street, talking. A house shaded them from the sun. Two young women wearing large straw hats were cutting the grass around the Kim Il-Sung monument with a small pair of scissors. On the stone construction, in dark red letters, was the motto "Forward workers!" The women placed the cut grass shoots in a bag. In the past they would have thrown the contents of the bag away in the hills. Now the women would probably take the grass home to make soup.

"Comrade Zhang, is that you? How was it in China, defector?"

Zhang swung around. It was Kim T'an Gong, the man who had robbed Zhang of his shoes during the criticism session, standing on the opposite side of the street.

"Good day!" Zhang crossed the street with an outstretched hand. T'an Gong took a step backward, his mouth fell open in surprise. But he quickly put on a sour face and refused the outstretched hand.

"Go away, traitor. I want nothing to do with you. Or do you want both of us to end up in the camp? I'm going to report you!"

"Bro . . . Comrade T'an Gong, I've got nothing to hide. After the death of my mother, I spent some time with family in the North."

"Yes, sure. And your father and sister as well then? We have not seen any of you in two years. We know you fled."

"And why would I come back then? Or more important, why would I leave our fantastic state and go to that terrible China? There is no reason to flee. The Dear Leader takes care of us here." *Not a lie*, Zhang laughed inside. *Jesus is my Dear Leader.* "Mind who you point your finger at, T'an Gong. You never know what consequences that might have."

"You haven't changed a bit, Kim Zhang," said T'an Gong. His eyes seemed to spit fire. "I'd be careful if I were you." T'an Gong turned his back on Zhang and walked off with huge strides.

So this was it. This was how people viewed Zhang, as someone who had probably fled to China. How long would it be before the police arrived at his doorstep? If he was not arrested immediately, he would have to keep a low profile for a while and make sure that his behavior was "socialist enough." This meant that Zhang would have to talk negatively about China. Zhang hated that. The Christians in China did not have an easy time either but compared to North Korea the Christians there enjoyed considerable freedom. More important still, China was the country where Jesus had saved him. Zhang loved China.

Suddenly he felt a pang of regret. He had expressed a veiled threat to T'an Gong: "Mind who you point your finger at, T'an Gong. You never know what consequences that might have." It was a remark from the old Zhang, the Zhang who hid behind the powerful family of Jin. Zhang asked God to forgive his rash words.

Two minutes later Zhang was standing in front of his parents' house. The dark brown paint had started to flake. Otherwise the outside of the house looked good. The windows were still intact, although the frames were clearly rotting. He could not remember if he had locked the door on the morning that he had fled. He walked cautiously to the wooden front door and found that it was unlocked.

Inside he stood in the dark, musty-smelling kitchen and then quickly opened the curtains to let in some light. The house was very dusty, but everything was exactly where he had left it. Zhang felt as if he had opened up a door to the past, as if he had left only an hour ago with Jin and Hyok.

He walked into his parents' bedroom and then into the living room and opened all of the curtains and windows. Suddenly his eye caught the portraits of Kim Il-Sung and Kim Jong-Il on the wall. His heart missed a beat. They were covered in dust!

No, he must not allow himself to think like that anymore. Of course he had to keep the portraits clean; otherwise his mission would be over within no time. But Kim Il-Sung and Kim Jong-Il no longer exercised any authority over him. They were not gods. Zhang served the one true God, the God who had made heaven and earth, the God who knows what it is to love.

He used a handkerchief to clean the portraits, rubbing until they were immaculate. He had not forgotten how to do that. After that he sat down on the couch. He looked around the room. His gaze stopped at Father's chair. Empty. It was quiet in the house, unpleasantly quiet, as if life in this household had been sucked away and thrown into space.

The loneliness hit Zhang hard. It made him think of a book he had read in China before his conversion; *Bitter Herbs: A Little Chronicle,* which through a series of brief anecdotes described the life of a Jewish girl during the Second World War. At the end of the book were words that Zhang would not quickly forget: "I miss the faith of my uncle. They would never come back, not my father, not my mother, not Betty, not Dave and Lotte."

They would never come back. Not Father, not Mother, nor Hea-Woo and Hyok. His chest moved up and down heavily. The sadness welled up inside him with the force of a volcano.

"You're a man now," his mother had told him, "a soldier. You're not allowed to cry. Your country needs you." She was right. A North Korean man does not cry. Yet Zhang felt overwhelmed with this wave of sorrow.

✪ ✪ ✪

"Jin!" Zhang jumped up from the couch where he had fallen asleep. The sound of the door had awakened him.

"Comrade Zhang!"

The two friends rushed to each other and hugged.

Then Jin grabbed Zhang by the shoulders and pushed him away. "Let me take a good look at you, old tramp," he said and then quickly added, "You look terrible, man!"

Zhang smiled as he took a good look at Jin. He had a moustache, which looked strange on him, but otherwise he looked good—better than most of the people Zhang had seen along the road.

"It's great to see you again, comrade!" Zhang said with real joy. "Fantastic that you survived your way back."

"The feeling is mutual, friend. Fantastic that you decided to come home!"

They crashed down together on the couch.

"How did you know I was here? I've not been here that long," said Zhang.

"Have you forgotten how small Unsung is? Most people saw you walking in."

"Really? No one greeted me."

Becoming serious, Jin said, "That hardly surprises me. The climate in our country has changed, Zhang. People no longer trust each other. Everyone is making these so-called visits to family. There is too little manpower to check whether everybody has an exit visa. Entire families are wandering through our country in search of food. Many people cross the river to look for food in China and then come back again. Or not. Small clubs of people are sprouting up everywhere to exchange food and other goods with each other. They want to keep everything for their own group and so they want nothing to do with outsiders. They won't trust you, Zhang. You were one of the first who left."

"We were two of the first who left," Zhang corrected his friend.

Jin laughed out loud. "Comrade Zhang, I went back to my studies!

147

I have not been anywhere near China. Who would dare accuse me . . . No, let me put it another way. Who would dare accuse the son of Lee Young-Nam, better known as Mr. Lee, of something so treacherous as fleeing the country?"

"Good point. So that is what you said? That you were back at school?"

"Of course."

"How did your father respond when you returned after months of being away?"

"I don't want to talk about that." Jin stared briefly into space and then his mood changed again and he smiled at Zhang. "And you? Where have you been?"

"At my aunt and uncle's in the north," Zhang responded quickly.

Jin frowned. "Not exactly original but credible enough. At least somewhat. And your father and sister?"

Zhang sighed. "I wish I knew. What do people in the village think happened to us?"

"They think that you fled. Everyone knew that sooner or later your father would flee the country. He was not as patriotic as you might have thought. But nobody thought he'd leave so soon after the death of your mother—just one day after the funeral!"

"No, it was the day of the funeral. That was my fault," Zhang said.

"Oh, yes, now I remember. You almost reported them."

"Let's not talk about that," Zhang said quietly.

Jin stood up, walked to the kitchen, took two glasses and rubbed off the dust with his sleeve. He placed them on the table and took a bottle of soju from his coat pocket. After filling the small glasses to the brim, he gave one to Zhang and raised the other. "To your return!" he said and downed the contents.

Zhang put the glass to his lips, smelled it and let the warm liquid flow down his throat. Jin refilled the glasses and put the bottle on the table. "You know you'll have to come up with a good story about your father and sister. Otherwise people will think that all three of you have been in China. Right now special camps are being built for such people. Mobile work camps they're called. You don't want to end up there. Not even for a few years."

"What should I say then about my father and Hea-Woo?"

"Do you think they will come back?"

Zhang looked at his friend. He wanted to cry. He shook his head, "I don't think so."

"Then the easiest thing to say is that they died from hunger—at your aunt and uncle's home. And that is why you finally came back—to live in this house once more. Does that sound good?"

"I guess. I don't really want to think about it. But, yes, perhaps that is the best story."

"As long as Hea-Woo and your father don't return, you should be okay. Nothing can happen to you with such a story."

CHAPTER 6

Zhang was washing his clothes in the river. Since no one was around, he hummed, "Silent night, holy night," a song he had learned in China. He thought it was a great hymn. The phrase "radiant beams from thy holy face, with the dawn of redeeming grace," sent shivers down his spine. He enjoyed spending many hours every day with God but he did so alone. He wanted to evangelize but he didn't get further than dreaming about how the whole village would be converted. In reality, he had not once said the word Jesus aloud since his return a few months previously.

A summer breeze came up. If it kept blowing so pleasantly, his clothes would soon be dry. If only it could be summer all year round. In the village there were seven children under the age of twelve. *Would they see another summer?* This thought alone broke Zhang's heart. He resolved to pray for them every day. Perhaps he would even be able to share some food with them.

"But You'll have to provide some food to share, Lord," he prayed silently.

He put his wet clothes into a bag and walked back home. On the way, he bumped into Jin.

"Hey, Zhang! I was just looking for you."

"What a coincidence! I was just on my way home." Zhang laughed.

"I've got some bad news."

Zhang stopped and studied his friend's face. "What's the matter?"

"Do you remember Soojin? She was in our class."

"Yes, I remember her, a pretty, cheerful girl. Not much of a star when it came to learning texts by heart, though. I didn't really have much to do with her. Didn't her parents die last year? I heard that recently from someone."

"That's right. More or less, that is. Her father went off after his youngest child died. Her mother died shortly afterward, because she was giving all the food to her children. Then Soojin was left to take care of her little brothers and sisters, but they all died last winter. Soojin's now sick herself. TB. She hasn't left the house in days now. I don't think she has long to live."

"Awful. Shall we go and see her?"

Jin stared at his friend in disbelief. Finally he said, "Are you mad? She's got a contagious disease. I think it's a great pity that she's alone, I really do, but the risk is too great. Anyway, she may have already died."

"She's been alone the whole time?"

"As far as I know she has."

"No one has been to see how she's doing?"

"No, Zhang, only someone who was tired of life would do that. And you're not going to tell me that you want to go there. Don't you dare go getting infected."

"Don't worry," Zhang said, starting to walk toward his house.

"I mean it!"

"I won't go getting infected, Jin. Sorry, but I have to go home."

Jin watched him go. "Wait a moment, comrade Zhang." He hurried to catch up with Zhang, put his hand in his coat pocket and took it out again. "Hold out your hands."

Zhang held out his hands. Jin dropped a handful of rice into each one. Zhang looked at him wide-eyed.

"Blood brothers, don't you know?"

"I'll never forget it, comrade." *Thank you, Lord.*

✪ ✪ ✪

"They will place their hands on sick people, and they will get well." The verse from Mark 16 echoed through Zhang's thoughts, while he paced back and forth in the living room. Was this the moment? Was now the time he was expected to step out in obedience? Did he have a choice? A hundred meters down the road, someone was dying and Jesus was asking Zhang to go there, to bring comfort and encouragement, to lay his hands on her, to pray and perhaps to say something about Christ. It was so simple. Simple, yes. Why was it then so difficult just to put his shoes on and go to Soojin? He had to stop thinking and go. "All right. I'll do it," he said aloud. He put on his shoes and his coat, took a hat belonging to his father and went outside.

The sun had disappeared behind the hills. The streets were silent. No one would see him. Just to be on the safe side, he put on his father's hat and pulled it down over his ears. Stupid, actually. With his height, any one of the villagers would recognize him right away.

Barely a minute later, he was at the door. He knocked gently. "Soojin!" he called. "It's me, Kim Zhang."

Not a sound. Zhang knocked on the door again, this time slightly louder. "Soojin! Are you there?"

Zhang turned the handle. The door opened.

"I'm coming in, Soojin," he called.

Cautiously, Zhang went into the dark house. It smelled as if it had not been aired for weeks. He walked across a room, assuming it was the kitchen. He felt around to find the counter and in the process knocked over some glasses. "Ouch!" he whispered as he grabbed his finger. He had cut it. He took another step and his foot kicked against an iron pan, which spun across the floor and crashed loudly into the

153

wall. Zhang shuffled on, into the living room. His eyes began to get used to the dark, but he was still not able to discern much. He took a candle and a match out of his pocket. By the candlelight, he was able to see around. The place was a mess. There were clothes, wooden shoes and empty drink cans scattered about everywhere. By the look of it, the cans were from China. She must have bought them on the black market. He held the candle up a bit higher and saw a portrait of Kim Il-Sung. Zhang was shocked. In the dust, a clear imprint of a woman's hand could be seen. If the Party Inspector were to see that, he might beat Soojin to death on the spot.

"Soojin?" he called quietly again. "Are you here? It's me, Kim Zhang."

No reply.

Cautiously Zhang made his way on through the house to the bedroom. The door to the room was open. The room smelled of vomit. Zhang held his breath for a moment and walked in. He held up the candle and could make out Soojin lying motionless on a thin mattress in the middle of the room. Her back was toward him. Her once jet black hair had become dull, as if there were a thick layer of dust on it. There was a thin blanket next to her. Her skinny arms stuck out like twigs from her working clothes, which were covered in stains of mud, blood and vomit. Zhang crouched down and put his hand on her shoulder. "Soojin?"

With a jerk, Soojin turned her head toward him. Her eyes, filled with fear, stared at Zhang. And then she began to cough violently. Spittle and blood trickled down her chin and onto her clothes.

Quickly Zhang stood up and took a step backward. He held his breath. *What must I do, Lord? Please let the coughing stop and tell me what I must do.*

The coughing slowly subsided. Soojin fell back against her pillow. Her fearful eyes dropped closed. Zhang picked up a dirty cloth from the floor, went to the kitchen and wet it. When he came back, Soojin seemed to be asleep again. Or was she unconscious? Zhang wiped her face as best he could. Suddenly her eyes opened wide, and Soojin grabbed his wrist.

"It's all right, Soojin. I'm not going to hurt you. I'm here to help."

"Who are you?" she groaned.

"Zhang. Kim Zhang. We were in the same class at school. Don't you remember?"

"Why have you . . ." Soojin was again overcome by a coughing fit. She let go of Zhang's hand.

"In Jesus' name, cough go away!" cried Zhang. He was shocked. *Where did that come from?* The coughing slowly died away.

"I've come to help you, Soojin."

"Why?" Soojin spoke softly with her eyes closed.

"I want to tell you something."

"Leave me . . . in peace."

Zhang laid the wet cloth aside. "Soojin, listen to me."

She opened her eyes again.

"I'm going to pray for you. I'm going to pray that you will be healed."

"Really? Is father Kim . . . father Kim Il-Sung . . . going to . . . make me better?"

"No, Soojin. He's not able to do that. He was never able to do that."

"Then . . . I'll die. Let me go."

"No, Soojin. You won't die."

"I want to die. Leave me alone."

"You're going to live."

"No."

"Shh. Be quiet. Let me pray for you."

Soojin closed her eyes again. Zhang, kneeling next to her, placed his hand on Soojin's shoulder. For a moment, he was silent. *What should I pray? What would Manchu do? Just start.* "Dear Lord Jesus, You are the beginning and the end. You have been given all power in heaven and on earth. You died for us—for our sins. You bore our pain, our illnesses and our sorrows . . ."

Soojin started to shiver. "I'm so cold. Give me a blanket."

Zhang covered Soojin with the blanket and continued to pray. "Faithful Lord, You instructed us to place our hands on the sick and to heal them. Lord, I can't heal anyone. I'm powerless. But You can, Lord Jesus. You can do it through us. Lord, I pray that You will touch Soojin."

Soojin stopped shivering.

"In Jesus' name, I command this illness, disappear from Soojin's body."

Zhang did not know what else to say. He pulled back his hand but did not dare to open his eyes. Only two words floated round in Zhang's thoughts. *Please, Lord.* Soojin did not move. Was she still breathing? Still Zhang did not dare to look.

Then he heard her murmur, "Who's Jesus?"

Zhang opened his eyes. Soojin was sitting upright and staring straight in front of her.

"How do you feel?"

Soojin turned her head toward him. Her eyes were bright.

"A bit better. I'm hungry."

"Have you got anything to eat here?"

Soojin shook her head.

"I've got an apple with me. And a bit of rice. I'll prepare something for you."

Zhang went to the kitchen, boiled the rice and cut the apple into small pieces. When he turned round, Soojin was standing behind him. She had changed her clothes.

Zhang put a bowl on the table and served up the apple and the rice.

"Aren't you having anything to eat yourself?" asked Soojin.

"No, thanks. I brought this for you." Zhang's stomach rumbled.

"How did you get hold of this rice?"

"Black market."

"Have you got so much money?"

Zhang smiled. "Some things you don't ask, Soojin."

She laughed. "No one ever brought me any food. Not even when I was sick. You're the first person to come anywhere near me in weeks. Everyone was keeping out of my way." With this Soojin began to cry. Zhang wondered what to do. Was it all right to put his arm around her? Hesitantly, he did so. Her sobbing became louder. "Everyone is afraid of me, afraid of getting sick, afraid of dying. Everyone except you. Aren't you afraid of me?"

"No."

"Why not?"

"Jesus is watching over me. He asked me to come to you."

"Who is Jesus? Is He a Party member? Does He work for the Dear Leader as a doctor?"

"No, Soojin." Zhang fired his words out at her and spoke much faster than he wanted to. "Long ago, a mighty God made the heavens and the earth. He made all the plants, trees, animals and people."

"Kim Il-Sung?"

"Let me finish. This God wanted people to be happy, but the people decided to turn their backs on Him. They did wrong things. Their decisions meant that they could no longer be with Him. That hurt God a lot. There was only one way in which He could save mankind. God had to send His own Son to the earth to die here. That Son is Jesus. He came two thousand years ago. He didn't do anything wrong, but only did good. Still He had to die. People murdered Him. But God made Him alive again. Jesus died in the place of the people. Instead of you and me. If we believe in Jesus and do what He says, we can belong to God again."

"Is Jesus now in North Korea?"

"No, Soojin. He's in heaven with His Father. But He can help us. He made you better."

Soojin was surprised. "Really? Am I no longer sick?"

"I believe you are well. Jesus will make sure you get over it. He loves you."

Soojin started crying again. "I don't understand. Where is He?

Why is He doing this? How can He love me if He doesn't know me?"

Zhang put his hand into his pocket and took out a small, black book. "May I read something to you?"

Soojin nodded.

Zhang opened the Bible to Mark's Gospel and began to read out long passages. He read the entire account of Jesus' death and resurrection. "... After the Lord Jesus had spoken to them, He was taken up into heaven and He sat at the right hand of God. Then the disciples went out and preached everywhere, and the Lord worked with them and confirmed His word by the signs that accompanied it."

He closed the Bible. "I came here to tell you the Good News, Soojin. That's what Jesus asked me to do. Perhaps it's difficult to understand everything, but in any case, please believe that Jesus loves you and that He has made you better. Do you believe that?"

Soojin nodded. "I've never heard of anything like that, but yes, I do believe it. I thought I was already dead, but I'm still alive. I believe that He's made me better."

Outside it was starting to get light. Realizing that he had been there most of the night, Zhang got up. "I have to go quickly," he said. "No one must know that I came to you at night. And don't tell anyone what I told you, all right?"

"All right ... but can't you stay longer? I want to know more."

"We'll talk about it later. Then I'll teach you how to pray, as well—how to talk to God."

"What should I tell people when they suddenly see me walking around again?"

"That you just got better."

"All right." She smiled at him, and Zhang headed for the door.

"Zhang?"

He looked round.

"Thank you."

Zhang smiled. "You know Who you should really thank."

✪ ✪ ✪

Zhang had tried to catch up on his sleep but he had not managed to. He was in a jubilant mood. To think that God had used him in such a powerful way! While he was looking for food in the woods, he had to watch out that he did not start singing songs of praise. Or at least not out loud. *Thank You! Thank You, Lord!*

All he could find for food was leaves and some grass. No rabbit in his trap and no berries to be found. It was getting cold, so he decided to go home quickly and make some soup from the leaves. He still had a little bit of rice from China but he wanted to keep that until the autumn. Once he was home, he made the soup and ate it quickly. It tasted awful. He gulped down two glasses of water to wash away the taste.

After closing the curtains and locking the door, he went into the bedroom and lifted up his mattress to take out the Bible. It was not there! Zhang was terror stricken and tried to think where he had last had the Bible? At Soojin's. And then? In his coat pocket. Oh, how he hoped it was still in his coat pocket! Suppose the Bible was still at Soojin's. Or worse still, suppose Zhang had lost it outdoors! Suppose someone had found it.

Zhang rushed to the hallstand and reached into his coat pocket. The Bible was there. *Thank You, Father.* How could Zhang be so stupid? He had to be more careful, especially with regard to his Bible.

He sat for a few minutes, holding his Bible and trying to regain his composure. Then sitting cross-legged at the low table, he started to copy out the first chapter of the Gospel of John on a grimy piece of paper. He wanted Soojin to be able to read the Bible too, but he did not want to give her his own Bible. He simply could not imagine life without his Bible. After an hour and a half of writing intensely, Zhang shook his wrist to loosen it up. It was time for a break. He stretched his back then looked at his work. He had written as neatly as possible, but it didn't really look very good. And the grimy, North Korean paper didn't help. He wished he had brought some paper with him from China.

There was a knock at the door. Zhang jumped up, picked up his Bible and papers and ran to the bedroom with his things and stuffed them under his mattress. *I must find a better place—or make one—to keep the Bible.*

Again there was a polite, patient knock on the door. That's what it sounded like anyway. Perhaps it was a trick. Perhaps in her naiveté, Soojin had said too much already and the police were at the door. He half expected the door to be kicked in. Taking a deep breath, he opened the door as calmly as possible. It was Soojin. Behind her stood another woman.

"Soojin?" Zhang was surprised to see them.

"Can we come in?"

Quickly Zhang inspected the dark street. No one to be seen. "Quick. Come in."

The two women slipped into the house.

"Would you like some tea?" Zhang asked.

"Yes, please," said Soojin. "By the way, this is my friend Seong-Eun." Seong-Eun bowed a low respectful bow.

"I'm Zhang." He too bowed and then went to make the tea.

"I told her about last night," Soojin said.

Zhang put the tea on the table and sat down. "Oh?"

"That I'm better and that it's because of Mr. Jesus," she continued.

Seong-Eun lifted her teacup with both hands and sipped it cautiously. Then she explained, "She tried to tell me about it, but I don't understand properly what it's all about. Jesus is the God of the Americans, isn't He? Why should He want to help us?"

Zhang let out the breath he realized he'd been holding. He didn't look at Seong-Eun. He kept his eyes on his tea and he prayed for wisdom.

"You mustn't be afraid. We're not going to betray you," said

Seong-Eun. No one spoke for a few minutes. They drank their tea in silence. "Come on; say something," Seong-Eun urged Zhang. "Where did you hear about Jesus? In China? In one of those houses with a cross on it?"

"Hey," said Soojin. "Take it easy. Zhang's not an enemy. He's a friend. Cut out the cross-examination."

"I'm sorry," Seong-Eun said. "I only wanted to know what it's all about. I'm curious."

"You really want to know what it's all about?" Zhang asked.

"Of course."

"It's dangerous information. If you report me, you won't be safe yourself. They may come after you too."

"I'm not going to report anyone. I wouldn't want to have it on my conscience that someone disappeared because of me—whoever it was."

"Just give me a few minutes," Zhang said. "I need to think about how I'm going to put it."

He went into his bedroom, closed the door behind him and knelt down. He prayed. Could he really trust them? And what should he say? In his mind, he could see himself in Beijing again, sitting on the sidewalk next to that church building, sure he was going to die. But Jesus kept him alive. That same Jesus had asked him to come back to North Korea to tell people about Him. He had waited for months before he had been able to share anything. Now two women were sitting at the table, wanting to hear more about the Kingdom of God. Of course he had to tell them what he knew. But what exactly should he say? After praying, he still wasn't sure.

He went back to join Soojin and Seong-Eun, who were talking in whispers. They stopped when they saw Zhang, and he did not pay any attention. He sat down again, ready to tell them about Jesus.

"What happened to Soojin was not an exception," Zhang began. And then the words just seemed to flow out of his mouth. "Every day Jesus is saving people from death. He saved me too."

Then Zhang told his life story—the death of his mother, the flight of his father and sister, his meeting with Hyok, his journey to China, the arrest of Hyok, how he had panicked and how Jesus had saved him in Beijing. Soojin and Seong-Eun listened attentively. Zhang wished he could tell whether or not they understood, but it remained completely unclear. So Zhang kept talking.

"Soojin, Seong-Eun, I am a bad person, and still Jesus saved me. My whole life long, He was looking out for me, even when I didn't know it. He saved me very often, even when I didn't ask for it. Now there is just one thing He asks of me. He asks me to believe in Him."

"Was this Jesus really dead and did He come back to life again?" asked Soojin. "How can you be so sure?"

"I believe it. And I see what He's done in my life."

"Dead and now alive again . . ." mused Seong-Eun. "Even Kim Il-Sung didn't manage that."

"Seong-Eun!" Soojin exclaimed.

Zhang smiled. "She's right, Soojin. Kim Il-Sung is dead, and one day Kim Jong-Il will die and not come back again. But Jesus Christ is always here and always will be here. There was no god before Him and there won't be any after Him."

Finally Seong-Eun asked, "What should we do now?"

"You must ask yourself whom you believe. Our leaders or our God?"

"I believe in Jesus," Soojin said. "He healed me. He saved me."

Seong-Eun was silent for a moment. Then she said, "I believe in Him too. Or at least, I want to."

"Then you have to do only one thing," Zhang said. "Pray to Him. In a moment, we'll kneel down and you can mention one by one all the things you have done wrong in your lives and then you can ask the Lord Jesus to forgive you. We'll say together that we want to belong to Him and that we need Him."

While they were kneeling, Zhang's eyes fell on the portraits of Kim Il-Sung and Kim Jong-Il on the wall. He thought they looked even more angry than usual. Zhang could not suppress a smile. Soojin and Seong-Eun did not need any guidance whatsoever in their prayers. Without the slightest hesitation, they asked for forgiveness for their wrong deeds. Silently, Zhang thanked the Holy Spirit for His presence.

We've finished," said Seong-Eun quietly. "What now?"

"Now we say, Amen. That means that we're in agreement with God's will."

"Just a minute," said Soojin, bowing her head again. "And Lord Jesus, please forgive us for having bowed down to the image of Kim Il-Sung. Amen."

Yes, thought Zhang, *forgive me and our whole people that we have bowed down to an idol.*

✪ ✪ ✪

Zhang was foraging on the bare hillsides. In the autumns that Zhang remembered, the hills had been covered with orange leaves. That time was in the past. The leaves were gone before the autumn came, eaten by the hungry population.

He wished there were work—anything. Even if he had to work in the mine, it wouldn't matter to him. He needed something to break up the daily drudgery. Of course he enjoyed spending so much time with God. During the day he prayed in silence or sang quietly. In the evenings he read his Bible and patiently copied out whole chapters for Soojin and Seong-Eun. But being among people had its value too.

Jin did have a job. He was working as a manager in his father's factory. Jin did not suffer from hunger, or hardly at all. Zhang thanked God that things were going well for his best friend and that Jin occasionally brought him some food. This made life more bearable for Zhang, even though he repeatedly gave the food away. Sometimes to Soojin and Seong-Eun, sometimes to vagrant children. The children were not grateful. They grabbed it from his hands. Some of them even tried to punch Zhang. They behaved like hungry wolves.

Recently Zhang had told Soojin and Seong-Eun how the Lord Jesus felt about children, that they were very special to Him and that they had to be brought to Him.

"Doesn't Jesus detest street children?" asked Seong-Eun. "They're dirty; they get in the way; they steal our food; they sleep in places where they don't belong . . ."

"That's precisely why Jesus loves them," Zhang said. "Because they are dirty, because they get in the way and have to steal food and because they don't have a home. Jesus wants to be a Father to them. He loves them, just as He loves you. And because Jesus loves them, we should also love them. Let us—Christians—try to do something for these children and treat them well—even if they're not grateful."

From then on Soojin and Seong-Eun also tried to find some food for the vagrant children who occasionally appeared in Unsung.

Zhang would have liked to teach Soojin and Seong-Eun so much more, but there were hardly any possibilities to meet together. No one in the village would understand if a young man went alone to the home of young women.

Zhang was drawn out of his thoughts by the sound of a branch breaking. He looked behind him. No one there. Was it a rabbit? Could he catch it? Cautiously he crept in the direction of the sound.

"Don't be afraid, Mr. Kim."

Zhang jumped and his heart skipped a beat. A few meters in front of him stood an older man in a black working uniform. A badge of Kim Il-Sung was pinned to his left lapel. His piercing eyes were looking at Zhang.

"Who are you?" Zhang asked.

"I'm a friend of Manchu."

Of Manchu? That wasn't possible. He was not going to establish contact for two or three years. Had he been betrayed?

"Who?" responded Zhang, as nonchalantly as possible.

"We can talk openly. We've not been followed. I'm a brother and I'm in touch with Manchu."

"Tell me your name."

"It's better if you don't know it. But you can trust me, brother Kim. I also belong to the Messiah. I've got something for you."

The man put his hand into his inside pocket and took out two small books with plain black covers. "Here you are."

Zhang took the books and opened one. He saw the words: "In the beginning God created the heavens and the earth." They were Bibles! Zhang gave them back. "These are forbidden books," he said. "Are you trying to trick me?"

The man was not put off. "Brother Kim, I've had these books in my possession for two years now. I got them from Manchu in the neighboring country, and all this time I've been praying about whom I should give them to. A month ago, someone brought a letter from Manchu. It said that you live in Unsung and might perhaps need some help. This was the answer to my prayers. I came yesterday and I tracked you down. Unfortunately, I had to wait until today before I could make contact with you. I had to be sure that no one saw me. These Bibles are for you. Give them to whoever needs them."

Soojin. Seong-Eun.

The man again held out the Bibles. With some hesitation, Zhang accepted the books. He felt goose bumps all over and he had a lump in his throat.

"Thank . . . thank you!"

"Don't thank me. Thank our Redeemer, the Lord Jesus Christ."

"How do you know Manchu?"

"Every year I leave the country for a short time to receive training from him together with a few others. I would like to tell you all about it, but it's better not to know any details. For your safety, of course."

"I understand. Can I offer you anything? You've taken such a risk for me."

"No, unfortunately not. I have to leave straightaway. It's better that we don't talk for too long." The man moved closer to Zhang and shook his hand firmly. Zhang looked into his fellow Christian's tear-filled eyes. Then the man pulled Zhang to him and hugged him, and Zhang wrapped his arms around him.

After a long moment, the man said, "I have to go."

"Can we first pray together?" Zhang asked.

"Yes, let's do so."

Still hugging one another, they each prayed for the other, for protection and for the gospel and they thanked God for their mutual friend, Manchu.

"We'll meet again, brother Kim." The man's voice broke as he spoke. "In this world or in the next." He patted Zhang's shoulder and then let him go. As he disappeared among the trees, he turned back and waved. Zhang looked down at the Bibles he was holding. He tightened his grip on them, as a tear rolled down his cheek and fell onto one of the covers.

✪ ✪ ✪

Sunday was the coldest day Zhang had experienced since his return. The advantage was that most people were indoors. But not Zhang. He was crouching down in the road, seemingly doing nothing. On the inside, he was laughing. In China it would be strange simply to hang around on your own. Here it was normal.

Not far away Soojin and Seong-Eun were leaning against a lamppost. It looked as if they were simply talking to one another. Zhang knew better. Occasionally they looked very briefly at Zhang to let him know that they were praying for him too.

This was their church service. If he were ever to meet foreign Christians, how would he explain this? Zhang wondered. Soojin and Seong-Eun and he were praying for one another, while no words passed their lips. They were singing songs but only in their thoughts.

Zhang thought it was a pity that he had not yet been able to teach

Soojin or Seong-Eun any songs he had learned in China. Fortunately they had thought of a system for Bible study. Every Sunday, in the morning they studied a chapter from John's Gospel. The next week it would be chapter twenty. Zhang looked around him. No one to be seen. He stuck up two fingers. Soojin nodded. After that he put up nine fingers. The key verse for next week's "sermon" had been passed on. It would be John 20:29. "Then Jesus told him, 'Because you have seen me, you have believed; blessed are those who have not seen and yet have believed.'"

During the week they would all meditate on this verse. God had to preach to their hearts. No one else could do so. Zhang missed Manchu. He missed the Chinese house church meetings—the teaching, the worship, the fellowship. He prayed that Soojin and Seong-Eun would one day be able to experience the blessing of a "real" Church.

Suddenly he had an idea. The next week, the autumn festival of Hangawi was to be held. In the evening, the whole village would turn out to tend the graves of their ancestors and to honor them. This provided opportunities. In the darkness, they might be able to slip away unnoticed and arrange to meet in a secret place.

✿ ✿ ✿

Zhang was panting. He had rushed up the hill to get away from the other people of the village. He hoped that no one had seen that he had not gone toward the graves at all. He hoped that Soojin and Seong-Eun would be able to avoid attention in the same way.

He blew on his hands and stuck them in his armpits to warm them up. It was horribly cold this evening, although winter had not yet come. It might even be freezing. But he was excited. This evening he was going to do something special. If only Soojin and Seong-Eun would come quickly! It felt as if his toes had frozen off.

Minutes passed. Zhang quietly hummed, "Silent night, holy night"—still his favorite. Every now and then, he rubbed the orange. It must not freeze.

"Zhang!" He heard the whisper. "It's me, Soojin."

"I'm here," Zhang whispered back.

Walking carefully, Soojin came up to him. "Isn't Seong-Eun here yet?"

Zhang shook his head. "I haven't seen her yet."

Soojin and Zhang didn't talk anymore. Ten more minutes passed. Finally they heard a voice. "Hello?" It sounded far away.

"Who's there?" Zhang whispered.

"Who do you think, joker?" Seong-Eun was smiling as she approached them. "I hope you have a good reason for arranging to meet here. I can't feel my feet anymore."

"Don't make such a fuss," Soojin chided.

"Follow me." Zhang began leading the way. He knew this area like the palm of his hand. So often he had played here with Jin. Together they had driven back so many attacks by the whole of the American army. This was the place where they had sealed their pact with an oath and where they had first called each other blood brothers. Zhang found the cave and indicated to Soojin and Seong-Eun where they were going.

"In there?" Soojin hesitated. "It's darker there than out here. Here there is a little moonlight."

"I've got a flashlight with me," Zhang replied as he walked into the cave.

The two women followed and they sat down on the hard, cold ground.

"Can we light a fire?" asked Seong-Eun.

Zhang started to say no but then said, "It is very cold, isn't it? Yes, let's light a fire—just a little one. I'll sit with my back to the opening of the cave so the light can't be seen outside. Make sure there isn't too much smoke. We don't want to suffocate."

When the fire had been lit, Zhang took his Bible out of his coat pocket.

Soojin was shocked. You brought your Bible? You're mad!"

Zhang smiled." Ah, perhaps I am a bit. But I thought it was appropriate. Let me read something from Luke 22."

The women looked confused. "Who's Luke?" Seong-Eun asked.

"Luke is a doctor from the time of Jesus. He had a lot to do with the other followers of Jesus and wrote down their stories. Listen. The evening before Jesus died, He had a last meal with His disciples. Luke tells us about that." Zhang began to read:

"When the hour came, Jesus and his apostles reclined at the table. And he said to them, 'I have eagerly desired to eat this Passover with you before I suffer. For I tell you, I will not eat it again until it finds fulfillment in the kingdom of God.' After taking the cup, he gave thanks and said, 'Take this and divide it among you. For I tell you I will not drink again of the fruit of the vine until the kingdom of God comes.' And he took bread, gave thanks and broke it, and gave it to them, saying, 'This is my body given for you; do this in remembrance of me.' In the same way, after the supper he took the cup, saying, 'This cup is the new covenant in my blood, which is poured out for you.'"

"Wow," Seong-Eun said. "And this was shortly before Jesus' death?"

Zhang nodded. "He told us to remember His death. By breaking and eating the bread and by drinking the wine, we remember His broken body and spilled blood."

"If only we had some bread and wine," said Soojin.

"I thought of that," replied Zhang. He beamed. "Only bread and wine were . . . eh . . . sold out. But I have got something else. Almost as good. Look."

He took out the orange and began to cut and peel it with a knife. "I cannot break bread, but I can break this piece of fruit." He put the knife back into his pocket and gave a piece of the orange to Soojin. "Soojin, remember the broken body of Jesus Christ. He died for you."

Soojin ate the fruit with her eyes closed.

Seong-Eun, too, received a piece. "Seong-Eun, remember the broken body of Jesus Christ. He died for you."

Then Soojin took a piece of orange from Zhang's hand, offered it back to him and said, "Zhang, remember the broken body of Jesus Christ. He died for you too."

Zhang closed his eyes. As he ate, he saw Jesus on the cross. *Thank You, Lord.*

It was time for the "wine." Zhang took the rest of the orange and squeezed some of the juice into a dish. He handed the dish to Soojin. "Soojin, Jesus' blood saved you from death."

"Thank you," she murmured and drank the juice.

Zhang squeezed more juice into the dish and gave it to Seong-Eun. "Seong-Eun, Jesus' blood saved you from death."

She nodded and took a sip. Then Seong-Eun squeezed the remaining juice from the orange into the dish and gave it to Zhang. "Zhang, Jesus' blood saved you from death too."

Zhang closed his eyes and drank. He saw a soldier stabbing Jesus in His side. *Thank You, Lord, that You were willing to suffer for me. Thank You that the dream that brother Lee had about me, in which I celebrated the Lord's Supper in secret, has now come true. Thank You that You always provide.*

Then Zhang realized it was getting even colder. He opened his eyes. The fire had gone out. Then he heard sobbing. It was Soojin.

"Poor Jesus . . . If I hadn't sinned, He wouldn't have had to die."

"He did it out of love," said Seong-Eun, her voice trembling too. "Of course, it isn't necessary, but if it were, Jesus would do it for you again tomorrow. He loves you so much. Doesn't He, Zhang?"

"That's right," said Zhang. Then smiling broadly, he shone his flashlight on his left coat pocket. "I've got another surprise!"

"Oh?" Both women leaned toward him.

"Yes. I not only brought my own Bible with me . . . but yours as well."

"What do you mean?" cried Seong-Eun. Zhang pulled his hand out of his pocket and revealed two small, black books.

"No!" Seong-Eun exclaimed.

"Goodness . . . it can't be . . ." Soojin clasped her hands over her mouth.

"Yes, it is," laughed Zhang.

Seong-Eun snatched a Bible from his hand. "Quick," she said. "Give me the flashlight." She didn't wait but grabbed the light, shone it on the book and began turning the pages and reading. "There is so much in it!"

Soojin still could not believe it. "No! This can't be true. Our own Bibles? Are they really for us, Zhang? That's not possible. How can this be? How did you get them?"

"We need to thank God. He did something miraculous."

"I told you, didn't I, Soojin?" Seong-Eun smiled at her friend. "He really does love us!"

"Let me have the flashlight," Soojin said. She snatched it from Seong-Eun and shone it on her own Bible.

"Hey there!" said Seong-Eun, but she didn't try to take the flashlight back again.

"Oh… it's fantastic!" said Soojin. But then her tone turned to shock. "Oh!" The Bible dropped into her lap.

"What's the matter, Soojin?" asked Seong-Eun.

"I suddenly realized that I've got God's Word in my hands!" Soojin said softly.

Zhang smiled at the enthusiasm of the two young women. *Thank You, Lord.* Then he warned them sternly. "Hide this book well. This book gives life but it can also cost you your life."

"Yes, comrade Zhang. Orders received and understood," said Seong-Eun. Soojin nodded.

✪ ✪ ✪

Should I tell him or not? For an hour now, Zhang had been walking with Jin near Unsung. Jin was chatting away about his work, the news from Pyongyang and especially about what was going on in the village. Evidently there were people who were trading illegally at night. A teacher from the primary school had left, because he was not receiving any wages from the government, and the villagers, in Jin's words, were too stingy to give him anything so that he could continue to teach. There had been a raid on someone who apparently had been to China. The family had been taken away.

Although they were alone, Jin did not refer once to the period in which Zhang and he had been together in China. It seemed as if Jin was trying to suppress the fact that he, too, had been there for several months and Zhang for nearly two years. He never asked why Zhang came back.

Perhaps Jin did not want to think about China anymore, but Zhang could not get the country out of his head. How could he forget that Jesus had saved him there?

Zhang wanted his best friend to know that Jesus was his Redeemer too! For a long time, He had been praying for a suitable moment to be able to explain the gospel to Jin. In his dreams, he saw Jin immediately coming to faith. Now he was finally alone with Jin and was outside Unsung, it was the perfect moment. And even now, Zhang did not dare to speak. Why was he afraid? Jin was his best friend. They had been to China together. Every now and then, he gave Zhang food. They were blood brothers.

I'm afraid of being rejected, Zhang thought. *What if Jin rejects Christ? If he does, he will reject me too. I will lose my best friend.*

"Zhang?"

"Um . . . What?"

"I was talking to you. Why are you so far away?"

"Oh, sorry." By now they were back in Unsung. "I'm tired, didn't sleep well."

Jin poked him, "Scatterbrain." Then he turned to the side and bowed.

At first Zhang was confused; then he realized what Jin was

doing. *Oh, no . . .* Zhang had made a terrible mistake. He had not paid attention to where they were going. They were standing in front of the statue of Kim Il-Sung. *Oh Jesus, save me! I don't want to bow down!*

"Hurry up," said Jin. "Then we can go to my place. I've got a whole bottle of soju."

"All right," said Zhang, wandering sleepily away from the statue.

"What are you doing?" asked Jin.

"What do you mean?"

"Why aren't you bowing?"

"Oh, sorry! I thought I already had." He walked over to the statue and nodded his head.

"Do you call that bowing? If my father were to see me bowing like that, he would kill me on the spot!"

Zhang felt helpless. "I can't do it, Jin." He could hardly breathe. Everything in him called for him to bow properly, but he had to resist that fearful voice within.

"Why not? Is there something wrong with your back? Stop messing about, guy! You're standing before the Great Leader."

Zhang took a step backwards. "I can't do it. Not anymore."

"Have you gone mad? Do you want to be picked up tonight by the secret police? Who knows who's watching us now?"

"Let's just keep walking. Then I'll explain."

"But . . ."

"No, Jin! We're going on now," Zhang said, turning and walking away.

Jin could hardly keep up with him. "Wait a minute!"

It took a while, but Jin finally caught up with him when they reached Unsung's main street, Zhang did not look at his friend but strode toward his house. Once inside, he leaned against the wall and slipped down to the floor. He pulled his knees up, formed a bridge with his arms and rested his head on them. His heart was still pounding.

Jin, completely out of breath, had come into the house with him. He was standing and studying Zhang. "What's going on, Zhang? You're putting us both in danger. I don't understand."

"What? What don't you understand, Jin?"

"What just happened! I still can't believe it."

"Jin, I can no longer bow down to a dead object."

"Pardon?"

"I can't bow down to a statue."

"I don't believe my ears! What's happened to my comrade? Have you been drinking? Has someone been giving you opium? What's going on?"

"Jin, you remember in China . . ."

Jin interrupted. "Stop it! I don't want to hear anything about China. I'm beginning to get really fed up with you wanting to have us dead." He turned his back to Zhang and then said in a whisper, "Do you know what it cost me to come back? And how I had to struggle to keep out of the prison camp?"

"No, I don't know. You would never tell me anything about it. You keep avoiding the subject."

"That's right, I don't want to talk about it."

"But I do want to talk about it, Jin. It's time you knew the truth. I now follow the God of the Christians."

Jin swung around and the expression on his face betrayed his shock. "No . . ." He shook his head frantically. "You were taken in by that seduction? That's exactly why I came back when I did. I should have dragged you along with me."

"Jin, please sit down. Let's talk about it—as comrades together. I want to tell you my story. You can bring yourself to listen to your best friend, can't you?"

Jin hesitated but then sat on the floor cross-legged opposite Zhang. He folded his arms across his chest and was silent.

Zhang began to talk, starting with the moment he and Jin had parted in China and finishing with his decision to return to North

Korea. Zhang couldn't tell whether Jin had understood everything. He said nothing and stared down at the floor. Zhang paused. "What do you think?" he asked.

Then Jin responded. "So why did you decide to come back? I don't understand. Wouldn't you have rather stayed with those Christians in China? Things were good for you there, weren't they?"

"Things were good. But I longed for my home country. And for you."

"Wouldn't you have been better off leaving that Jesus in China then? Here Kim Il-Sung is the president and Kim Jong-Il the secretary general. Here Juche reigns and there's no room for any American religion."

"Jin, Jesus died for you too."

"Kim Il-Sung lives for me and for you."

Zhang leaned back. He could not fight this. Jin would not allow himself to be convinced. *I can't change him or convert him, Lord. Only You can.*

"Think about it, Zhang, and come to your senses—preferably before someone reports you. If they catch you, they'll soon be after me too. Jesus takes care of you? So how come it's me who gives you food? Why doesn't Jesus do it?"

"Are you afraid, Jin?"

"I don't want to be branded as a criminal and spend the rest of my life in a camp, if that's what you mean." Jin got up. "I suppose that you won't be wanting any soju anymore now that you're a 'Christian'! I'll finish off the bottle at home on my own."

CHAPTER 7

Z hang and Soojin were doing their best to follow Seong-Eun. In the dark and with so many trees, they were barely able to keep up with her. Seong-Eun seemed to slip easily through the brush, while Zhang and Soojin kept tripping and stumbling over branches or tree roots.

"Hurry up," whispered Seong-Eun. "Otherwise we'll be too late."

Smack. A low-hanging branch hit Zhang in the face. Soojin giggled. "Look where you're going, guy."

"Shh," Seong-Eun warned. "Come on."

They reached the edge of the wood and looked out over a small village. "Sit here," Seong-Eun whispered. "I'm going to see if it's safe."

Seong-Eun did not wait for an answer. She sprinted to the houses just beyond where they came out of the woods.

Zhang studied the village. With regard to size, it was comparable to Unsung. He estimated the number of people to be at most three hundred. He was not able to see if the houses were well maintained. He tapped Soojin on the shoulder. When she looked at him, he folded his hands. She understood and nodded. In silence they prayed to God.

The signal was a quiet whistle. The coast was clear. Zhang and Soojin got up and walked as calmly and discreetly as possible. Seong-Eun was standing a little farther on waving. Zhang and Soojin followed her to a house in the middle of the village. Seong-Eun knocked on the door. They heard a thud.

"Who's there? It's past eleven," said a woman's voice from behind the door.

"It's me, Seong-Eun."

Cautiously a woman opened the door a crack. She looked at Seong-Eun. "What are you doing here so late? And who's that with you?"

I brought some friends, Auntie Mae. Good people."

Still the woman hesitated.

"Come on, let us in, Auntie Mae. We want to help Uncle Joo-Chan."

Gently Seong-Eun pushed the door open a bit wider. Mae did not resist. Now that Zhang could get a better look at her, he saw that she was very thin, with unkempt, gray hair and deep lines in her sunken cheeks. She made Zhang think of a walking skeleton.

Mae spoke in a monotone, without emotion. "Your uncle can't be helped anymore. There's no medicine in the world that can still help him. Tonight he'll die. But then, that's what I said yesterday and the day before that. And last week. And he's still here. Ah, I've already buried two children and four grandchildren. It's a matter of time before we're all gone. The question is only in which order. I . . ."

"Shh, Auntie Mae," Seong-Eun interrupted. "Hush. There is hope, Auntie. There is hope."

Mae led the way to the living room. "It's sweet of you to say so. I hope that there is still hope." She laughed a hollow laugh. "What am I saying? Perhaps there is hope for you. You're young and strong. The Great General will watch over you. He's always watching over us." Again the hollow laugh. "That's what my mother always says."

"Grandma's not alive anymore, Auntie Mae."

"Isn't she? Ah well, it's a matter of time before we're all gone. The question is only in which order we're put into the ground. It's not my turn yet. Evidently my husband has to go first. I hope that I won't have to wait long now. It'll be so quiet without him."

"Mother, don't talk like that." A man's voice came from the living room. Then he appeared and seemed surprised to see them. "Cousin Seong-Eun! How nice of you to come. And who is this?"

"Hello, cousin. These are my friends Zhang and Soojin." They all bowed to one another.

In the living room, Joo-Chan and Mae's children and grandchildren had gathered. There were about ten people in all. Zhang was thirsty, but no one offered them anything to drink. He could not ask. That would be rude.

"We'd like to see Uncle Joo-Chan, Auntie," Seong-Eun said.

Mae stayed seated and without looking up she said, "He's in the bedroom. Go quietly. He's asleep."

Just as the three started to go to the bedroom, the electricity went off. One of the relatives lit a few candles and gave one to Seong-Eun, so she led the way into the bedroom and knelt down by the bed.

"Uncle Joo-Chan," she said softly.

Joo-Chan groaned, and Seong-Eun leaned closer to him. The light of the candle revealed his pale face and thin, gray hair. *Hunger is claiming its next victim*, thought Zhang. *Unless you intervene, Lord.*

Seong-Eun spoke quietly. "Uncle Joo-Chan? We've come to pray for you, Uncle Joo-Chan."

"Shut the door, will you?" Zhang asked Soojin. She did as he asked.

"Will you pray, Zhang?"

"You do it, Seong-Eun."

"What should I say?"

"What you heart tells you."

Seong-Eun was silent for a moment and then slowly began to speak. "Dear Lord, when you were on the earth, You healed so many people. Even today, You still heal the sick. You made Soojin better too, for which we are very grateful. Dear Lord, will You now also perform a miracle for my uncle? Will You touch him with Your healing hand and save him from death? I pray this all in Jesus' name. Amen."

Minutes passed. Zhang looked at the motionless Joo-Chan and placed his hand on his forehead. He felt warm.

"Why is nothing happening?" asked Seong-Eun. "Why doesn't God do something?"

"Have faith, Seong-Eun." Zhang touched her shoulder. "God knows what He's doing. Let's keep praying."

Now Zhang prayed for healing. Again minutes passed. Then the old man said something.

"Pardon?" Seong-Eun leaned closer.

"Tea," he mumbled.

Seong-Eun looked at Soojin. She nodded, got up and left the room.

"We're getting you some tea, Uncle," Seong-Eun said. "How do you feel?"

Joo-Chan spoke in a hoarse voice. After every word, he had to swallow. "Who are you?"

"It's me, Uncle, Seong-Eun, your niece. And this is a friend of mine, Kim Zhang."

"Let me . . ." He swallowed. ". . . have a good look at his face."

Seong-Eun held the candle in front of Zhang's face. The old man gave him a penetrating look and pointed at Zhang with his index finger. "You, you prayed to Jesus. Are you a Christian?"

"Yes. Yes, that's right, sir. I am a follower of Christ. Have you heard of Him?"

Joo-Chan turned his gaze to Seong-Eun. "And so you . . . you are too?"

"Yes, Uncle." Zhang thought she sounded guilty and wondered whether she now felt ashamed of her decision.

Joo-Chan closed his eyes and mumbled something incomprehensible. Zhang and Seong-Eun bent toward him. "What did you say, sir?" Zhang asked.

"Thank You. Thank You, Jesus," Joo-Chan repeated.

"'Thank You, Jesus'? Is that what you said, Uncle? 'Thank You, Jesus'?"

Joo-Chan's eyes had become moist. He pointed at the wardrobe behind Zhang. "Open. Look."

Zhang took the candle from Seong-Eun and opened the cupboard. "What am I looking for?" he asked.

"Look. Look." Joo-Chan seemed agitated now, though he still lay flat on his bed.

Despite the poor light, Zhang could see that there were hardly any clothes in the wardrobe. He lifted up a pile of shirts and underneath saw a little book without a cover. The words were printed on very fine paper. It could not be true! He looked at the contents: Genesis, Exodus, Leviticus, Numbers, Deuteronomy, Joshua. It was a Bible!

"What is it?" asked Seong-Eun.

Before Zhang could answer, Soojin opened the door and came back with a cup of tea. In her wake followed the rest of the family, several of whom had lit candles. Zhang quickly put the Bible into his trouser pocket.

"Husband, are you awake?" asked Mae. "Come, take some tea one more time."

"Regret," whispered the old man.

Seong-Eun heard him and asked, "What do you regret, Uncle?"

"Never . . . told . . . about Jesus."

One of Joo-Chan's sons took the cup of tea from Soojin and held it to the old man's lips. He took a sip and then looked around for Zhang. When he found him, he said pleadingly, "You . . . Psalm 23."

Zhang hesitated and looked around at the others. "Are you all Christians?" he asked.

"What?" a young girl responded.

Joo-Chan's son looked confused. "No idea. What's Psalm 23, Father? Here, have some more tea."

Joo-Chan put out his hand, keeping the cup of tea away, and shook his head. He kept staring at Zhang. "Read Psalm," he said as forcefully as he could.

Zhang took the Bible out of his trouser pocket.

The young girl was curious. "What's that?" she asked.

"Just listen," said Seong-Eun.

Zhang turned to Psalm 23 and began slowly to read.

The LORD is my shepherd, I lack nothing.
He makes me lie down in green pastures,
he leads me beside quiet waters,
he refreshens my soul.
He guides me along the right paths
for His name's sake.
Even though I walk
through the darkest valley,
I will fear no evil,
for you are with me;
your rod and your staff,
they comfort me.

You prepare a table before me
in the presence of my enemies.
You anoint my head with oil;
my cup overflows.
Surely goodness and love will follow me
all the days of my life,
and I will dwell in the house of the LORD
forever.

Joo-Chan gasped and beckoned to Zhang, who leaned toward him. The old man spoke so quietly that Zhang could hardly hear him. "Tell them where I'm going. Tell them about heaven."

His son was trying to hear what he was saying. "Pardon, Father?" he said.

Then Joo-Chan tried to sit up. Zhang and Joo-Chan's son helped him, supporting him on both sides. Suddenly he pointed at Zhang and spoke loudly and forcefully. "Listen to him!" Then he coughed and closed his eyes. In a murmur, he said, "Father . . . forgive me that I never dared to speak about You."

Zhang, still supporting him, said, "You are forgiven. He who prays, will receive. The Lord Jesus is waiting for you."

Joo-Chan tried to reach up to place his hand on Zhang's head, but he could not lift his arm high enough. He managed only to brush across Zhang's face. "You're . . . a courageous boy . . . Don't . . . make . . . the mistake . . . I made . . . Keep . . . talking about . . . Jesus . . . until . . . death."

With that his head fell backwards, and no more breath passed through his lips.

Two young girls started crying and moved close to their mother. Joo-Chan's son laid his father's head gently on the pillow.

"The old man is so tired. He's gone to sleep again. Let's go quickly into the living room," said Mae, but no one moved.

Joo-Chan's last words resounded in Zhang's mind. *"Don't make the mistake I made. Keep talking about Jesus until death." This man was a brother and had never dared talk about his Redeemer. None of his children or grandchildren had ever heard about Jesus—until tonight.*

"I have to tell you something." Zhang broke the silence. He held up the Bible. "Do you know what this is?"

"That crazy book?" Mae said in disgust. "He was always reading that when no one else was around. His parents gave it to him before they died."

"Were his parents . . . I mean, were my granny and granddad Christians?" asked Seong-Eun.

"I don't know, my dear. They may have been. What's that?"

"If Uncle Joo-Chan was a Christian, my mother may have been too!" Seong-Eun beamed with excitement. "Perhaps she's now in heaven with Father and Uncle Joo-Chan!"

"And your granddad and granny!" added Soojin.

"So tell us about being a Christian," Joo-Chan's son said. "What does it mean?"

Zhang began to speak slowly. He told about how God had made the heavens and the earth, how mankind went wrong and why Jesus had to come. He explained that He had saved people from death if they decided to follow Him. Then he told his personal story. At the end of his monologue, he was out of breath and even more thirsty. No one had interrupted him.

"So if you believe in Him, when you die, you go to heaven?" asked one of the children suddenly.

"Yes, you do." Zhang smiled.

"And is Granddad there now too? With Jesus?" the same child asked.

"That's right."

"Then I believe in Jesus too!"

Her father knelt down beside her and put his arm around her. "And if you believe and are going to heaven later, then I believe it too."

"I believe it too," said the girl's mother.

A warmth began to flow through Zhang's body. He realized that the Holy Spirit was touching one after the other of Joo-Chan's family.

"It's wonderful!" said another. "What a wonderful, loving God this is! I want to belong to Him. Then we'll see Father again."

Zhang looked at Seong-Eun and Soojin. Seong-Eun was crying with joy. Soojin put her arm around her.

"And you, Mother, what do you think about it?" asked one of her sons.

"So my husband is in paradise?"

"Yes, Mother."

"Then we must give thanks." She shuffled in her slippers into the living room and the rest followed her. In the middle of the room, she stopped. She turned a quarter and bowed. "Thank you, Father Kim Il-Sung. Thank you for your wonderful deeds."

Zhang sighed. *Could this woman still be saved? Or was she too far gone? For God, nothing is impossible.* He had to remember that.

A couple of the adults started to explain to Mae what they had understood about God, but her eldest son said, "Leave her alone for now." Then turning to Zhang he asked, "What should we do now? Does Jesus expect something of us?"

Zhang nodded. "Jesus did instruct us to do something. He said that everyone who wants to belong to Him should be baptized. Being baptized means going under water and saying that you believe in Him. When you decide to follow Jesus, a new life starts. By going under water and being baptized, you're actually telling the Lord Jesus that your old life is passed and the new life, a life with Him, has started."

"Should we do that now?"

"No, that would be too dangerous. It won't be long now before it's light. But I think that it would be good for you to be baptized. Let's make a good plan for your baptism. God will provide a way for us to baptize you."

Another of Joo-Chan's sons asked, "How can we get to know more about Jesus?"

Zhang held up Joo-Chan's Bible. "By reading this book. And I'll come and see you occasionally and teach you things that are in here. Seong-Eun and Soojin will help me do that."

Soojin was surprised. "Us? We still know so little."

"God will give you the words. It's too dangerous for me to come often. That would be too conspicuous. We'll have to take turns."

Zhang looked around at the family. "Sometimes you'll have to come to Unsung and sometimes we'll come to you. Let's also agree to meet regularly by the brook to wash our clothes. Then we can also talk in secret."

Outside, it was getting light. Soon the sun would be up. "We have to go. We mustn't be seen."

✪ ✪ ✪

Jin was pacing. He did not look up once. Zhang tried to see his face, but the candle shone dimly and did not provide enough light.

"Jin?" Zhang said.

Jin stopped pacing and for a moment he looked at Zhang but then immediately turned his face away again.

Zhang sighed then said, "Jin!" more loudly.

Jin folded his arms across his chest. "So what about this Jesus? Why do you believe in a dead Man?"

"In China I almost froze to death, Jin. I cursed Jesus and still He saved me. He's still alive. That's reason enough. Besides that, it was Christians in China who took care of us, don't you remember? They did that because they love Jesus. And Jesus loves us."

The silence hung like a thick curtain between them. Zhang prayed that Jesus would get through to Jin's heart.

"How do you know that?" Jin asked.

"Know what?"

"That Jesus loves you."

"He's like a father to me. He . . ."

"My father doesn't love me. He thinks I'm a failure."

Zhang got up and put a hand on Jin's shoulder. "I'm sorry about that, Jin. Your father is indeed not easy on you. But God is a very different Father, full of love. He gave up His life for you."

"He lost His life, you mean. He was murdered. What God allows Himself to be murdered? President Kim Il-Sung risked his life, too, in the fight for our country, but he won every battle. No one was able to kill him."

"Still, Kim Il-Sung is no longer alive. Jesus is."

"Prove it then."

"I believe it. Anyway, I know that He is alive because He works through Christians. The Christians in China provided us with accommodation and helped us. By doing so, they risked fines, prison sentences and closure of their church."

Jin turned his back on Zhang. "Here you're risking death, being locked up in a camp, disgrace for your family. Here you run the risk that everyone who has anything to do with you will be branded for the rest of his life. Or worse still, that they'll disappear. Oh man, if my father were to know that we're having this conversation."

"Are you afraid of that?"

"Of course, you know what he's like!"

"In the Bible it says that Jesus has been given all power in heaven and on earth and that He will always be with us. He makes sure that we do not lack anything and . . ."

"Oh, sure! Don't Christians die of starvation?"

Zhang made no reply. How difficult this was! *Only You can get through to him, Lord God.*

Then Jin said, "You've allowed yourself to be misled, Zhang. The Chinese Christians have distorted the truth. Come to your senses before you infect anyone else with that contagious language. Or have you already told anyone else?"

"Whether I've told anyone or not and what the effect of that might have been doesn't make any difference, Jin. What matters here is the decision you make. If you choose Jesus, you're choosing the truth. If you choose Kim Jong-Il, you're choosing a lie. Don't you remember anymore that we were always told that China was so bad? That people there were dressed in rags, that there was so much misery, that people were dying of hunger? And what did we see? Brand new cars, beautiful houses, cafes, restaurants, clubs, sports centers, supermarkets, stalls with food, drink, clothing and even jewelry along the sides of the streets. People have work and they can buy food. For breakfast every day we ate more than we do here in weeks. Here we have maize, grass soup and porridge made from tree bark. In China they eat vegetables, fruit, meat and eggs. They drink milk, juices, tea and coffee. Tell me now, who is living in a lie, Jin?"

Jin took a couple of steps and stood by the window. He peered outside. It seemed as if minutes passed before he said anything.

"All right," Jin said.

"What do you mean?"

"All right, I believe it."

"You do? Really?" Zhang could hardly believe his ears. In the darkness, he could hardly see his friend. "You're not messing around, are you?"

"No, comrade. I've been thinking about Jesus for a long time. Ever since China. Now you've convinced me."

"If you're convinced, it's not me who's done it, but Jesus."

Jin came back to the table. His face was glowing. "Then we'll give Him the credit. That's all right too. How do I become a Christian?"

"By praying."

"Can you do it for me?"

"No. I can tell you what you should say, but I can't do it for you."

"Let's do it now."

Zhang slowly led in prayer, and Jin repeated every sentence.

"I want to give my heart to You, Lord Jesus. I want to follow You. In Jesus' name. Amen."

The adrenaline rushed through Zhang's body. *Thank You, Lord! Thank You, Lord!* "Now state your sins and say that you are sorry. Ask for forgiveness."

"What do you mean by 'sins'?" asked Jin.

"Things that you have done wrong in God's eyes."

"How do I know what God thinks is wrong? By the way, I have to be home in a few minutes."

"All right," said Zhang. "Soon I'll explain to you what sins are. Then we can continue the prayer."

"Do you by chance have a Bible I could have?"

"No, sorry, not yet. But God will provide one. Just you wait and see."

✪ ✪ ✪

Zhang wished that he had a video camera with him. How would he manage to describe this scene to Manchu? The Christians abroad, who according to Manchu were praying so faithfully for North Korea, had to know what was happening here. Then they could pray more specifically.

In his mind, he tried to put into words what he saw. A typical North Korean illegal market on a Friday morning. A long line of women, old and young, were taking heavy bags off their backs and setting out things on the street.

A "distinguished" lady—certainly related to a high-ranking party member—was setting out some iron tools, obviously acquired from a state factory. She arranged them in groups and squatted down to wait for customers.

A young mother in a worn-out pink shirt and black trousers with torn trouser legs put a bag of potatoes on the ground. Her children, two boys of about seven, were quarreling. Their mother kept an eye on the pair but did not intervene. It seemed that she could hardly keep her tired eyes open. Probably she had walked many kilometers early that morning with her two children and her goods. Perhaps she had even stolen the potatoes that night from a state farm.

A middle-aged woman, with unkempt gray hair and deep wrinkles, was gesturing instructions to her husband. On the sack, which the man was opening, were written in big letters "World Food Program." Zhang did not know what the letters stood for, but it did mean that the food in the sack came from abroad. It was not meant to end up on the black market. But then, better on the black market than the party elite keeping it for themselves. Her husband was not moving quickly enough, and she raised her hand threateningly. For a moment it looked as if she were going to hit him.

Zhang went up to the man and woman. He still had a bit of money left from China and wanted to buy a small bag of rice with it.

"A man coming to buy food?" reacted the woman. "We don't often see that. Here at the market there are usually just women. The men go to the factory, and do you know what they do there? They hang around. There's nothing to do. They're not paid. We women have to provide for our children somehow."

Her husband looked in the other direction, as if he were not there and did not hear anything.

"I force my husband to help me, sir," the woman continued. "Otherwise he won't do anything and we'll all starve to death."

"A bit of rice, please, madam."

She handed Zhang a little bag of rice.

"Things will get better, woman," her husband said. "Kim Jong-Il will turn the situation round for the good."

She frowned in his direction. "Ah, you're living in a dream world. What's important is the here and now."

"We're not living for today. We're living today for tomorrow," said her husband.

The woman again addressed Zhang. "That's what I have to put up with. I've been hearing the same thing for three years. We're living today for tomorrow. Do you know?"

"Do I know what?" asked Zhang.

"When it is finally going to be tomorrow?"

"When the sun comes up, madam," Zhang replied. "One day the darkness will be over." Zhang swallowed. He wanted to tell her about Jesus' return, but this was not a good moment.

The woman accepted Zhang's payment. "You sound just like my husband," she said and turned away.

Zhang thanked her and went on. At the end of the street, he saw two police inspectors talking quietly to a young vendor. She handed them something—presumably money—and they went on to the next vendor.

Then in an instant, from an alleyway, a group of gotchabees, street children, swarmed across the market like birds of prey. The vendors jumped for their goods and hit any children that came toward them. The inspectors took out their batons and stormed after the children, shouting. All around Zhang there was screaming.

Two boys of about ten dove onto the World Food Program sack. "Get off, you filthy kids!" screamed the woman. Her husband remained motionless. Suddenly the woman leapt backwards. One of the boys had pulled out a knife. He cut the bag open and the rice flowed out onto the street like water. The two boys filled their pockets and hands and made off.

Screeching, the other children, too, rushed to help themselves to the rice. Behind the group hopped a girl of about six. She was wearing a pink tracksuit and her face was dirty. Under her left armpit, she held a crutch. Her left leg had been amputated at the knee.

She was too late. The inspectors had reached the sack and were trying to knock the children to the ground. The woman who had been selling the tools launched an attack with a large hoe.

Zhang felt a hand in his trouser pocket.

"Hey!" he called.

The little girl hit Zhang's shin with her crutch.

"Oww!"

Then another child was pulling on his bag of rice. Zhang felt compassion and let it go. The barefoot boy looked around nervously and fled into an alley. Two bigger boys ran after him. "Ouch! Ouch!" a girl screamed. The inspectors were roughly holding her and a boy.

"Let me go! Let me go!"

Someone smacked the boy. "At the orphanage, they'll know what to do with you."

"Get that girl there!" The inspector looked at Zhang and pointed to the girl with the crutch who was rushing away.

"No point," Zhang replied. "Let her go." He walked off.

"If it were your goods, you'd have a different attitude," said one of the vendors. "Traitor! They took your rice too. Don't go thinking that you can buy anymore from us!"

Zhang shook his head. *How could I ever tell anyone outside North Korea about this country?*

❂ ❂ ❂

"Are you sure you want to do this?"

"Yes, Rabbi."

"Don't call me that."

"Sorry, but it's in my father's Bible, you know. Rabbi means 'teacher,' doesn't it? What should we call you then?"

"Simply by my name perhaps?"

"That doesn't feel right."

Zhang sighed. "Seriously though. This is an important moment. Let's be quiet and pray," he whispered to the three men behind him.

Lying in the damp grass, he prayed for Soojin and Seong-Eun, who were with the women a few kilometers away. They had the same mission that night, a perilous mission. Tonight Seong-Eun's uncles and aunts were to be baptized—if everything went well.

"Here they come," whispered Han-Me, the youngest of the brothers.

Zhang held his breath. He heard the sound of marching boots. The nightly patrol from the army barracks near Unsung always passed by here at about two o'clock. When he had been a soldier himself, these patrols had seemed so important. Just imagine that some American parachutists had landed! Or that there were spies moving around the country to destroy the harvest! Such nonsense— that permanent state of war!

Since the famine, there had been another reason for these patrols. Disobedient inhabitants—"deserters and saboteurs"—had to be detained.

Zhang heard the soldiers march on briskly. They were invisible in the darkness, but their loud, even paces made it clear where they were. They marched along the river, the only place in the woods where the soldiers could walk three abreast. The sound slowly died away. Zhang's neck hurt. He had to relax.

"Let's hurry up," said Han-Me. "In about forty minutes, they'll come past again."

"That's plenty of time," said one of his brothers.

Zhang stood up and tried to brush some of the dampness from his coat. Then, pushing aside branches, he cautiously made his way to the brook. When he got there, he took a handful of the water. It was still icy cold. In only a few weeks, it would be spring again and the water would begin to warm up. Zhang called the others, asking them again, "Are you sure that you want to do this?"

"Of course!"

"Of course, Rabbi!"

"Han-Me . . .!"

"Sorry!" Han-Me said with mock regret. He had already taken off his coat. He took off the rest of his clothes too except for his underwear. Zhang did the same and stepped into the dark water. The cold cut through his flesh like a knife. The moon broke through the clouds a bit. *God's spotlight provides some pretty illumination*, thought Zhang.

He waded out to the middle of the brook. Han-Me was the first to approach him.

"Oh, this water is cold. But I don't mind putting up with it, you know."

"Neither do I," Zhang smiled. "But let's hurry up."

Zhang placed his hand on Han-Me's forehead and asked, "Do you believe that Jesus Christ is the Son of God, that He came to the earth, lived among us, died and after three days rose again? Do you believe that He took your sins on Himself?"

"Yes," Han-Me answered loudly. "I believe that. And I believe much more too."

Zhang smiled at the childlike faith of this forty-year-old man.

"Han-Me, I baptize you in the name of the Father, the Son and the Holy Spirit." Gently he pushed Han-Me under the water.

Han-Me came up again shivering but smiling. "Thank You, Father."

Zhang baptized the other two brothers and then quickly got out of the water. His lower body was so cold that he could hardly feel it.

As he walked onto the grass, Han-Me reached out to him. "Rabbi . . . ah . . . Zhang, I thank God every day that He sent you to us."

"And I thank Him for each of you, Han-Me."

As Zhang walked back home, a blissful feeling came over him. *Lord, You are good.*

❁ ❁ ❁

Panting heavily, Zhang sat down on a fallen tree. Had he been running that fast? The winter and the lack of food had weakened him. Still he was enjoying the spring here in the woods. The trees were getting their leaves; the grass was growing; the birds were singing again. Since he had baptized Han-Me and his brothers, it seemed as if Zhang had been living on a cloud. The hunger did not bother him—most of the time, anyway. God was using Zhang in a wonderful way. And not only him but Soojin and Seong-Eun as well. They had baptized Seong-Eun's aunts.

Ocasionally Zhang managed to meet Soojin and Seong-Eun, teaching them from the Bible. More accurately, he told them what he knew. There was so much that was still unclear to Zhang. Why was there a hell? Why did Jesus go back into heaven after His resurrection? What did the prophecies in Revelation mean? If only he could telephone Manchu occasionally or simply write to him with his questions.

It was hardly ever possible to visit Seong-Eun's family. They had agreed not to go to one another's place very often, to the great disappointment of Han-Me and the others. Still Zhang saw them growing spiritually. Reading the Bible regularly was clearly doing them good. Zhang was surprised that they learned so quickly from God's Word. But they had to be careful. Seong-Eun's Auntie Mae was, in the words of Han-Me, "not quite all there." They could read the Bible and pray only when Mae was not around. The risk that she would say the wrong thing was far too great.

Zhang picked some leaves from the trees so that he would be able to make some soup later on. He put them in a bag and walked back to Unsung.

On the way, he prayed for Jin, who was perhaps already waiting for Zhang at his place. Jin came to Zhang three times a week to read the Bible. He asked Zhang questions, and they discussed the faith. If God called Himself Father, what did that mean? Why did Jesus have to die such a painful death? When Jesus said that the gospel should be taken to the ends of the earth, was He talking about North Korea?

"Shouldn't other people know this, Zhang?" Jin had asked.

"Yes, everyone should hear the gospel."

"Then why aren't you doing anything? I mean, why aren't you telling others about Jesus?"

Zhang was silent.

"From what I can see it's a clear commandment." Jin looked at Zhang. "Isn't it? We should tell everyone about Him."

"But that's not easy in our country."

"What are you afraid of? Surely Jesus will protect you."

"That's right. But He also calls us to be vigilant."

"If I want to tell other people about Jesus, how do I do it then?"

"Allow yourself to be led by God. Pray about it and let Him make it clear to you who is ready—whom you should share the gospel."

"Is that what you do?"

Zhang nodded. "I try to. I try to follow Him as much as possible."

"Interesting. We must talk about this again soon. I've gotta go." Jin put on his coat and hurried out the door for home.

✪ ✪ ✪

How wonderful it would be if Jin were right, that only North Korea still had to be won for the gospel. All other people had already heard about Jesus' death, had they not? Imagine that Kim Jong-Il and the other leaders were to see the error of their ways. Perhaps all over the country Christian "seeds" would suddenly blossom. Perhaps there were even Christians in Unsung whom Zhang did not know about.

Tears of joy, of hope, came into Zhang's eyes. *Oh Lord, I long so much for that time, the time when the country opens up to Your gospel, to Your message, to Your love.* Zhang was walking through his village. As he turned a corner, he felt the wind in his face. It reminded Zhang of when God spoke to Elijah in a gentle breath of wind. *You are good,* he thought.

On the horizon, the sun was already going down. It would not be long before it was dark. Fortunately he was nearly home. Indeed, Jin was already waiting for him.

"So," said Zhang, "you're early. Or am I late?"

Jin nodded and they went inside.

"Sit down Jin and I'll get the book from the bedroom."

Jin turned on the radio. The commentator was describing a visit of Kim Jong-Il to a state farm in the central part of the country. Zhang went into the bedroom and took the Bible out from under his mattress. He opened it and took out the family portrait that Hea-Woo had drawn. As he did so often, he stroked her face with his thumb. *Dear Hea-Woo, where are you? When will I be able to tell you I'm sorry?*

Zhang put the paper back in his Bible and went back into the living room.

Jin was standing at the window.

"Here you are." Zhang gave the Bible to Jin, which he took without looking at Zhang.

"What's the matter?" Zhang asked. "You seem so distant. Don't you feel well?"

Jin shook his head and let the Bible fall to the floor.

"Jin, what's the matter?"

Jin bowed his head. "You should never have gone on with this." He sounded tired.

"What do you mean?"

"I warned you. You knew. You knew!"

"Jin? I don't understand. What did I know?"

"You should have known. You didn't have the right. You simply didn't have the right!"

Jin bit his lip.

Zhang had an unpleasant feeling in his stomach. "Jin! What are you saying, man? I don't know what you're talking about."

Jin turned around abruptly and held his index finger under Zhang's nose. "You know my father, don't you? You know what he's like. He never has a good word for me. He's always running me down at home. He runs me down in front of the family. In the factory he runs me down in front of my colleagues. And my mother? She only listens to him!"

Zhang put his hand on Jin's shoulder. "I know, Jin. Shall I pray for you?"

"It's too late for that."

Just then there was a pounding on the door. "Kim Zhang!" someone yelled.

"Jin?" Zhang grabbed his friend's arm. "Jin! What have you done?"

"You don't know what it's like. You don't know what it's like to have my father. I had to do it. He forced me."

The pounding on the door continued.

Now Zhang was holding Jin by the shoulders. He shook him. "Forced you to do what?"

"To go with you to China and to make a report."

Zhang was stunned. "Jin, no!"

Crack! The wooden door broke into pieces. Six men in uniform stormed into the living room. They looked at Jin and Zhang.

"Kim Zhang?" demanded the leader.

Jin nodded in Zhang's direction. The men grabbed Zhang and one punched him in the stomach. Zhang dropped to his knees. Two of the men grabbed Zhang by his elbows and pulled him to his feet. Zhang tried to catch Jin's eye, but his friend was again staring out of the window.

"Jin," Zhang gasped.

Then Jin's father, Lee Young-Nam, came in. He looked at Zhang disdainfully. "Well, well, well. I'm pleased to see the pest control has got here in time. Before you know it, we'll have a plague of rats here!"

"Mr. Lee, I'm innocent!" Zhang pleaded.

Standing with his back to Zhang, Lee lit a cigar and looked slowly around the room. Finally he asked, "Didn't your father and sister try to flee? Didn't you defect and go to China yourself? You had that sweet little orphan with you, didn't you?"

"And your son, Mr. Lee. Jin was there too."

"Of course, he was there. I sent him with you myself."

Lee turned around and blew smoke in Zhang's face. Zhang coughed, which made the pain in his stomach worse.

"As always, I first had to convince him of the use of it. In the end, he uncovered quite an operation. The network of that . . . What were they called, Jin?"

"Brother Lee and sister Ping," replied Jin.

"That's it, brother Lee and sister Ping. In collaboration with China, we were able to roll up their network nicely. Pity that you had already gone."

"And Hyok?" Zhang asked, turning toward Jin, "did you betray him too?"

"Silence!" screamed the officer. He slapped Zhang in the face. "Traitors like you have no right to speak."

"I didn't have anything to do with Hyok," Jin answered.

"Enough of that talking," said Mr. Lee. "Take this vermin away." Then he reached for his son and put his hands on Jin's shoulders. "Well done, son, well done."

The soldiers pulled Zhang outside. Looking back, Zhang called, "Jin, we were brothers!"

"Take him away," Lee growled.

Jin turned to Zhang and said, "I never knew you."

CHAPTER 8

It was as if burning acid had been injected into his muscles. Zhang tried to focus his thoughts on something other than the pain in his thighs and knees. He could not. The pain was becoming more intense by the second. His head was also beginning to itch. Lice, perhaps? Already? How long had Zhang been kneeling in this cell? Two hours? Six hours? Was his first day in prison already over?

Out of the corner of his eye, he could see the other prisoners. All in the same position as he. They were all kneeling on the hard floor, their hands bound with ropes on their laps. Their necks were bent. Only the cell leader, a fellow prisoner, was standing up, like a soldier standing to attention. Everyone in the cell of barely six square meters was motionless.

Some light shone in from the fluorescent light in the corridor. Without moving his head, Zhang tried to count the number of prisoners. He estimated that there were more than thirty of them. *Ow!* Another shot of pain through his thigh.

An elderly man, sitting in the middle of the cell, suddenly began to shake uncontrollably. "Stop it!" screamed the cell leader. He strode over to the man and kicked him in the side. The old chap groaned and sobbed in waves.

Zhang straightened his back and wanted to say something.

Without looking at him, the prisoner next to him anticipated his reactions. "Shh," he whispered. Zhang knew the man was right—he had to control himself if he was to survive.

"Ooow!" the old man cried as he was kicked again.

"Keep quiet!" shouted the cell leader. "Quiet!"

The lock on the cell door rattled and then, with a jerk, the door opened and officers came in. One of them hit the cell leader, who fell groaning to the floor.

"Keep the prisoners under control," screamed a guard. "Otherwise I'll let them get you."

"Yes, sir," the cell leader responded.

"Silent!"

The guards pulled the old man out. He did not resist. Perhaps he was no longer alive. The cell door slammed shut again.

Father, please be with this man. Will You . . . Oww! Zhang felt a cramp in his neck. *I can't keep this up.* He stretched his neck, and his eyes met those of the cell leader. A warm glow passed through Zhang's chest, but the man remained impassive. Probably he did not want to take a chance that the guards would come into the cell again.

Zhang tilted his head back again. He tried to focus his attention on something besides his pain. Recently he had learned Psalm 23 by heart. *The LORD is my shepherd . . . I lack nothing. He makes me lie down . . . ohh . . . in green pastures . . . and leads me . . . beside . . . oww . . . leads me beside . . . quiet waters.* Zhang took a deep breath. *Think of the Psalm. Think of the Psalm. He refreshens my . . . ohh . . . soul. . . . He . . . He . . . oww . . . guides me . . . along the right paths . . . ohh it hurts so much . . . for . . . His name's sake.* Now Zhang's favorite part. *Even though I walk . . . oww . . . through the darkest valley . . . I will fear no evil . . . Oh, Lord, I'm so afraid . . .*

Zhang was shocked by his own groan. No one reacted. *Go on. For You are with me . . . Your rod and Your staff . . . they comfort me . . . What's next? Oh God, what's the next part?*

Again there was the sound of a key in the lock of the cell door, and it opened again.

Please let them be coming for me!

Two guards walked toward Zhang. *Please let them be coming for me!* They seized Zhang's arms and pulled him up. Zhang stretched his legs to stand up, but they had turned to rubber, so the guards dragged him across the cell.

The long corridor was barely lit. The floor was a dark green color and was covered with a thin layer of dried mud. Zhang's face was hanging barely twenty centimeters above it. In the mud he could see the boot prints and the marks where others had been dragged along.

On both sides of the corridor, there were cells. Some had solid doors with closed peepholes; others had bars. Some of the cells were empty; others crammed full. Not a word was being said.

The waiting room of hell. Yes, this must be the waiting room of hell.

They turned to the left. A steel door opened. The guards now grabbed Zhang by his trousers and threw him into the room. He felt a shooting pain in his head and right shoulder as he hit something. He felt his head with his hand. Blood stuck to his fingers.

He raised himself to his knees, and the pain that shot through his thighs made all the other pain fade. Zhang clenched his teeth so as not to scream and fell on his side. With difficulty, he stretched his legs.

The fluorescent light was flashing irregularly and every few seconds plunged Zhang into darkness. The room seemed to be completely empty except for two chairs on either side of a desk. Zhang rolled toward the desk, pulled himself up and flopped down on a chair. Standing was too painful.

The flashing light irritated him, so Zhang held his hands in front of his eyes to shield them from it. With his finger, he rubbed his right temple. The blood was still flowing down his cheek.

The door opened. Zhang bowed his head. A tall man in uniform with medals on his chest sat down on the chair opposite Zhang. Zhang heard more footsteps. Guards were taking up their positions behind him.

Their leader took a sheet of paper and a pen out of a drawer. The man began to write slowly. Minutes passed. Zhang wanted to pray but could only manage one word, *Lord! Lord! Lord!*

"I am Captain Choi," the man said so suddenly that it made Zhang jump. "Who are you?"

"Kim Zhang."

A baton pressed against Zhang's throat from behind. The guard held it there for a few seconds and then let go again. Zhang gasped for breath.

"Who are you?" the captain asked again.

"I really am Kim Zhang."

A pain shot through his right shoulder as the guard slammed him with his baton. Zhang closed his eyes so tightly that they became moist. *I'm not going to get through this if they hit me that hard,* he was thinking.

"Look at me," the captain said calmly.

Zhang opened his eyes.

"You're not very bright. Let me spare you any further punishment for the time being, because it may take a long time before you give the right answer to my simple question. You have no name. You are a worthless piece of vermin. You have betrayed the Dear Leader Kim Jong-Il and your country, an unpardonable crime. Nothing gives you the right to eat our food, to drink our drink, to breathe in our air. A rat is a more useful being than you. You no longer have any right to exist."

Rage overcame Zhang. The words hit him like poisoned arrows. People were valuable in God's eyes. How did this man dare to say that Zhang had no right to exist?

The man paused for a moment. "Now, who are you?"

Zhang made eye contact with his inquisitor. "A child of Jesus," he said.

Zhang braced himself, but the blow did not come. The captain started to laugh. "I've never got such an easy confession. So you admit to being a Christian?"

"Yes."

The captain laughed. "Wonderful. You're even more stupid than I thought. Or cleverer. It depends on how you look at it. We've known for a long time what you've been up to. For example, that you were in China. Tell me, what was it like with brother Lee and sister Ping? You left very suddenly, didn't you? Why was that? Wasn't some dirty street child involved?"

He took a file out of a drawer and leafed through the papers. "Oh yes, here it is. Hmm. Stupid enough to beg at the same hotel every day. Do you know what I think? That brat simply missed our country and wanted a free return ticket."

Zhang's rage increased. "He's called Hyok."

"Not anymore," Choi replied. "He's buried in an unmarked grave. It'll reassure you to know that yours is already prepared for you. Let's see, what else does it say? Oh, yes. Almost forgot to ask. How is your dear little sister Hea-Woo getting on? Did you meet her and your father in China?"

Zhang was silent. *Jin told them everything.*

The captain took a deep breath and continued to leaf through the file. "Oh, this is nice. That's what I was looking for." He pulled a sheet of paper out of the file and nodded as he read it silently. "Oh, yes, I see. No wonder you never came across them in China. They never got there. The party leadership correctly reported that they had left. We were able to stop them in time."

"Jin!" *Did I say that out loud?*

"What did you say?"

"Jin," Zhang repeated.

"Jin? Ah yes, of course, Lee Jin. If only you'd followed his example. He has more regard for the Dear Leader than for his so-called friend. Did you know that agent Jin was the only reason that you got to China? We let you through, as it were. That's a good one, don't you think? Do you still remember Uncle Sung and his daughter Young-Soon? They helped you get across. They are very faithful members of the Party."

The only reason? That was a lie.

The captain got up from his chair and with a grin sat on the corner of the desk. Zhang wanted to ask if he was enjoying this.

He stared at Zhang. "You Christians have always been interested in the truth, haven't you? I'll tell you the truth. Thanks to agent Jin, we've been able to pick up twenty defectors. He had to work for months in a mine for it, but in the end, as we cooperated with the Chinese police, all the North Korean workers were rounded up. Of course, we let Jin go. He still had to map out who exactly was in contact with Lee and Ping. Unfortunately we had to recall him because Christian groups were beginning to suspect that a spy had infiltrated them. We told China about Lee, Ping and you. Pity that the Chinese authorities waited so long before intervening. Then you would have been brought to justice much sooner."

The captain paused and there was silence. Zhang felt numb. He had been betrayed. Everyone had betrayed him. *God too?* Zhang was a traitor himself. He had betrayed Lee and Ping by taking Jin with him. He had dragged Hyok to his death. *Where are You, Lord?*

"I am always straightforward," Choi continued as he lit a cigarette. "I go straight for my goal, if you know what I mean. I tell you what I want to know. I will go away for ten minutes, and when I come back, I want you to tell me where you went after you left Lee and Ping, with whom you had contact, which churches you went to, who's helping you in our country and what espionage activities you carried out."

Again that silence. Still that flashing light and filthy cigarette smoke.

"If you cooperate, next week you'll be hanging from the gallows and it'll all be over—for you. If you resist, we'll exterminate you like a weed. And your sister too."

Zhang's eyes darted to the captain's face.

"You heard me right. Your sister's doing well—so far. At the moment, she's being reeducated. If things go well, she'll be returning to society in a year. You don't want to let her down again, do you? You don't want to betray her again."

Zhang shook his head. "My father?" he asked tentatively.

A guard hit Zhang hard on the back of the head.

"Aaah!" Zhang fell to the ground.

"From now on I only want to hear you answering my questions," the captain growled. "People speak to one another. You are more worthless than vermin. You don't have the right to ask me any questions. I'm going away for ten minutes now. Think carefully about your answers. My colleagues will make sure you don't get bored."

Choi left the room. The chair was pushed aside. Zhang felt a blow in his back and almost lost consciousness. The men kicked him and beat him with their clubs. They worked down from top to bottom and seemed not to miss any part of his body. Zhang slipped out of consciousness.

When he awoke, he felt cold and wet. He opened his eyes and hoped he would awake from this nightmare. The light was flashing. It was not a dream. He was still in prison.

Water was thrown in his face. Zhang shook his head to get the water out of his eyes. He had a thumping headache, pain in his neck, stabbing in his side and legs. Everything hurt.

"Aaah." Zhang was roughly thrown onto the chair.

The captain was again sitting across from him. "Who did you have contact with in China?"

"Brother Lee and sister Ping."

"Who else?"

"No one."

"Stop playing games."

Zhang was silent.

"Move that chair," the captain directed. Zhang was pulled to his feet but was not able to stand. They let him fall.

"Who did you work with?"

"With Jesus."

Choi looked at his watch. He put the paper and pen away in the drawer and went to the door. "Two zero one," he said on leaving the room.

The guards grabbed Zhang and dragged him along through the seemingly endless corridor. They turned left and then right. Zhang had completely lost his sense of direction. Then he noticed "201" above a brand new steel door. The door swung open, and two other guards took charge of Zhang. One man opened what looked like a cat flap in a narrow, rusty cell door.

"Get in!" he yelled.

Zhang crawled in through the hole as one of the guards kicked him. The door swung shut and Zhang sat in complete darkness. His head was throbbing and trickles of blood ran down over his face.

Could there be other prisoners in this cell? He could not hear anyone. He wanted to lie down and felt the floor around him to find a place. He stretched out his left hand—wall. Right and behind him— wall. His legs were not stretched out and still his feet rested on the cell door.

This cell is no bigger than a meter and a half by a meter and a half. How can I stand this? I can't even lie down!

He heard a scream coming from a distance, the sound of a person in mortal fear.

✪ ✪ ✪

Zhang panicked. He wanted to go up, up out of the water. Or up out of life. Suddenly the hand that was pushing his head underwater grabbed hold of his hair. With a jerk, the guard pulled him out. Spluttering, Zhang gasped for air. He felt a punch on his cheek. It was as if he were dreaming. The figures in front of him no longer seemed real. Another blow. Even the pain felt far away.

"Who did you involve in your treason?" It was Captain Choi

screaming at him, but Zhang could hardly hear him. "Who else in your village are Christians? Speak up!"

Then he was pushed underwater again. Zhang gave up. He could not fight anymore. *Father, here I come.* The world turned black.

✪ ✪ ✪

Father, will You save Soojin, Seong-Eun and the others? Lord, will You bring them to safety? If they come to get me again, I won't be able to stand it anymore. I'll tell them everything they want to hear. I have fallen short. I'm not strong enough. I realize that You did not betray me. Lord, give me the strength so that I will at least not betray You. Come and get me quickly. Let this soon be over. Will You take the lives of Hea-Woo and of Father in Your hand? I hope to see her again in Your heavenly Kingdom. In Jesus' name, amen.

✪ ✪ ✪

There's a woman screaming. Oh, Lord, let that interminable screaming stop. It's driving me mad. I can't stand it. Take me out of here.

✪ ✪ ✪

Zhang shivered. Outside it was summer, but in this damp cellar it felt as if it was freezing. Zhang had been kneeling there naked for hours. Every so often, a guard threw cold water over him.

All Zhang could think about was the cold and Jin. *Thanks to him, you're here. He betrayed you.*

It was the voice from within that Manchu had warned him about—that fearful voice, that accuser, that scoundrel who could not tell the truth. How was he to fight against it in these circumstances? Recite Bible verses! That was what Manchu had taught Zhang. He tried to think, but nothing came to mind. The only thing in Zhang's mind was Jesus on the cross.

A door opened. There were heavy footsteps. Another wave was coming. The water was thrown over Zhang's head. *A wave of forgiveness.* The door shut.

A wave of forgiveness? Why did I think of that? God wants to tell me something. Jesus. Cross. Forgiveness. I have to forgive Jin. "No, Fa-Father, I c-c-can't do it."

The laughing voice of Manchu was in his head. *"If God asks you to do something, you'd better do it. Otherwise there will only be more conflict."*

"F-F-Father, I d-d-don't know how, but I w-w-want to forgive Jin. I-I-I forgive him. Amen."

✪ ✪ ✪

Zhang had lost all concept of time. He had no idea how long he had been in prison. Weeks? Months? He had thought that he would never again see clouds or the sun. Now he was breathing in the fresh morning air. He thanked God that he could at least experience this again.

The truck stopped. Zhang heard people outside talking to the driver. Evidently a barrier was opening. The vehicle drove on.

He looked around the truck. Next to him there were two men of over fifty. Just like Zhang, they were wearing dark, torn clothing and shivering from the cold. Their faces had deep scars. In front of Zhang there sat a small woman of Zhang's age, with her hands folded in her lap. She had been staring down all the way. On Zhang's right there sat two severe looking soldiers of about eighteen.

The canvas at the back of the truck occasionally blew open a bit, which meant that Zhang was able to see something of the surroundings. They were driving along a narrow road. On both sides of the road there were high fences with barbed wire along the top.

Occasionally there were watchtowers where soldiers were keeping guard.

The vehicle slowed down and stopped. The soldiers jumped out of the truck and beckoned urgently for the prisoners to follow. Zhang was the first to get out, then the two men. The young woman kept staring at the floor of the truck. Her hands were shaking. A soldier got back onto the truck and pulled her out roughly.

"Line up!" roared the guard. The four of them stood next to one another.

Then the door of the cab opened and an officer got out. Zhang recognized Captain Choi. He came and stood in front of the prisoners.

"Surprised?" he asked. "I visit the prison occasionally, but here, this camp, is my domain. Have a good look at it. On this land, you will spend the last days of your lives. You have proven to be of absolutely no value anymore. Every other being, dead or alive, is worth more than you. Don't expect any humane treatment from us or from other prisoners. You are no longer human beings. You never were."

Choi stood immediately in front of Zhang, and his head came only up to Zhang's chest. He kicked Zhang's right knee hard. Zhang uttered a cry and fell to one knee. "Some may think that we cannot break them, that they can keep information to themselves, that they don't have to admit that Kim Jong-Il is a superior god." He leaned toward Zhang's ear. "A matter of days or weeks, runt. Then you'll be begging for mercy and will acknowledge that Kim Jong-Il is supreme."

The captain signaled to his driver, got in the truck and drove off. The other soldiers began to pull Zhang to his feet.

"Jesus loves you," Zhang blurted out. Immediately the soldiers pushed Zhang's face down onto the road and kicked him in the ribs. Then they yelled at him to get up. He stumbled after the other prisoners. They went through another gate. On it was written in large characters: "Village 17." Zhang looked up at the cloudy sky. He hoped to see the sun. A soldier pushed him on with the butt of his gun.

Something ran past Zhang. He wanted to follow it with his eyes, but something else bumped into him. What was it? A dwarf? Zhang's heart skipped a beat. These were not dwarves. They were prisoners. Some of them were missing one or two ears, had broken noses or only one eye. They were dressed in filthy rags. It seemed as if they had no flesh on their bones, only a thin layer of skin. Several prisoners were going around on crutches. Someone passed by who was walking on his hands and feet. No, on two feet and one hand. If the prison was the waiting room of hell, this was hell itself.

Zhang and the other men were pushed into a hut. The woman was made to go on farther.

"Get undressed," one of the soldiers yelled. Quickly Zhang took off his clothes and placed them in a corner of the room. There was nothing on the walls, not even a portrait of Kim Il-Sung. There were doors without glass on the right and left sides of the room.

"Sit down."

Zhang sat down on a stool. A soldier knocked on one of the doors and shortly afterward two other soldiers came in. Not officers, by their look. One began to cut off all the hair of the prisoners; the other tattooed numbers on their lower arms. Zhang looked at the blue dots which formed the number.

The soldier doing the tattooing followed Zhang's gaze. "189178. Remember that. That number is who you are."

No, Father. You determine who I am.

The door through which the prisoners had entered opened and a cold draft blew in. Then a man dressed in a doctor's coat walked past them. He set out his stethoscope and some other medical instruments, which Zhang had never seen before, on a table. An assistant in military uniform held a paper.

The doctor began to examine the prisoners. He did not trouble himself much. He listened with his stethoscope, looked at the teeth and in both ears. He pointed to the men next to Zhang. "These two are class B." His assistant wrote down the indication. And pointing at Zhang, he said, "He is young. He can do hard labor. Put him in class A."

Zhang felt weak. His arms and legs were like twigs. How could he do hard labor?

"Get up and get dressed," ordered a soldier. He opened a bag and threw some overalls on the floor. "You will be allocated a barracks. Have a good rest there. Starting tomorrow, you'll have to work."

"Come with me," said one of the young soldiers to Zhang. Zhang followed the soldier outside and to his barracks. From the outside, it looked like a very long, drafty barn, one in which cattle might be kept. The walls were a dirty white. The roof tiles were dark green. There were no windows. Zhang was pushed inside.

"Roll call tomorrow at 5:30," said the soldier, closing the door. Zhang was left behind in the semi-darkness. The barracks was lit by a number of small lightbulbs. There were no beds, only thin mattresses—hundreds of mattresses.

"Is there anyone here?" called Zhang.

No reply. Zhang stumbled to a dark place in the middle of the barracks.

"Oh, Lord Jesus, give me strength," he prayed.

"Can you pray for me too?" said a soft voice at the other side of the barracks.

Zhang held his breath.

"Can you come over to me?" the voice said.

"Yes," said Zhang. "Where are you?"

Then he caught sight of a silhouette at the far end and a hand raised up for a second before it dropped out of sight. Zhang walked toward the figure. His knee, ribs, and arms still hurt so much. When he got to the man, he sat next to him and took his hand. The man began to shake. From his throat came a sound that was soft, but like that of an animal. It took a moment before Zhang realized that the man was crying.

What's the matter?" asked Zhang.

"I can't remember when someone last held my hand," the man sobbed.

Zhang tried to soothe the man by patting his hand. Finally he asked, "Are you a Christian?"

"That's why I'm here." The man tried to swallow.

"What are you called?"

"Jesus," he whispered.

"Are you called Jesus?" Zhang stroked the man's forehead.

"No." The man shook his head. "Only Jesus knows my name."

"How long have you been here?"

The man was silent for a moment. "I don't know."

"It's been a long time since I prayed with anyone," said Zhang. "I can't remember when it last was. What should I pray?"

Silence.

Then Zhang prayed briefly for strength, blessing and God's presence with this man. Praying aloud gave Zhang a feeling of hope. Was it possible to serve God in these circumstances?

"Remember, in Psalm 23 it says that the LORD is our Shepherd."

The man started crying again. "I … I'd forgotten the Psalms," he whispered.

Zhang didn't know what to say.

Then the man asked, "Why aren't you working?"

"It's my first day here."

The man grabbed Zhang by his collar and tried to pull him closer. "Did you see my wife, comrade? Is she outside? Outside the fences? She must be there somewhere. We were to wait for one another. Whatever happened. We were to wait for one another . . . on the other side."

"Sorry, but I don't understand what you mean."

The man looked terrified. "The Americans are coming. Our liberators. We have to get away. To the south. My wife . . . I can see her. I can't reach her."

Zhang swallowed. "Did you try to flee to the south when the Americans came? That was . . ." *Decades ago.*

The man let go of Zhang and lay his head down on his thin

mattress. "In the camp, you're not allowed to look at the sky." The man seemed to be back in the present. "Not if you're a Christian. Always look at the ground. Never at the clouds. If you want to live, do what you're told. Listen to the guards. In their hearts, they're not . . . bad children. They were brought up badly. Yes. Their education was no good. You know, the guards are still children. Here in the camp they can earn a place at school. If they shoot you dead, they're allowed to go to school. So don't ever look at the clouds, because then they'll shoot you. What are you called?"

"Zhang."

"Comrade Zhang . . . They nearly shot me dead too. I can still see him . . . I can still hear him . . . The Frog . . . Yes, comrade, we called him Frog. He walked like a frog. Until they saw him stealing tomatoes. They beat him until he didn't walk anymore. I heard him screaming all night. Until I couldn't stand it anymore. I went to him and carried him on my back. They saw me. And shot." The man made a laughing sound. "They shot. I pretended I was dead." He laughed again. "But they hit Frog and he finally stopped screaming." He laughed but it soon turned into uncontrollable weeping. But then the weeping stopped as suddenly as it had started. The man grabbed for Zhang's hand. "Comrade Zhang, God is with you, even in this camp."

"Are there any more Christians here?"

"Yes, lots, lots . . . but they're not allowed to look at the sky, because that's where God is. And there are lots more rules. Comrade Zhang?"

"Yes?"

"Promise me that you'll keep the rules! The Ten Commandments of this camp, I call them. Thou shalt not escape. Camp inhabitants must not form groups of three. Thou shalt not steal. Thou shalt obey the orders of the guard. Thou shalt immediately report suspicious people or things to the camp commanders. Thou shalt immediately report unusual behavior of fellow prisoners. Thou shalt carry out sublimely every task imposed on thee. There shall be no contact between men and women. Thou shalt sincerely repent of thine own deeds. Anyone who comes in view of the camp commanders shall immediately fall to the ground and turn away his face." The man was out of breath. Reciting the rules had taken a lot of energy. Finally he said, "Keep these rules or you'll end up in front of the firing squad."

Better sooner than later, thought Zhang, *then at least this will be over.*

Suddenly more light shone into the barracks. A tall, thin guard stood in the doorway and looked around until he saw where Zhang was sitting. Zhang got up and fixed his gaze on the floor. The guard strode over to him. At a distance of three meters, he came to a halt and threw a parcel in front of Zhang's feet. "You never saw me, rat," he growled then turned and left.

Zhang bent down to pick up the parcel. *Lord, please let there be food in it.* The package had been loosely wrapped in thin, grimy brown paper. Zhang undid it.

"Oh dear Lord . . ."

"What is it?" asked the man.

"Oh, Lord . . . that's impossible. This can't be true . . ."

Zhang walked to where he could stand under one of the small lightbulbs. He stroked the cover of the little book. He lifted it up to the light so that he could see it better. A note fell out of it.

"We are thinking about you all the time, SJ." *SJ?* Zhang swallowed. *Soojin! She had managed to smuggle his Bible into the camp! Did she perhaps have influential family members? Who knows how much money this had cost Soojin and the others!*

His Bible was still resting in his hands on the paper it had been wrapped in. Suddenly Zhang realized that it was the paper on which his sister had drawn the family. The portraits of Father, Mother and Hea-Woo stared at him. Zhang pressed the paper against his heart.

He opened the Bible to the place marked by the ribbon. His eye immediately fell on the underlined words. "I, even I, am the LORD, and apart from me there is no savior."

❂ ❂ ❂

Zhang felt Sergeant Shin's gaze piercing his back. He did not treat Zhang or the other prisoners leniently. Over the past weeks, Zhang had watched him. It did not take much to enrage the tall Shin. Habitually he tapped his baton nervously on his knee as though just waiting for a cause to beat someone.

It had taken some time before Zhang had recognized Shin. He was the guard who had given Zhang his Bible. He knew that Zhang had a Bible and Zhang knew who had given him the Bible. That must make Shin uncomfortable. Zhang must not give Shin any reason to kill him.

With a crash, the bricks fell onto the pile and dust flew into Zhang's eyes. He stretched his arms. *A moment's rest.* He took a second, turned round and ran back to the truck where he had to get the next load.

"Run!" screamed Shin. "Faster, rat!"

Zhang did not speed up. He was not able to go any faster, even if he wanted to. His legs were heavier than lead. They might snap at any moment. Zhang's arms had no strength left in them. Only one thought filled Zhang's head. *Keep going.*

He stood behind the truck and was handed another stack of bricks. The row of prisoners formed a long, moving rectangle with the trucks carrying the bricks at one end and a barracks under construction at the other. On one side, prisoners ran toward the building with bricks in a bucket. On the other side, they ran back to the vehicle, where they were given another load of bricks.

Someone was shouting, "Get on with it! Who's holding things up?" Zhang froze. They didn't mean him, did they? Fortunately not.

It was someone in front of him. A young man, probably around Zhang's age, had fallen over and was being pulled out of the line by the guards. Zhang turned away from the scene.

"Are you a Christian? I saw you looking up. That's forbidden!" Sergeant Shin was questioning the young man.

"Yes," he replied.

Then he was kicked. The young man screamed. "Again," yelled Shin. There was another heavy kick followed by another long scream. "Oh, Lord! Oh, Lord! Oh, Lord!"

Shin looked down at the young man with contempt. "Water," he yelled. "I'll give you Christians what you deserve."

Out of the corner of his eye, Zhang saw two guards walk off and after a moment come back with a big bucket of water. It was steaming. Zhang closed his eyes tightly and wished he could do the same with his ears. The victim screamed horribly. And then a shot brought an end to it.

Rest in peace, thought Zhang. *Your suffering is over. You didn't betray Jesus.* But in Zhang's mind, the boy was still screaming.

"Look at him!" Sergeant Shin was suddenly screaming in Zhang's ear. "That's the fate of Christians."

Zhang did as ordered and looked at the mutilated corpse.

"Put the bricks down and bury that derelict."

Alone? Zhang wanted to ask but he held his tongue. He dragged the body across the grounds and up the hills a bit. A guard followed him but did not lift a finger to help.

Zhang knelt down and began to dig a hole with his hands.

✪ ✪ ✪

The light went out. Ten o'clock—bedtime for the inhabitants of the camp. *At last.* Zhang had come to like the night. It meant not being beaten, not being sworn at and not working. But the night had two enemies: hunger and that nightmare. Every night it seemed as if

Zhang could dream only one thing. He was at home with Father, Mother and Hea-Woo. He was telling them about China, about Jesus, about the prison and about the camp. But they were not listening. It was as if he did not exist.

Zhang dug some clay out of the wall. His fingers sought for the paper. Carefully he took the Bible out of the hole. The Bible was damp. The paper was stiff and wrinkled. He stumbled to a corner at the back of the barracks. Here there was a hole in the wall. When there was a full moon, it was not completely dark outside. There was just enough light to be able to read the Bible for a few minutes unnoticed.

Comfort me, Lord. Please comfort me. He opened the Bible to John 15 and read: "If the world hates you, keep in mind that it hated me first. If you belonged to the world, it would love you as its own. As it is, you do not belong to the world, but I have chosen you out of the world. That is why the world hates you."

The Bible is right. Of course it is right! The state hates me because I have become a citizen of a heavenly kingdom. But the world can still hurt me, Father. Can hurt so much. Please grant that I will not betray You.

✪ ✪ ✪

Sergeant Shin raised the chain.

"Aaah!" Zhang's wrists were pulled up sharply. His feet were now dangling twenty centimeters above the floor.

"You've held out for a long time, but you've become my personal project," said Captain Choi. "The longer you keep it up, the worse it is for my reputation and that of Sergeant Shin. It's time to put an end to this. We're going to break you. This week you will declare that Kim Jong-Il is your god."

Maize. Zhang was always given a handful about this time. *How can I work tomorrow if I miss my daily portion of a hundred grams? Impossible!*

"Did you hear the captain?" roared Shin.

Maize. Those delicious, yellow, round grains. So tasty and nourishing. Impossible to believe that in China I sometimes left them or gave them to the birds. A wicked waste. You can never have too much maize. A man needs maize. Otherwise he doesn't survive.

"You vermin! Scum!"

And what about rice? What did that taste like? Delicious! Yes, very delicious. Especially with pieces of chicken in it. What a good cook sister Ping was. If I ever go back to China, I'll go straight to her.

A sharp pain penetrated his side. Shin had taken a swing with his baton and was ready for the next blow.

"Wait," said Choi. "Let us first take good care of our guest." He got up from behind his desk, went over to a trolley on wheels and removed a cloth from a large, copper dish. He took the time to fold up the cloth. Then he took the lid off the dish. Steam rose from the rice. There were also six small dishes with spices and sauces and small dishes of meat and fish.

The captain pushed the trolley just in front of Zhang, but far enough away so that he could not reach it with his legs. "Bon appétit! We'll come back in a while."

Zhang turned his body as it dangled from his wrists. He hoped that the ceiling would come down. He would eat that rice with dust and all, even if it was his last meal on earth. The ceiling did not give way. The only thing Zhang achieved was causing the flesh to be scraped off his wrists.

As the steam from the food rose up, Zhang felt his stomach twisting into knots. He closed his eyes and began to pray intensely. In his mind, he went through the story of Jesus' life. He saw His birth, he saw Him rebuking the storm, walking on water, preaching on the mountainside, praying in Gethsemane and standing in silence before the judgment of Pilate . . .

The door opened again. "Aren't you hungry?" asked Choi. "Then you won't mind if we eat, will you? You see, the sergeant and I need it. We have to work very hard today. For example, in a moment, we have to deal with a stubborn prisoner. Do you know what the worst of it is? That runt still thinks he's a human being. While I have stated quite clearly this is not the case. But that's all right, he'll soon find out."

Choi and Shin sat down and ate slowly.

Zhang's whole body was sweating. "Maize," he said. "I must have maize. And water."

The officers stood up and took iron rods. With the very first blow, Shin knocked Zhang out.

❂ ❂ ❂

"Brother, brother . . ."

"Stop . . . stop. Get off me . . . Aaah . . ." Every movement hurt.

"Eat. You must eat."

"Let me . . . sleep . . ."

❂ ❂ ❂

Zhang woke up. He was back in the interrogation room. For the umpteenth time. He had lost count and no longer knew how often he had been there. Sometimes Captain Choi was there. Sergeant Shin was always there now too.

Shin was sitting back in a relaxed position in his chair and smoking a cigar. There was a newspaper on his lap. He saw that Zhang, who was chained to the wall, had come round. "The revolution is doing well. Did you know that? Food production is already in full swing again."

Zhang became angry. "A lie."

"I know. I know. You're not interested in the revolution, are you?" He blew smoke into the room. "Only in that Jesus. Tell me about Him."

Zhang was silent.

"Go on. It's not as if you will be beaten for it, or anything!"

Still Zhang was silent. Shin took his feet off the desk and stood in front of Zhang. "Do you know, I am not a filthy rat like you? Actually, I'm quite a good person. Faithful to the revolution, faithful to the Great Leader Kim Il-Sung and the Beloved Leader Kim Jong-Il." Shin laughed.

"I've got children. You didn't think so, did you? Those children have to have a good education. My father was not as faithful as me. That's why I have to work my way up here. And you can help me. You only have to say that Kim Jong-Il is the true god. Is that so difficult now? Your suffering will be over, and I'll get a bonus. Captain Choi too. Everyone will be happy."

Zhang looked into Shin's eyes without saying anything.

"How dare you look at me?" Shin growled. He hit Zhang everywhere he could and started to scream at him. The screaming seemed to come from a different world. As if someone were roaring through thick glass.

✪ ✪ ✪

"Let him down," said Choi. Shin took his key and opened the shackles that chained Zhang to the ceiling. Zhang fell to the floor.

"Take him outside," said Choi. "We're going to play the car game."

Shin dragged Zhang outside. With ropes, his arms were bound to two different cars. Zhang did not feel any fear. *Oh Lord, let it soon be over. Will You please protect Hea-Woo?*

Soldiers started the cars and slowly drove in opposite directions. Zhang's arms stretched. The burning pain all over his body was terrible. Just a little while and it would be over.

"Admit it!" screamed Shin.

Darkness surrounded Zhang.

✪ ✪ ✪

Stink. Terrible stink in his nose. Faces. Choi. Shin. It was not over yet. Don't wake up. Voices. Louder and louder.

"Admit that Kim Jong-Il is your god."

No.

"Say it!"

I don't want to.

"Say, Kim Jong-Il is god."

Such pain. I want to die.

"Say it!"

"I . . . I admit it . . ."

"What do you admit?"

"Kim Jong-Il is . . . god. Let me die."

CHAPTER 9

Zhang was alone in his barracks. He had been given a piece of paper and a pen to write out a profession of love for Kim Jong-Il. Zhang could barely raise his arms. With a lot of pain, he managed to get his Bible out of the hiding place in the wall. He opened the book to the first page and read the familiar words. "In the beginning . . ." Zhang looked away. He dared not read God's Word now. He had betrayed Him. He was too weak, too weak to survive life in the camp and the torture. Why had God not let him die sooner—as a victor? And what was to become of Hea-Woo?

Zhang took the pen and wrote—scratched—a few words in his Bible. He lay his head back against the wall again. *Sleep.* Tomorrow was his last day. The day of his final betrayal.

❂ ❂ ❂

The three thousand people on the square were deathly quiet. Only the sound of the birds could be heard. For weeks, or months, Zhang had not seen the sky. Would God still want to have him? Even after what he was going to say?

Zhang looked over the square at the crowd. He could not see any faces. They were too far away or Zhang could not see clearly anymore. He longed for the end. It was good that Hea-Woo could not see him now. She would be ashamed if she saw her brother bound to this pole.

He did not deserve any better. First, he had betrayed his father and Hea-Woo. Then Kim Jong-Il and his country. Then Jin and Hyok. And also brother Lee and sister Ping in China. Zhang had taken Jin into his confidence and had himself been betrayed. Through his naiveté, he had betrayed Soojin, Seong-Eun and the others. And now he was going to commit the ultimate betrayal. He was going to betray God.

The face of Captain Choi came into focus. Behind him stood Sergeant Shin. "I said we would break you. In the end, it wasn't so difficult, was it, Sergeant?"

"No, sir," replied Shin.

"Right. Let's not waste any time. Fetch the microphone and let him read out his declaration."

"He hasn't written anything down, Captain."

"Never mind. Nothing good is going to come out of vermin like that. Let him read from this paper." Choi gave Shin a typed declaration.

Zhang wanted the cloud to pass on from in front of the sun. It was cold. Was it still summer? How wonderful to see the sun one more time! His stomach rumbled. That would soon be over too. *Just a little longer, Zhang.*

Choi walked away, while Shin fixed the microphone in front of Zhang's mouth. It was attached to the pole by a hook. Shin said, "This way the firing squad will at least have a clear shot. I understand that especially for this occasion they have only one marksman instead of three. I hope for your sake that he hits the first time."

"Ready Sergeant?" called Choi through his microphone from the other side of the square.

Shin took a few steps backward and raised his hand.

Choi turned around and addressed the prisoners. He pointed at Zhang. "There on that pole hangs a being who was not worthy to be born. He chose to betray his country and . . ."

*The young Zhang was running across the green hills of Unsung. Jin
caught up to him and jumped on his back. They rolled down the hill.*

". . . He followed this so-called Christ, but has come to his
senses . . ."

Hea-Woo snuggled up to Zhang on the bed.

"Later, when we're big, will you marry me?"

"I would want to marry only you, my sister."

"Will you protect me then too?"

"Yes, as long as I live, nothing will happen to you."

". . . This scoundrel has been sentenced to death . . ."

Zhang and Jin pressed their blood-smeared index fingers together.
"Promise that you will never let me down, comrade Jin."

"I promise, comrade Zhang. Blood brothers forever."

"Forever."

". . . But first the prisoner wants to make his own declaration.
Sergeant Shin!"

Shin switched on Zhang's microphone and held the paper in
front of his nose. "Speak clearly."

My last betrayal. The characters danced before his eyes. Zhang
squinted to see more clearly. Slowly the characters turned into words
and sentences.

"Prisoner," called Captain Choi, "who is your god?"

Zhang began to speak. "My god is . . ."

"Louder," said Shin.

"My god is the eternal, the inviolable, the loving, the . . ."

A cloud again passed in front of the sun and covered the square
in a gray light. A sudden wind cut through Zhang's thin overalls.
Zhang shivered.

I, even I, am the LORD, and apart from me there is no savior.

"Go on," Shin snarled at him.

Zhang turned his mouth away from the microphone. "Do you
want to know who my God is, Shin? Listen carefully."

Then Zhang addressed all who were standing in the square. He felt himself gaining strength. "My God was born a King. He is the King of righteousness. He is the King of heaven. He is the King of kings and Lord of lords. He is strong, supreme and merciful. He is God's Son and the Savior of mankind."

Shin grimaced. "What are you doing? Stop!"

"He gives strength to the weak. He is there for those who are tempted and tried. He heals the sick. He forgives sinners. He discharges the guilty of their guilt. He cleanses lepers. He frees the prisoners. He defends the weak . . ."

"Shin!" screamed Choi, gesturing violently. "Make him stop!"

But Shin didn't. He was staring at Zhang with his mouth open.

". . . He blesses the children. He serves the unfortunate. He respects the elderly and rewards the meek. His goodness is boundless and His grace is eternal. His love is great and unchanging. The earth is His footstool. He is so great that the highest heavens cannot contain Him, and no man can explain Him . . ."

"Shin! Microphone! Off!"

Shin reached for the microphone.

". . . The leaders of His time could not stand Him, but they couldn't stop Him. The governor couldn't find any guilt in Him. They killed my God, but the grave could not keep Him. He rose again to bring salvation to everyone present here . . ."

"Firing squad, take aim! Silence him!"

". . . In the West, people shall fear His name, and in the East His majesty. Because He will come with the power of a river along a narrow bed . . ."

Shin was still standing next to Zhang, his arm stretched to the microphone; his finger was on the on-off switch.

"Shin! Get out of the way! Move to the side!"

". . . And He came. To bring good news to the poor, to provide hope for the downhearted, to set prisoners free and to release those in chains, to declare the year of the Lord's favor and the day of vengeance for our God, to comfort all those who mourn . . ."

"Shin, move away! We're going to fire!"

". . . He is the true vine and we are the branches. If we remain in Him and He in us, we will bear much fruit. But without Him, we can do nothing. One day, every knee shall bow before Him and every tongue confess Him as Lord. You cannot outlive Him and you cannot live without Him. He has no predecessor and no successor. Before Him, no god was formed and after Him there shall be no god."

"Who are you talking about?" Shin asked.

From behind the clouds, the sun came out again. Zhang was completely happy.

"Soldiers! Fire!"

"Jesus, You alone are Lord! Apart from You there is no one who saves!"

EPILOGUE

Hea-Woo held her mug of tea tightly between her hands. She allowed the steam to rise up to her nose. "Ohh . . . nice and hot," she said aloud. When it was this cold in the past, when she was little, she would simply climb into bed with her brother. They would cuddle and he would tell her thrilling stories—more violent than she really would have wanted, but she liked to listen to his voice. He made her feel safe. She missed him. She missed her parents. She missed the village of Unsung, where she had grown up. She missed their house. It was so different from this bare, empty, cold, drafty, dull house in which she now lived. She giggled. It was time she added another adjective to that list. Perhaps, *bare, empty, cold, drafty, dull, boring house*?

Hea-Woo took a sip of tea, got up and took a piece of paper out of the cupboard, a reminder of the past. It had become a daily ritual to study this drawing carefully. Her brother had only three crayons when he drew it: green, red and blue. On the left, drawn in red, there were two figures who represented two brave friends. On the right, in green, an army of Americans, who were being defeated by the two Koreans. At the top of the paper, carefully drawn with a blue pencil was a girl, who was watching, full of admiration. Above that, it said in big letters, "My dear sister Hea-Woo." Fortunately, Father had packed this drawing when they had fled.

If only she could see her silly, dear, funny brother once more. She remembered the day when she saw him for the last time. He must think they were in China. But they had not managed to get there. It had taken them a week and a half to reach the border, where they had been picked up.

Father had been taken away and she did not see him again. It was a good thing that Zhang had not gone with them. He might no longer be alive. If only they had stayed in Unsung. Again she could see herself walking through the labor camp.

Hea-Woo closed her eyes tightly. When would there come a day on which she did not have to think about the labor camp? The things which she had seen there—people dying of starvation, executions, cruel guards, cruel prisoners. Zhang would probably not understand such suffering.

Was he still alive? And would she ever be allowed to leave this village for former prisoners? Unsung was not even that far away. Two hundred kilometers separated her from her brother—if he was still alive.

Outside it was already almost dark. It would be another moonless, cold winter night. Hea-Woo drank her tea and took a blanket, which she wrapped tightly around her. With small steps, she went over to her mattress.

There was a hard knock at the front door. Who could that be? Quickly she walked through the living room and opened the door. The tall, thin man facing her towered above her. For a fraction of a second, she thought that Zhang was there. But this man looked nothing like her brother. He was wearing civilian clothing, but he stood bolt upright, like a soldier at attention, with his hands behind his back.

Hea-Woo gasped, her heart beating in her throat. "Can I help you?"

"Kim Hea-Woo?"

"That's me."

The man smiled for a split second, barely visible. Then his face became serious again. "I've found you at last. My name is Shin Hyo.

I've been looking for you for months. I had to draw on all my contacts to get here."

"What have you come for?"

"I have a message for you from your brother."

"Zhang? Zhang, is he still alive?" she screeched and grabbed Shin's arms with both hands. "Tell me he's still alive!" she begged.

The man took Hea-Woo by the shoulders and shook his head. "I'm sorry," he said gently and dropped his hands from her shoulders.

Hea-Woo covered her eyes with her hands and screamed. She had felt so sure that someday she would see her brother again.

"But I have a message for you," Shin said.

Hea-Woo moved her hands away from her eyes and looked up at Shin. He stood awkwardly for a moment, looking as if he were going to cry. He breathed heavily. With his left hand, he reached into his inside pocket. He took out a small, black book and gave it to Hea-Woo. The cover was loose and some of the pages were wrinkled.

"What's this?"

"Open it please. The first page."

Hea-Woo opened the book. Something was written there—more like scratches than writing. Hea-Woo studied the words and made out what it said:

Dear Hea-Woo,

If God wants, this book will one day reach your hands. I do not know what state this book will find you in, but whatever the circumstances are, these words will give you life, eternal life.

For eternity,
your Zhang

P.S. Forgive me for everything.

Hea-Woo looked up at Shin and mumbled, "Thank you." Then she turned around as if in a daze and stumbled through the doorway.

Images of the past rushed through her mind. She could hear Zhang's voice. *Forgive me.*

"Your brother changed my life, Miss Kim," Shin called after her. "He was a good man. Please read this book."

She nodded and continued walking into the house. Shin closed the door.

Hea-Woo opened the book at the place where there was a note slipped into it. She took out the note and recognized the drawing she had made five years ago. Mother and Father were sitting on chairs next to one another. Zhang and Hea-Woo were standing behind their parents. Zhang's right arm was on Hea-Woo's shoulder.

At the bottom of the page, there was a sentence. She recognised Zhang's handwriting. It said, "God says, 'I, even I, am the LORD, and apart from Me there is no savior.'"

Who was Zhang talking about? About himself? Hea-Woo had to know. She threw the blanket off her and ran outside.

"Wait!" she called.

Shin stopped and turned around. When Hea-Woo reached him, she grabbed his wrist with both hands.

"Tell me everything! Tell me Zhang's story!"

"I don't know everything," said Shin, "but the story of comrade Zhang is a story of pure victory."

AFTERWORD

Let us, then, go to Him outside the camp,
bearing the disgrace He bore. For here we do not have
an enduring city, but we are looking for
the city that is to come.

-Hebrews 13:13–14

This book was largely written at the dining table in my living room. But this is not where the book came into being. I did not make up comrade Zhang. He sought me out at two specific moments in my life, even though I did not yet recognize him.

The first time was on my first night in North Korea. Kim Il-Sung Square in Pyongyang was completely crowded. Ten thousand children of between, I suppose, five and twelve years of age were practicing to honor the Beloved Leader. Through loudspeakers, fearsome, incomprehensible orders rang out. Some of the children were marching like fully fledged soldiers. Others were sitting on the ground and resting their heads on their knees. They were slapped if they did not stay awake. I fell on my knees and could only pray two things, "Why, Lord?" and "Please bring an end to this madness."

The second defining moment was later in Seoul, the capital of South Korea, where I was to talk to North Korean refugees. I met

233

Kim Tae-Jin, a potential speaker for our Open Doors day. He had been in the Yodok concentration camp for years. I clearly remember the first thing he told me as it has stayed with me years later. He said, "If you say that I have to move a chair ten times from one side of the room to another, I'll do it without asking for any explanation. But if I can choose between two lectures, I don't know what I should do. I can't make my own decisions."

Since then I have spoken to many refugees from North Korea. Comrade Zhang was born out of all those conversations. I have tried to reflect the atmosphere in North Korea as best as possible and to sketch a picture of the dilemmas that North Koreans face every day, including the feelings of utter despair.

Walking around in North Korea, one imagines that one is in a spiritual desert. It is as if God has withdrawn from here and has allowed Himself to be replaced by statues of Kim Il-Sung, which rise up high above towns and villages. In a certain sense, North Korea is much like the Old Testament. Read the book of Isaiah and chapter after chapter seems to be applicable to this country with its authoritarian regime. God's promises and warnings provide either a great support or great uncertainty. For instance, "I will not yield my glory to another or my praise to idols" (Isaiah 42:8). Does God not keep His Word or is this promise still going to be fulfilled?

And what can a North Korean do with Jesus Christ? In Kim Jong-Il's "paradise," God's name must not be glorified. Where is Jesus to be found? Anyone who trusts in Jesus risks a stay in a heinous concentration camp comparable to the death camps of the Nazis. There are no free churches or evangelistic campaigns, as there are in the West. From conversations with Christians, we know that dreams and visions are not occurring as they are in the Muslim world. Every year, thousands of people are still dying of starvation. Children, often little more than toddlers, are wandering around the country looking for food. Countless people are locked up in prison camps with their families. The God of the Old Testament is much more attractive than

Jesus because however hard you look in the Gospels, nowhere do you find that Jesus Christ came to overthrow earthly kingdoms.

Anyone looking for Jesus in North Korea is quickly inclined to point out the miracles that are taking place. For example, Open Doors helped a couple who had literally walked out of their prison cell in North Korea, because the doors were suddenly unlocked. Surprisingly many North Korean Christians have received the gift of healing.

But every day, North Korean Christians are dying in prisons and concentration camps. Most Christians are not released. Because of this, it is shortsighted to seek Jesus only in miracles. Just as in Jesus' time, miracles are rare. The tragedies that occur here are sometimes unbearable.

Eleven-year-old Jong-Cheol fled without his parents to China. There he came to faith. Fate hit hard. With a group of other children, he was arrested and deported back to North Korea. There they were questioned, pressured and beaten. One boy was no longer able to stand it and betrayed the fact that Jong-Cheol had become a Christian. The soldiers killed Jong-Cheol. The character Hyok is based on this brave boy, Jong-Cheol.

But this book has not been written only to show how difficult it is to be a Christian. It was written to glorify God and to demonstrate Jesus' supremacy. He is worthy to be followed radically, even in the most difficult circumstances, even when following Him means that it costs you everything.

The writer of the Letter to the Hebrews says, among other things, the following about Jesus:

- He is God's ultimate revelation, through Whom the world was created (1:2).
- He is the radiance of God's glory and the exact representation of Him (1:3).
- He purified us from our sins (1:3).

- The angels honor Him (1:6).
- His kingdom will last forever (1:8).
- He is crowned with glory and honor (2:9).
- He has destroyed the one who holds the power of death, the devil (2:14).
- He is a merciful and faithful priest (2:17).
- He is the source of eternal salvation (5:9).
- He appears for us in God's presence (9:24).
- He is coming a second time to save those who are waiting for Him (9:28).
- He is the same yesterday, today and forever (13:8).

This is all summed up in the word "Him," when Hebrews says in chapter 13, verses 13–14: "Let us, then, go to him outside the camp, bearing the disgrace he bore. For here we do not have an enduring city, but we are looking for the city that is to come."

Zhang, and the many Christians whom he symbolizes, live in relative security. He was as fortunate as a person could be in his situation. But God always has a higher plan for us. God wants us to have deep, satisfying fellowship with Him. This is why He asks us to give up our certainties and our comfortable lives, to join ourselves to Him and to bear His humility. After all, our city is not enduring. A far better city is coming.

He asks us to follow Him radically, with risks and with a sacrificial love. But it is not a path that we take alone. If all is well, on this road we will find many other Christians who share in one another's suffering. Even if this is not the case, even if it seems as if we are walking alone on this path, still we are not alone. Jesus is waiting for us outside the camp. He says to us, "Go out and do My work!" He issues us an invitation: "Leave your safe home. Come to Me. I am here. Share in My suffering."

The omnipotence of Christ exists not only in His perfect capacity to bear our sin or in the precious future reward that will liberate us from fear, greed, pain and illness. But Christ has also become our personal Treasure, around Whom the universe turns.

So let us learn from persecuted Christians in North Korea that Jesus is issuing us with an invitation: Go outside the camp (what is your camp—your "safe" environment?), join Him and share in His reproach. After all, our city is not enduring. Rather we are looking forward with longing to the city that is coming, a city that is built by God and is lit up by His Son, Who learned obedience through suffering and proved that He is worthy to be the radiant Focus of everyone's life. Even if it costs you everything, He is more than worth the price.

Jan Vermeer

Get Involved!

Open Doors started in 1955 when a Dutch missionary discovered that Christians in Communist countries were desperately longing for Bibles and supplies—and so he began to take Christian literature behind the Iron Curtain. He became known as Brother Andrew—'God's Smuggler'—and the founder of a ministry still rooted in a passion to follow God's call and release His Word into the lives of believers in the world's most difficult areas.

More than fifty years later Open Doors continues to serve persecuted Christians in around fifty countries, whether the oppression comes in the name of Communism, Buddhism, Hinduism or Islam. Where the people of God are under pressure, Open Doors stands with them, responding to their cries for help and shaping its response under their guidance.

Prayerful involvement with Open Doors is a great way to strengthen the Persecuted Church, not just to face the onslaught of pressure, but to continue to reach out with the Gospel of Jesus Christ.

Right now Open Doors is ready to give you information for your prayers—the authentic voice of the Persecuted Church brought to you in print, by email, and on the web, so that your prayers are timely, informed and effective weapons in the spiritual battle.

Open Doors can channel your gifts to where they will make a significant difference to our sisters and brothers in the Persecuted Church, not least in providing the Bibles and other Christian literature they have requested. You will be helping to train pastors and congregations so that they can stand strong through the storm, to strengthen the Church in its commitment to mission, to make sure that those who have lost so much can receive material help and spiritual encouragement.

Many Christians around the world also volunteer to bring the Persecuted Church into the life of their own church family, sharing news for prayer and exploring the lessons to be learned from our sisters and brothers.

Perhaps you would allow Open Doors to become your link to the Persecuted Church, so that together we can all play our part in God's great plan and purpose for His world. For further information, simply contact the national office listed below—and discover more of the miracles that come in obedience to God's call.

Open Doors AUSTRALIA
PO Box 6237
Frenchs Forest NSW 2086
www.opendoors.org.au
Email: ODAustralia@od.org

Open Doors CANADA
8-19 Brownridge Rd.
Halton Hills, ON
L7G 0C6
www.opendoorsca.org
Email: opendoorsca@od.org

Open Doors INDONESIA
PO Box 5019 JKTM 12700
Indonesia
www.opendoorsindonesia.org
Email: Indonesia@od.org

Odmal Services Berhad
P. O. Box 216
41720 Klang
Selangor
MALAYSIA
Email: Malaysia@od.org

Open Doors NEW ZEALAND
PO Box 27630
Mt Roskill
Auckland 1440
www.opendoors.org.nz
Email: OpenDoorsNZ@od.org

Open Doors PHILIPPINES
PO Box 1573
QCCPO 1155
Quezon City
www.OpenDoors.ph
Email: Philippines@od.org

Open Doors SINGAPORE
8 Sin Ming Road
#02-06 Sin Ming Centre
Singapore 575628
www.OpenDoorsSG.org
Email: Singapore@od.org

Open Doors SOUTH AFRICA
PO Box 1771
Cresta
2118
www.opendoors.org.za
Email: southafrica@od.org

Open Doors UK & IRELAND
PO Box 6
Witney
Oxfordshire 0X29 6WG
www.OpenDoorsUK.org
Email: inspire@OpenDoorsUK.org

Open Doors USA
PO Box 27001
Santa Ana, CA 92799
www.OpenDoorsUSA.org
Email: USA@OpenDoors.org